"You believe in love overcoming all, then?" Pippa asked.

"Of course. Without it, the world would be a poorer place."

"Have you ever fallen in love?"

"My dear, I do it all the time. At least once a month."

"Now you are roasting me."

"Perhaps."

"What other attributes?" she continued.

"Why, she must be good-natured, generous, sympathetic to others, well-read, able to converse properly without simpering, and she must love me, of course."

"And have you found such a one?"

"No. Which is why, once a month, I am disappointed."

"Perhaps you do not come up to the ladies' expectations. Have you thought of that?"

* * *

Sir Ashley's Mettlesome Match
Harlequin® Historical #308—May 2011

Author Note

Sir Ashley's Mettlesome Match is the fourth in my series about law and order in Georgian times. Each has a hero dealing with a different crime. Sir Ashley is concerned with smuggling, and of course Pippa, my heroine, is mixed up in it—albeit innocently. The idea came to me when I was reading *The Lawless Coast* by Neil Holmes, which deals specifically with the trade on the north Norfolk coast. Smuggling was not the romantic pastime that many imagine it to be, and many tried to thwart the smugglers at their peril. If duty conflicted with love, it became even more difficult—as Sir Ashley discovers. I hope you enjoy reading it.

If you would like to find out about the other novels in the series, or any of my books, visit my website, www.marynichols.co.uk.

Sir Ashley's Mettlesome Match

MARY NICHOLS

TORONTO NEW YORK LONDON
AMSTERDAM PARIS SYDNEY HAMBURG
STOCKHOLM ATHENS TOKYO MILAN MADRID
PRAGUE WARSAW BUDAPEST AUCKLAND

ISBN-13: 978-0-373-30617-6

SIR ASHLEY'S METTLESOME MATCH

This edition published by arrangement with Harlequin Books S.A.

For questions and comments about the quality of this book please contact us at Customer_eCare@Harlequin.ca.

www.Harlequin.com

Printed in U.S.A.

Born in Singapore, **Mary Nichols** came to England when she was three, and has spent most of her life in different parts of East Anglia. She has been a radiographer, school secretary, information officer and industrial editor, as well as a writer. She has three grown-up children and four grandchildren.

Available from Harlequin® Historical and MARY NICHOLS

The Incomparable Countess #156
Lady Lavinia's Match #163
A Lady of Consequence #169
Mistress of Madderlea #177
The Hemingford Scandal #196
Marrying Miss Hemingford #199
Bachelor Duke #204
Dear Deceiver #213
An Unusual Bequest #218
The Reluctant Escort #226
Talk of the Ton #236
Working Man, Society Bride #244
A Desirable Husband #251
Runaway Miss #262
Rags-to-Riches Bride #270
The Earl and the Hoyden #281
Honorable Doctor, Improper Arrangement #288
**The Captain's Mysterious Lady* #302
**The Viscount's Unconventional Bride* #304
**Lord Portman's Troublesome Wife* #306
**Sir Ashley's Mettlesome Match* #308

*The Piccadilly Gentlemen's Club

Chapter One

The night was inky black and the wind, coming off the German Ocean, was biting into Pippa's bones, numbing fingers and toes and making her huddle into her cloak and wish herself back home and in the warm. The summer, coming on top of the worst winter anyone could remember when the rivers and even the sea froze, was wet and cold. It was a foolish idea to come out. The sea was rough; huge breakers were rolling up to the sandbanks just off the shore, so perhaps they would not land, or she might have been mistaken in thinking that there was going to be a delivery in Narbeach this night. The signs had all been there earlier in the day: everyone whispering and hurrying home after evensong; no one showing any lights; dogs chained up, stable doors left unlocked and a ship hove to half a mile out to sea. It was a beautiful vessel, long and sleek, rigged fore and aft with a long bowsprit to take a jib sail, intended to outrun the revenue cutters. Now the sails were furled and it was simply a dark outline against the horizon.

She wanted to witness a landing, to watch the cargo

being brought ashore, to find out where they hid it and how many men were involved. What could she learn that reading the reports of smuggling trials in the news sheets would not tell her? she asked herself. The atmosphere of the landing, she supposed, which dry-as-dust accounts could not give: the drama and tension, the sheer volume of goods piled up on the beach, the essence of danger, which she had to feel in order to convey it in writing. But if she were seen…

She pulled her dark hood over her head and huddled even farther into her cloak, crouching down behind a sand dune, as much to shelter from the wind as to hide herself. If she were seen and accosted, they would not hesitate to kill her. They had too much at stake to let her live.

As she watched she heard the jingle of harness and the rumble of wheels on the lane behind her and threw herself down into the sand and prayed they would pass by without noticing the dark heap almost at their feet. She dare not look up and expose her pale complexion, which would easily be seen even on so dark a night. From beneath her shadowing arm, she could just see their feet as they passed, leading horses and carts down onto the beach. There were dozens of them, silently tramping past the spot where she lay. No one spoke, not even a whisper.

At last they were gone and she risked lifting her head. The beach, which a few minutes before had been empty, was swarming with men, pack mules, horses and carts. It seemed as if the whole male population of the village was there. Someone struck a flint and lit a lantern and swung it to and fro. It was answered in similar fashion from the darkened ship. Now everyone was facing seawards and Pippa dared to stand up and watch. Two boats were lowered and two men scrambled down into each to receive and stow the goods being slung down to them in nets. She could not see what the cargo was, but when the boats were riding low in the water the oarsmen began pulling for the shore.

When the boats were within wading distance, those on the beach went to help haul them out. Almost before they grounded, the unloading began. Soon the sand was littered with kegs, barrels, boxes and bundles and the boats went back for a second load. The carts were filled and some of the kegs were roped in pairs and slung, fore and aft, on the shoulders of the strongest men. Stooping under their weight, they made their way inland past Pippa. It was time to fling herself down on the sand again.

The boats returned from the ship and more contraband was deposited on the beach, put in carts or slung on backs. They had unloaded each boat three times when a single warning shot rang out. The men on the beach had been working quickly before, but now there was desperation in their movements. The rowers set off back to their ship, leaving the land party to salvage what they could and make themselves scarce. Some of them carried what they could inland, or on to the marshes to the east of the village, others whipped up the horses and left with carts only half-loaded. There were still a few men on the beach when a party of dragoons, led by a Captain and a Customs Officer, appeared on the lane and began firing on the stragglers, who fired back. Pippa, her heart in her mouth, watched the skirmish, her frozen toes forgotten. She dare not move.

Some were injured and were hauled away by their mates, others ran, dodging the bullets. One of the dragoons was winged, resulting in a more frenzied attack of retribution. It was too much for the remaining smugglers and they threw down their weapons. As Pippa watched they were roped together none too gently by their captors. There were six of them and a boy. Some of the dragoons stayed to guard what contraband had been left behind, others marched the prisoners off the beach, prodding them with their riding crops to hurry them along. It was then Pippa recognised her cousin, Benjamin, dressed in a dark belted tunic and breeches, his face smeared with dirt. Fifteen years old and he had been caught smuggling! Her first impulse was to rush out and try to reason with his guards, but common sense prevailed. She would not save him that way and might very well be taken up herself. She watched them go, unable to move until the coast was clear. Then she ran.

Hampered by her skirts, she raced up the lane and along the coastal path to Windward House, which stood on a slight promontory at the north-eastern edge of the village. She must find Nat. Her brother would know what to do. He would find out where the prisoners were being taken and speak for Ben, who was only a boy looking for adventure and hadn't realised the seriousness of what he was doing. There was no one abroad in the village, either on foot or driving horses and carts. The houses, cottages and hovels were dark, their occupants seemingly abed. The land party had arrived and disappeared like ghosts. The captured seven would pay for the crimes of fifty. Out at sea the smugglers' cutter had sailed off and was disappearing over the horizon.

Philippa Kingslake, twenty-six years old, unmarried and, in her Aunt Augusta's eyes, unmarriageable on account of the life she led, was also known in the literary world as Philip King, whose adventurous stories were avidly read by all and sundry, especially by young lads like Benjamin, who had no idea their author was a woman. Had she inadvertently led him into danger, writing tales with heroes he might aspire to emulate? Aunt Augusta would almost certainly think so.

The lane from the village to the house dwindled into a track as she began the uphill climb to the house, arriving so breathless she had to stop and lean against the stable wall to recover before going indoors. The horses were restless; she could hear them snorting and pawing the ground. Had they been startled by the shots which must have been heard clearly by everyone in the village? She went into the stable where her own mount and Nat's, together with two carriage horses, were housed. Going over to stroke and calm them, she realised they were sweating. They had been out recently and there was only one place for them to have gone. The sheer impudence of the smugglers astounded her. Where was Joe, the coachman, who had quarters above the stables? Had he been sleeping so soundly his charges had been led out under his nose? Or was he involved? Was he even in his bed? Torn between finding out and reporting Ben's arrest to Nat, she chose the latter and hurried indoors and up to her brother's room.

And then she was in for another shock. He was not in his bed, had never been to bed by the look of it. Had he also been out with the smugglers? She had not seen him, but then she had not dared show her face—recognising anyone would have been impossible. He had certainly not been one of the seven who had been arrested and herded so close to where she was hidden. Now she was in a quandary. Should she wait until Nat came home or alert her aunt?

She went back to the stables and climbed the ladder to Joe Sadler's quarters, banging on his door loudly enough to rouse him. After a few minutes he opened the door. He was wearing a hastily donned nightshirt over his breeches, his hair was ruffled and he was pretending to yawn as if woken from sleep. She was not deceived; the bottoms of his trousers were wet. 'Miss Kingslake!' he exclaimed, genuinely surprised. 'What are you doing up in the middle of the night?'

'Never mind what I am doing. Do you know where my brother is?'

'No, ma'am. Is he not in his bed?'

'No. Was he on the beach with you?'

'On the beach?' he queried, feigning ignorance. 'What do you mean?'

'I am not stupid, Joe. I know what has been going on. I saw you all down there, unloading cargo.'

'You should have stayed indoors, ma'am.'

'Then I would not have known what had happened to Ben, would I?'

'Ben? Master Whitehouse?'

'Please do not be obtuse, Joe, you know whom I mean. He was taken by the dragoons along with six others. I need to rescue him and I cannot find Nat. Am I right in thinking he was one of the land party and he sanctioned the use of the horses?'

'Oh, Miss Kingslake, you was never supposed to know about any of it. Someone tipped off the Customs and we had to scatter. Mr Kingslake will be home d'rectly.'

'I hope so,' she said. 'In the meantime, you had better rub down the horses and settle them before the Customs come searching for goods and see they have been out.' She paused as a new thought struck her. 'You are not hiding any of the contraband here, are you?'

'No, Miss Kingslake.'

She was not sure whether to believe him or not, but went back into the house. It was beginning to get light and Mrs

Sadler, Joe's mother, was busy in the kitchen, raking out the fire, ready to cook breakfast.

'Lord a-mercy, Miss Pippa,' she said as Pippa entered from the yard. 'Whatever are you doing up so early?'

'I went out to watch the boats come in.'

'You never did! Whatever next! Don't you know no one goes out on landing nights unless they have business with the free traders? They'd as soon kill you as let you go...'

'The revenue men and dragoons came upon them with half the cargo still on the beach. Seven of the landing party were arrested...'

The plump woman, whose apple-red cheeks came from constantly working over a kitchen fire, turned pale. 'Joe...'

'He is home. I've just seen him.'

She let out a long breath. 'Thank God for that.'

'But my brother is out and my cousin has been arrested.'

'No?' She crossed herself. 'Oh, Lord have mercy, for the justices won't.'

'We will have to get him out somehow. I was hoping Nat would be back by now. I wish I knew what had happened to him. I cannot believe he would leave Ben to his fate.'

'He would not, Miss Pippa, you can be sure of that. Something prevented him.'

It was that which was worrying Pippa as she climbed the stairs to her aunt's room to break the news to her. Where was Nat? Was he holed up somewhere safe, waiting for the furore to die down before coming home, or was he lying bleeding, perhaps dying, in one of the numerous channels across the marshes, unable to move? She dreaded the confrontation with her aunt, who would undoubtedly blame Pippa and Nat for the arrest of her beloved son.

The widowed Mrs Augusta Whitehouse had come to live at Windward House six months after Pippa's parents had died leaving a seventeen-year-old Philippa and thirteen-year-old Nathaniel orphans. Aunt Augusta did not like Windward House; it was exposed to every wind that blew down from the Arctic, as she so often pointed out. It invaded every nook and cranny of the building and she never felt warm in spite of huge fires in every room, but nothing and no one would persuade her to leave her niece and nephew to their own devices, even though Pippa had said she was well able to manage with the servants they had.

'Leave a seventeen-year-old not yet out in society to manage a household and her brother who seems not to know the meaning of discipline is not to be thought of,' she had declared. 'I would be failing in my duty if I did not take you both under my wing.' And so she had shut up her own house and come to Narbeach, bringing her six-year-old son with her. Benjamin, unlike his mother, loved Windward House and was soon into mischief with the village children and doting on his cousin Nat.

And look what it had led to, Pippa mused, as she rapped on her aunt's bedchamber door and, bidden to enter, went in to find her aunt sitting up in bed, her long grey hair on her shoulders over which she had draped a thick shawl. The room was lit by the embers of the fire of the night before.

'Philippa, what in heaven's name are you doing up and about? It is the middle of the night. Has something happened?'

'It is almost dawn,' Pippa said. 'And, yes, something has happened or I would not have wakened you. There was a landing last night…'

'Everyone knows that. I keep my head under the blankets when I know the free traders are about. It has nothing to do with me.'

In spite of her concern, Pippa smiled. 'Have you never drunk untaxed tea or taken a nip of illicit spirits, Aunt?'

'Everyone does that. I ask no questions.'

'Then ask yourself what Ben does when the gentlemen are about.'

'Ben? I should think he sleeps, as I do.'

'Not last night. I saw him arrested and taken away by the dragoons.'

'Never.' Augusta scrambled out of bed in one swift movement. She flung a dressing gown over her nightrail and dashed from the room, along the corridor to her son's bedchamber. His bed had not been slept in. Then she rushed to Nat's room, though Pippa could have told her he was not there.

'Tell me,' she demanded of her niece who had followed her. 'What did you see?'

Pippa recounted exactly what had happened. 'I was hoping Nat would know what to do, but he has disappeared,' she finished.

'I might have known. Nathaniel has led the boy astray. Ben didn't know what he was doing. We will have to get him out somehow. You had better ask Sir Felix to intervene. The dragoons will take the captives to him; he will be the one to decide whether to send them for trial. He will help, I am sure.'

Pippa knew all that, but she was reluctant to go to him. Sir Felix Markham was the local squire and magistrate. He was twice widowed and made no secret of the fact that he had his eye on Pippa for wife number three. She did not like him. He was fat and over fifty and could not keep his hands to himself when they found themselves in the same company. Being beholden to him for a favour went against the grain. 'I would rather wait for Nat to come home. He can do it.'

'We dare not delay.' Augusta was hurrying back to her own room as she spoke, followed by Pippa. 'Once Ben has been sent to the Assizes, it will harder to get him set free. Where is Nathaniel anyway?'

'I do not know.'

'Was he on the beach?'

'I did not see him.'

'A fine kettle of fish this has turned out to be. I am beginning to wonder why I ever bothered to come here to live. You and your scapegrace brother both go your own way, whatever I say. You should have been wed by now and bringing up a family, not rushing all over the countryside like a hoyden and writing books. That is no occupation for a lady. No wonder Edward Cadogan changed his mind about marrying you.'

'Aunt, that was six years ago and long forgotten.' It wasn't forgotten, not by Pippa, but the memory was too humiliating to talk about and it was better to pretend it was of no consequence.

'Hmph,' was her aunt's reply to that. 'Why did you go out anyway?'

'I wanted to know about the smugglers for my next book. Reading about them is not the same as seeing them on a dark and windy night with danger all around.'

'No, I do not suppose it is,' her aunt said repressively. 'Had you thought of what might happen if you had been arrested too?'

'It would be an experience,' Pippa said, more to bait her aunt than because she welcomed the idea. She realised almost at once that she was being unkind when her aunt was so anxious about her son. 'I was well hidden.'

'No doubt that is why you have sand in your hair and all over your clothes. Go and change. If the Customs Officers come here, they will see at once where you have been. And dress respectably. We are going to pay a call on Sir Felix. I think a demure, frightened young woman will fit the bill.'

'Aunt, I am neither demure, nor frightened.'

'Well, you should be. Off with you, while I dress.' She clapped her hands to summon her maid from the adjoining room, still addressing Pippa. 'Go and tell Mrs Sadler we will breakfast early, then tell Joe to harness the carriage. We have not a moment to lose.'

Sir Ashley Saunders was breakfasting with Sir Felix Markham. Having been alerted by his informers that a cargo of contraband was to be landed at Narbeach on the north Norfolk coast, he had jumped at the chance to leave London for a while. His latest mistress, Arabella Thornley, was becoming more and more demanding and had broken the explicit condition of their relationship and was hinting quite openly that he ought to marry her. It was the last thing he wanted. At thirty-four, he was a confirmed bachelor and intended to remain that way. His previous mistresses had understood and agreed to bide by that and it annoyed him that Arabella should think she was any different. He had once been fond of her, appreciative of what she provided, but the prospect of making her his wife filled him horror.

Norfolk was far enough from the capital to afford him some respite; as it was currently being plagued by smugglers who were openly defying authority, he had taken the opportunity to investigate their activities. Arriving in Narbeach, he had made himself known to Sir Felix, who had invited him to stay at Narbeach Manor. 'Can't have someone of your rank staying at the Cross Keys,' he had said, when Ash told him he was spending a holiday in the area.

Ash did not tell his host that he belonged to the Society for the Discovery and Apprehending of Criminals, popularly known as the Piccadilly Gentlemen's Club. They had their headquarters in Piccadilly at the home of Lord Trentham, who had encouraged James, Lord Drymore, to set up the group twelve years before and it was now well established. Its principal members, besides James and Sir Ashley, were Viscount Jonathan Leinster; Harry, Lord Portman; Captain Alexander Carstairs and Sam Roker, Lord Drymore's servant, who had been recruited in the early days because he was familiar with the cant of the criminal fraternity and could gain access to places where a gentleman would have stood out like a sore thumb. Not all of them were such masters of disguise as Harry Portman.

Each had their own area of expertise and each was required to promote law and order. They were not empowered to arrest anyone, but they would track them down and alert the watch or the parish constable or the army, who would apprehend the criminal, preferably with incriminating evidence on him. They were not paid for their services, but did it for love of their country and in a spirit of adventure, so it was important that each was of independent means. Ash had inherited a property and some money from his grandfather and had managed to increase it severalfold with judicious investment and was now prodigiously wealthy. He had joined the Piccadilly Gentlemen's Club because the ever-increasing crime in the country was something that needed addressing and membership gave him something useful to do.

Lately he had turned his attention to the smugglers who operated along almost every coast of the British Isles. Like the coiners whom Harry Portman investigated, their activities were depriving the government of thousands of pounds of revenue and threatening to destabilise the country's finances. With the army away fighting a war there were not enough troops to deter them and they mocked the efforts of the Customs and Excise men to catch them. The war, which had been waging in Europe for seven long years, had ended the month before, but the troops had not yet been brought home and only a handful of dragoons helped patrol the coast.

Ash was not concerned with the village men who took part out of necessity. There was little labouring work to be had in the winter months and what there was did not keep a man and his family in food, let alone other things they might need, like fuel, clothes and medicines, and the smuggling barons paid them well for their services. It was these barons who were the focus of Ash's attentions. He suspected that Sir Felix knew more than he was admitting, but it served Ash's purpose to pretend he believed him innocent, if not exactly ignorant.

They had almost finished their leisurely breakfast when a footman appeared to say Mrs Whitehouse and Miss Kingslake had arrived and wished to see Sir Felix on an urgent matter.

'What can they want at this hour?' Sir Felix murmured to Ash. 'It is hardly a civilised time to make calls.' To the footman he said, 'See that the ladies are made comfortable in the withdrawing room. Tell them I will join them directly.' Then to Ash. 'I must go and change. I cannot receive them in a dressing gown. You will wait for me here?' He did not wait for a reply before dashing from the room.

Ash left the table and wandered about the room, idly looking at the ornaments and pictures. There was one of Sir Felix with his family grouped about him: a wife, upright and unsmiling, and three girls, which must have been executed some years before because he had been told Sir Felix was twice a widower and his daughters were all adults with families of their own.

The door behind him was flung open and he swivelled round to face a middle-aged woman dressed in widow's weeds, who had determination written on every feature of her lean face. She was followed by a younger woman, who was endeavouring to restrain her. 'Aunt, you should not come in here. We were asked to wait in the withdrawing room—' She stopped suddenly when she caught sight of Ash. 'Oh, I beg your pardon.'

She was tall, he noticed, wearing a blue wool gown with an embroidered stomacher that emphasised a slim waist and an enviable bosom. Her hood had fallen back from her cloak and it was her hair that struck him most. It was a fiery red and so curly it had defied all attempts to confine it. It spilled from the combs that were supposed to hold it in a knot on the back of her head and stuck out in all directions. He took his gaze from her hair to her face. It was a perfect oval, with high cheekbones, well-shaped brows and the most brilliant green eyes he had ever seen. He was reminded of a ginger cat and wondered if this one had claws.

'Think nothing of it,' he said, sweeping her a bow. 'Sir Ashley Saunders at your service.'

She curtsied. 'Sir Ashley, how d'you do. I am Philippa Kingslake and this is my aunt, Mrs Whiteside.'

He bowed. 'Your obedient, ma'am.'

'We have come to see Sir Felix,' the lady said, bowing her head in response.

'He will be with us directly. In the meantime, may I help you? I am spending a few days with Sir Felix.'

'No, we must speak to Sir Felix,' Augusta said. 'He is the magistrate and only he can help us.'

Sir Ashley was a handsome man, Pippa decided. There was a glint of humour in his dark eyes as if he would burst out laughing at the least provocation. It might have been that she had not had time to see to her *toilette* properly and her hair had escaped from the combs and pins she had hastily dug into it. Knowing she was visiting Sir Felix, she did not care that she was looking less than her best. If it served to put him off, so much the better! And their errand was urgent. But to find herself confronted by a vision of elegance in a superbly tailored suit of burgundy velvet, whose own dark hair was sleeked back into a queue with not a strand out of place, was disconcerting. He wore no make-up and his face was tanned as if he spent long hours out of doors in all weathers.

'Ah, then, am I to suppose you have come to report a felony?' Although Ash was addressing the older woman, his gaze was on the younger. He could not take his eyes off her. She intrigued him. He saw the slight expression of impatience she did not bother to hide and added on a sudden flash of inspiration, 'Or has someone close to you been taken up?'

'How did you know that?' Augusta demanded. 'Have you seen him? Do you know what happened? Where have they been taken? Are they still here?' She fired questions at him, allowing him no time to answer.

'Madam,' he said, lifting his hand to stop her in full flow, 'calm yourself and tell me what has happened.'

Whoever he was, Pippa would rather talk to him than Sir Felix; as her aunt had been forced to stop for lack of breath, she decided to explain. 'My young cousin has been apprehended by the Customs, Sir Ashley. He is no more than a boy with a love of adventure and went down to the beach to watch a landing last night. He was not involved, simply a spectator, but the Customs arrived with a troop of dragoons and rounded some of the men up, and Ben along with them.' She decided to say nothing of her brother whose presence on the beach, if he were there—and she could not be sure of that—could not be explained away in the same manner.

'There was a landing of contraband last night?' he queried, annoyed that he had missed it and wondering if Sir Felix had known it and kept him talking over supper to distract him from his purpose.

'Yes,' she said. 'Sir Felix is the local magistrate; the prisoners would have been brought to him to deal with.'

'I heard nothing of it,' he said. 'Though my room is at the back of the house and Sir Felix might not have wished to disturb me.'

His host came in at that point, dressed in a suit of purple satin and a long matching waistcoat with huge pearl buttons. On his head was a hastily donned bag wig. He made a flourishing bow to each lady, before taking their hands and kissing them. He lingered over Pippa's just too long for her comfort and she quickly pulled her hand away and surreptitiously rubbed it against her skirt, a gesture that was not lost on Ash. So, she did not like the gentleman, though he was obviously taken with her. 'Ladies, I gave orders you were to be made comfortable in the withdrawing room…'

'Sir Felix,' Augusta said, having recovered herself a little, 'we need your help.'

'Anything, dear lady, anything within my power.'

'You are aware there were smugglers on the beach last night and some of them were arrested?'

'No, I was not,' he said, affecting dismay. 'Is there no end to their lawlessness? Have they harmed you or yours? If so, I will pursue them to the full extent of the law.'

'No, they have done us no harm,' Augusta answered him. 'But Ben was out there watching them and was taken up with them. I did not know he had gone or I would have stopped him. You have met him, Sir Felix, and you know he is very young and easily led. I suppose he thought it would be exciting, he would not have thought of the danger. I felt sure the dragoons would have brought their prisoners here.'

'No, they did not,' he said. 'I know nothing of it. Of course if they had, I would have rung a peal over Ben and sent him home. As it is…' He shrugged.

'Where would they be taken, if not here?' Pippa asked.

'Hunston, Lynn, Heacham—it would depend where the soldiers were based and the nearest magistrate. I will endeavour to find out for you.'

'By that time it will be too late,' Augusta wailed. 'They will be sent to the Assizes and God help my poor boy then. What am I to do?'

'I heard one of them say the goods they had seized were not worth turning out of bed for,' Pippa put in. 'He mentioned a chambermaid at the Standard in Wells who was keeping his bed warm for him.'

'You heard them talking?' Ash asked her in surprise. 'Where were you at the time?'

Pippa grinned. 'Face down in the sand,' she said. 'Hiding behind a dune.' When she smiled her whole face came alive and her emerald eyes sparkled. She was, in Ash's eyes, a remarkable woman and, in spite of his avowed intention to take a rest from the ladies, he found himself wanting to know more about her.

'Miss Kingslake!' Sir Felix remonstrated. 'I am surprised at you. You are lucky you were not seen. The free traders would have had no compunction about bringing an end to your existence, especially if they thought you had informed on them.' He paused. 'Did you? Inform on them, I mean.'

'No, of course not. I was simply an observer.'

'They would not have believed you,' Ash said laconically. 'I am not sure that I do.'

She faced him, the humour in her eyes turning to anger. 'I do not lie, Sir Ashley. I, like my young cousin, was simply watching.'

'What on earth for?'

'My reasons are my own.' She did not tell him about her writing, which her aunt abhorred. *'It would not be so bad if you wrote about feminine things, like housekeeping or embroidery or collecting sea shells or such like,'* she had said, more than once. *'But to make up stories about war and pirates and highwaymen and things a real lady should know nothing about is not something to noise abroad. It will give society an aversion to you. It has already cost you one suitor.'*

The fact that Edward had been horrified when she told

him about her writing and insisted she stop it at once was only one of the reasons they had parted. They had met at her come-out year, introduced by a close friend of her aunt. He was handsome and attentive and before long was escorting her to functions all over town and had sworn his undying devotion. Her other suitors faded from the scene. Everyone said it was an ideal match and, not being versed on the ways of the world, she believed them, but after a while little things began to give her doubts. He seemed to want to change her, to make her into a one of those insipid, timid young ladies, without an idea in her head of her own. His insistence that she conform made her realise he did not understand her one iota and caused dissension, which was surely not right between two people supposedly in love.

'If I could have rescued Ben, I would have done,' she said, mentally shrugging these unconstructive musings from her mind. 'But they would not have taken any notice of me.'

'What are we to do?' Augusta asked, impatient with the way the conversation was going.

'I had better go to Wells and see for myself,' Sir Felix said with a sigh that indicated a reluctance to do anything of the sort. 'Lord Borrowdale is the justice there. If I can persuade him to let the boy go, I will.'

'Oh, please do,' Augusta said. 'We will be for ever in your debt if you can effect his release, won't we, Pippa?'

'Yes,' Pippa murmured.

It was obvious to Ash that the young lady was as reluctant to be in the baronet's debt as he was to confront his judicial colleague. 'If you wish, Sir Felix,' he ventured, 'I will go to Wells and make enquiries on your behalf. I am acquainted with his lordship. A request for the release of one of his prisoners might come better from me, since you know the boy and your action might be wrongly interpreted. What do you say?'

'Capital idea!' Sir Felix said with great relief. 'I should hate to be accused of being in league with smugglers.'

'And that would never do,' Ash said with a barely concealed smile. 'I shall need one of the ladies to accompany me to identify the boy and lend weight to my argument. As Mrs Whiteside seems overcome, perhaps you would come with me, Miss Kingslake?'

'Of course,' she said. 'How shall we travel?'

'I have my carriage,' Ash said. 'It will take but a few minutes to have it harnessed and ready.'

'You cannot go unchaperoned,' Augusta said, suddenly recovering some of her usual aplomb.

'Oh, Aunt, what does it matter? This is not London, nor even Norwich. I go out and about here unchaperoned and no one thinks anything of it. You take our carriage home and have Mrs Sadler make up a tisane for you. You need to rest. After all, you had little sleep last night.'

Ash found himself smiling again. He did not know how much sleep the matron had had, but Miss Kingslake, on her own admission, had been out on the beach, burying herself in sand while the smugglers did their work. How much sleep had she had? And what did she know that she was not revealing?

'Yes, you are right,' Augusta agreed. 'I should not be of any use to you if I came.'

This arrangement did not please Sir Felix, but he could not object since he had said he was glad of Ash's help. Instead he sent word that Sir Ashley's equipage was to be made ready.

Twenty minutes later Pippa found herself sitting beside her escort in one of the most luxurious carriages she had ever seen. It had steel springs and padded rich blue velvet cushions, and it was pulled by a pair of matched white horses. Sir Ashley was evidently very rich, as well as handsome and agreeable. If she had not been so worried about Ben and Nat, she would be enjoying the outing.

'Why do you suppose the dragoons took their prisoners so far?' she asked as they made their way along the narrow coastal road that joined the villages and towns of north Norfolk. 'Sir Felix usually deals with Narbeach matters.'

'Perhaps they thought he would be biased in the prisoners' favour,' he said. 'Especially if they were local men, known to him. On the other hand it might simply be that they were anxious to get back to their warm billets. There again, they would want to be sure they received their share of the prize money.'

'Most of the contraband had left the beach by the time they turned up,' she told him. 'It was amazing how quickly the men scattered with their loads, leaving only the stragglers and a few kegs and bundles behind. I would be very surprised if they reached the Customs House...'

'Tut, tut, Miss Kingslake, you are surely not suggesting the Customs men are corrupt,' he said, but he was laughing.

'The boats went back to the ship and it sailed away,' she said, her own lips twitching. 'How much was still on board, I could not say.'

'We could probably calculate that if you can describe the ship and remember what you saw landed. If there was anything left on board, they will undoubtedly make another run.'

'It was a cutter, but as to the cargo, I do not know if I can be accurate.' She paused to frame her question, risking a rebuff. 'What is your interest in smugglers, Sir Ashley? Are you a Revenue man?'

He thought of telling her the truth about the Piccadilly Gentlemen, but decided against it. He had no idea how deeply she was involved in lawlessness. 'No. I, like you, am an ordinary citizen curious about how law and order is maintained.'

Her mind flew to Nat and Joe and the other village men. Smuggling was a crime punishable by death and yet all the coastal villages indulged in it. Wherever there was a suitable place to land and places to hide the goods until they could be taken inland and sold, men were prepared to risk their lives for the rich rewards on offer. People like Sir Ashley Saunders were a serious threat to them. 'Did you come to Narbeach on purpose to catch smugglers?' she asked, endeavouring to hide her dismay.

'It is a huge and profitable business and is depriving the Exchequer of many thousands of pounds every year, Miss Kingslake,' he said, evasively. 'Its perpetrators are violent and not above murder and intimidation, as you, who live on the coast, must surely know.'

He had not answered her question, but she let it go. 'Yes, but some of the men are forced to join in for fear of reprisals on their families and, besides, the lure of money to a poor man with a wife and family to support is irresistible.'

'I am aware of that, Miss Kingslake. But think of this. If there were no smugglers and everyone paid their proper dues, the country would be better off and that includes the poor man in his cottage, who would not be afraid of a knock on the door in the middle of the night.'

She did not like the sound of that, not with Ben in the hands of the law and Nat missing, though she was careful not to let it show. 'If you are not a Revenue man, then who are you?' she asked. 'I cannot imagine an ordinary citizen setting out to change the world single-handedly.'

'Change has to begin somewhere.'

She had to concede he was probably right, but her main concern was to protect Ben and Nat as far as she could. The fact that her companion was a handsome man with a ready smile, who made her heart flutter in a way it had not done for six years at least, was a distraction she must overcome. 'Why Narbeach?' she asked.

He paused to turn and face her. She was looking somewhat anxious, which probably meant she knew some of the smugglers; it would be strange if she did not, living in the village as she did. And was her cousin as innocent as she pretended? 'Why not? Narbeach is only one of many such places. Taken together, they represent a threat to the economy of whole country.'

She was not prepared to argue that point and turned away from him to look out of the window at the countryside through which they were passing. On the inland side it was grazing land, dotted with cattle; on the seaward side the salt marshes were intersected by narrow channels of open water. Only local people dared venture on those, and she did not doubt there were hiding places for contraband in its creeks if you knew where to look. She was not thinking about the view or the contraband, but whether to consider Sir Ashley Saunders friend or foe. 'Smuggling has been going on for centuries,' she said. 'You would have a challenge on your hands if you tried to put a stop to it. Others have tried and failed.'

'I know.'

'I think you would only cure them if you offered them an alternative way of earning a living that would take them out of dire poverty.'

'I know that, too.' He paused. 'Enough of that. What about you?'

'Me?' She turned to face him. 'I am no smuggler. They would not have me even if I wanted to become one. You need strong muscles and an even stronger determination and I have neither.'

'You may be right about the muscles,' he said with a smile, which she found unnerving. 'But I am not so sure about the determination. What were you doing on the beach at night when all respectable and law-abiding ladies should be safely in their beds?'

'Enjoying a midnight walk.'

'Do you often do that?' he asked mildly. 'Or only when a cargo is coming in?'

'I often do it,' she said. 'It helps me to think.'

'Can you not think at home?'

'Yes, but sometimes I cannot sleep and then it is best to go out and feel the wind on my face and see the moonlight shining like a silver ribbon on the water and the tide swirling about the rocky pools. It makes me feel humble and thankful for the life I have.'

He would not describe her as humble and fancied that like most people of her colouring she had a fiery temper. 'There was no moon last night.'

'No.'

'Were you not afraid when you saw what was happening on the beach?'

'Not until the dragoons arrived and then I was fearful for the men.'

'Did you know any of them?'

'It was dark and I was not close enough to identify anyone.'

'But you did recognise your cousin.'

'He was brought close to where I was hiding.'

'What does your aunt think of you going out at night? I assume you live with her.'

'Not exactly. She lives with us.'

'Us?'

'My brother and me. It is my brother who is the householder.'

So, she was not Mrs Whiteside's companion as he had at first surmised. He found himself looking at her in a different light. 'Where was he last night when you were out watching smugglers?'

She was afraid he might ask that and was reluctant to tell him she did not know. He would undoubtedly jump to the conclusion that Nat was involved with the free traders and he might possibly be right. 'He is away from home at the moment.'

He was aware of her wariness in answering, but he did not pursue that line of enquiry. 'And your parents?'

'They were drowned in a boating accident nine years ago. Aunt Augusta moved in with us soon after that.' She gave a wry smile. 'She seemed to think we could not manage on our own.'

'From what I have learned I can understand that,' he said with a teasing smile. 'If you make a habit of wandering about at night to help you think. Most ladies I know would be terrified of doing such a thing.'

'Of thinking?' she queried, laughing.

He laughed, too. 'That, too, but I meant walking out alone.'

'Then the ladies you know must be mean-spirited.'

He had not thought of that, but on reflection decided she was probably right. Even his mistresses obeyed the rules of convention. Arabella liked to pretend she was a lady, but

Miss Kingslake, who undoubtedly was one, did not care. He wondered what had made her like that. 'I begin to feel sorry for your aunt,' he said.

'Oh, I know we are a handful, but she is very fond of us.'

'Us being you and your brother?'

'Yes. He is four years younger than I and took it very hard when Mama and Papa were drowned. I tried to look after him and, if that meant being strong and independent, then that is what I was, what I am. We are very close.'

'It is perhaps a pity that he is from home at the moment.'

'Yes, it is,' she said. 'He might have prevented Ben going to the beach last night.'

'Am I right in supposing your cousin is always into mischief?'

'He is fifteen years old, Sir Ashley—all young men of that age are into mischief. Ben has been somewhat spoiled by his mother, but there is not a malicious bone in him. I do hope you can persuade the magistrate of that.'

'I shall do my best, when I have spoken to the boy.'

'Oh, I see,' she said, suddenly angry. 'He must tell all he knows in exchange for his freedom. Don't you know that turning King's Evidence is as good as a sentence of death hereabouts?'

'Smuggling is punishable by death—'

'Innocent as he is, he cannot win,' she stormed. 'If the law doesn't get him, the smugglers will. It is not fair and I shall make sure the world knows it. And don't think I can't.' She was looking at him with such fury in her green eyes, he found his earlier question answered—this ginger cat had claws and he had better watch out.

Her question had been answered too. Sir Ashley Saunders

was almost certainly a foe. Her bitter disappointment in him made her want to weep. But she had not shed tears for over six years and no man, however attractive, was going to make her cry again. She turned her face resolutely from him and looked out at the countryside again.

Chapter Two

Ash had detected the moisture in her eyes, though it was disguised by anger. Until now she had been perfectly composed, answering his questions, apparently hiding nothing and unperturbed by his disclosure that he was on the side of the law. He had been prepared to believe that her young cousin had been innocent and he only wanted to speak to the boy to verify that, not to have him turn King's Evidence. If the lad had simply gone down to the beach to watch, there was nothing he could tell him, certainly not the name of the real smugglers, the ones who paid for the goods and organised their sale. If they could be brought to book, the smuggling might be curtailed; he did not flatter himself he could bring it to an end. All this he had intended to explain to her, but before he could so, she had flared up like a glowing fire suddenly stirred into flame.

In some strange way, her anger made her more attractive, not less, because under it he sensed a vulnerability he realised she would never admit. It made him feel protective towards her. But supposing she was involved with the smugglers—would he still want to defend her? It was a question he could not immediately answer.

'I am sorry to find you in sympathy with lawbreakers,' he said, probing.

'I am not in sympathy with lawbreakers,' she snapped. 'How can I be when I have seen what they can do? They hanged a man on a homemade gibbet last year because he warned the Excise of a landing and as a result some of the free traders were caught red-handed. His body hung there for weeks as a warning to others. I do not want that to happen to Ben.'

'Naturally you do not, but had you thought that travelling with me to visit a magistrate might be construed as informing? You were, after all, in a position to see what went on.'

'I saw nothing that could be of any help to the Customs and Excise,' she said. 'Apart from Ben, I could not identify a single one of them. In any case, no one knew I was there. As far as the public is concerned, I am a simple female anxious to obtain the release of my innocent cousin.'

'Why were you really on the beach?' he demanded, smiling at the idea that she was simple. There was nothing simple about Miss Philippa Kingslake, except, perhaps, her clothes. He wondered why she had so little regard for her appearance. Most of the ladies of his acquaintance would not venture out unless they had spent at least two hours dressing in the latest mode and having their hair done and face covered in paint and powder.

'I have told you. I often walk out at night.'

'And do your smuggling friends know that?'

'I have no smuggling friends. At least, none that I know of.' There was a hint of a humour in her voice; she had evidently overcome her tears. 'One can never tell who they are these days.'

He smiled, too. 'My involvement in securing your young relative's release might also be misconstrued.'

'Then I must face Lord Borrowdale alone. I will be broken-hearted, pleading for mercy for my cousin.'

He laughed aloud. 'Have you met his lordship?'

'No.'

'He is not one to be swayed by broken hearts and feminine tears. He is famous for his harsh punishments. He takes a pride in them. Being even remotely associated with free traders will be enough to condemn you.' He put his hand briefly over hers. 'I think, my dear, you had best leave it to me.'

She did not answer, not even to tell him she was not his dear, not his anything, because they were turning in at the gates of Lord Borrowdale's country mansion and she needed to gather her wits for the confrontation to come.

Ten minutes later she realised Sir Ashley's summary of his lordship's character had been correct when a very superior servant in full livery announced them and she found herself facing the man himself. He was a big man, both in height and breadth, with bushy brows and a full brown wig. His grey eyes surveyed her from top to toe, taking in her plain wool gown, her wild red hair and lack of a bonnet as if wondering how this person had had the effrontery to invade his house. She was glad of Sir Ashley's steadying hand under her elbow.

Ash had used his considerable reputation and standing in society to gain them admittance and was not going to let a little thing like the other's superior rank intimidate him. He gave the man a flourishing bow. 'Your servant, my lord.'

'Sir Ashley.' The bow was returned. 'I have not seen you since your late lamented father went to his Maker. How many years ago was that?'

'Ten, my lord.' He turned and drew Pippa forwards. 'May I present Miss Kingslake of Windward House, Narbeach.'

Pippa gave him a curtsy. 'My lord.'

'Narbeach, you say?' his lordship queried, taking his eyes from Pippa and turning to Ash. 'There was a landing of contraband goods there last night and the Revenue alerted. All but seven of the devils got away, though.'

'Six,' Pippa said, resolutely. 'The seventh was an innocent bystander.'

'Innocent bystander!' his lordship scoffed. 'On the beach in the middle of the night when cargo is being brought ashore and you call that innocent!'

She refused to be intimidated. 'I do, my lord. He is but a child, full of childish curiosity. He simply followed the others down to the shore. He was never part of the illegal activities.'

Ash nudged her. She turned to look at him. His eyes were telling her to be silent. She did not feel like obeying him; she wanted to scream and beat her fists upon the bigoted Lord Borrowdale's chest and demand he set Ben free.

'Sir Ashley does well to silence you,' his lordship said. 'You are incriminating yourself with every word you utter. How do you now what was in the muckworm's mind unless you were party to it?'

'Ben is not a muckworm! And I know his mind because I have known him since he was in leading strings.'

'My lord, may I have a private word with you?' Ash asked, gripping Pippa's elbow so hard, she almost cried out. 'I think I may be able to throw some light on the matter.'

'Oh, very well, but make it quick. I am about to go out.'

'Miss Kingslake, would you be so good as to wait in the carriage?' Ash said. 'I shall be but a moment.'

Pippa was reluctant to obey. She wanted to hear what was being said. What could Sir Ashley tell his lordship which she did not know? But when a footman was summoned to escort her to the carriage, she was obliged to follow him from the room, her annoyance plain in her posture and the way she swept her skirt up in her hand and threw back her head.

Ash watched her go, smiling a little, then turned back to Lord Borrowdale. 'Miss Kingslake is naturally upset. She is very fond of her cousin and cannot understand why he was taken up in the first place.'

'He was with the smugglers. Good God, man! If I let off every young varmint whose females swore his innocence, no one would ever be arrested. How can you be sure she is telling the truth?'

'I cannot,' Ash admitted. 'But if I could talk to the boy, I am sure I should learn something from him. I would deem it a favour if you would give him into my custody. I will undertake to see that he is dealt with according to the law.'

'And what is your interest in smugglers? Not a Revenue man, are you?'

'No.' Ash smiled. 'Have you ever heard of the Piccadilly Gentlemen's Club, my lord?'

'No. Are they a band of smugglers?'

He laughed. 'No, on the contrary, they are gentlemen

dedicated to upholding the law of the land. They have been doing it for the last twelve years. I am one of them. We brought the O'Keefe gang of coiners to justice and the murderers, Black, Randle and Smith, not to mention putting a stop to a possible Jacobite rebellion. Wherever we see crime, particularly organised crime, we investigate it and bring the perpetrators to book.'

'Don't the Bow Street Runners do that?'

'To a certain extent, yes, but their force is small, their resources limited, and they rarely operate outside London. We are a roving band and go where we are needed and we have access to people and places denied to the Runners.'

'I understand that, but why Piccadilly?'

'The headquarters of the Society is there at Lord Trentham's home. You may check my credentials with his lordship, if you wish. As a member of the government he is particularly interested in combatting smuggling.'

'But you are asking me to release one of my prisoners—surely not the action of a law-abiding citizen?'

'Into my custody.' Ash smiled again. His face was stiff with smiling. 'I intend to make a friend of the boy through his cousin. By gaining his trust, I might find out more. Where are the prisoners being held?'

'I had them in the Customs House overnight, but this morning I sent them under guard to Norwich gaol. They will be safer there than anywhere until the Assizes in Thetford later this month.'

Ash understood him to mean safe from being set free by their friends. 'Then I must go to Norwich. Will you furnish me with a letter ordering Benjamin Whiteside's release into my custody? It will save me having to explain myself all over again. The fewer people who know my intentions the better.'

'And Miss…' his lordship waved his hand in the general direction of the door '…Miss Whatshername—does she know your purpose?'

'Miss Kingslake. No, she does not. She went to Sir Felix Markham for help when I was there and I offered to do what I could to bring about the release of her cousin.'

'Then I hope she is suitably grateful.'

'Oh, I am sure she will be,' he said lightly, perfectly aware of his lordship's meaning.

His lordship left the room and came back a few minutes later, waving a sheet of paper in his hand. 'Here you are. And I hope I may not live to regret this.'

'Thank you, my lord.' Ash took the paper, checked the wording and signature and folded it before putting it in his pocket and bowing his way out.

Pippa was in the carriage, impatiently drumming her fingers on the door edge, when he returned and gave orders for the coachman to proceed. 'Well?' she demanded as soon as he had settled in his seat beside her. 'What happened? Where is Ben? Is he to be released?'

'Your cousin has been sent to Norwich Castle to await the Assizes and, yes, he is to be released into my custody.'

'Then we must go to Norwich at once.'

'No, Miss Kingslake, we cannot go at once. It is becoming late and we should need to stay in Norwich overnight. Even you must realise the impropriety of that. I am going to take you home and acquaint Mrs Whiteside of our progress so far, then I shall go and fetch your young cousin tomorrow. It won't hurt him to have a taste of prison for a night or two.'

'Then you will quiz him all the way home, I suppose. You will be wasting your time. He knows nothing.'

'Then he has nothing to fear.'

'Have you no heart?' she demanded.

'Oh, yes, my dear. My heart beats as everyone's does. Here.' Before she could stop him he had grabbed her hand and laid it flat over his heart, where she felt its solid beating beneath her palm. It had a strange effect on her own heartbeat, which suddenly became erratic and unduly loud, as if to prove it was every bit as efficient as his. It took her breath away and, for a moment, she could neither move nor speak. She was hurtled back in time, to the days before Edward Cadogan turned his back on her. He had made the same gesture to prove his constancy. 'Two hearts beating as one,' he had said. And what an empty gesture that had been! She would not succumb again. She would not! She pulled her hand away and made a pretence of fumbling for her handkerchief in the pocket of her cloak.

'Allow me,' he said, handing her his own pristine square of cambric. She took it and squeezed it into a ball in her fist. She did not speak, not even to thank him.

They journeyed in silence for several minutes but they could not go all the way to Narbeach without speaking; the atmosphere was tense enough without that. 'Let us call a truce,' he said. 'After all, we both want the same thing—freedom for your cousin, the end of crime and bloodshed. And a peaceful life. Do you not agree?'

'Yes,' she murmured.

He held out his hand. 'Then let us shake hands on it.'

She took his hand. It was warm and dry and his grip firm. 'I am sorry, Sir Ashley. It is only my anxiety that makes me flare up,' she said. 'I do it far too often. It is all on account of my hair...'

'Your hair?' he queried, 'What has your hair to do with it?'

'It is red,' she said.

He pretended to study it. 'So it is,' he agreed mildly.

'Red hair is supposed to denote a quick temper,' she said. 'I am afraid, in my case, it is true. It is also said to be unlucky. Some people of a superstitious nature turn away from me. Some go as far as to say it is the mark of the devil and cross themselves.'

'Then they are ignorant bigots.'

'Are you married?' she asked suddenly.

'No.'

'I'll wager you would not marry a red-haired woman.'

'My dear Miss Kingslake,' he said with a wry smile, 'are you proposing to me?'

Her face turned nearly as red as her hair. 'Certainly not! I have no wish to marry you or anyone.'

'Oh, dear, that has put me in my place.' But he was laughing.

'My question was purely hypothetical,' she said.

'Then I will answer it. Purely hypothetically, of course. The colour of a lady's hair would not influence me if all her other attributes were favourable. And if I were in love.'

'You believe in love overcoming all, then?'

'Of course. Without it the world would be a poorer place.' He didn't know why he said that. Love had never entered his head before. Desire, perhaps, but that was not the same thing at all; one involved the physical senses and the other the emotions, and he had schooled himself not to become emotional. In his mind he related it to weakness. Still, his contemporaries James, Jonathan and Harry were far from weak and yet all three loved their wives at a time when being in love with one's wife was considered eccentric.

'Have you ever fallen in love?'

'My dear, I do it all the time. At least once a month.' His flippancy hid his confusion. Confusion was something else he did not allow himself.

'Now you are roasting me.'

'Perhaps.'

'What other attributes?' she asked, going back to his reply.

'Why, she must be good-natured, generous, sympathetic to others, well read, able to converse properly without simpering and she must love me, of course.'

'You say nothing of her colouring, dark or fair, or coming from a good family, or having a generous dowry...'

'A woman with all those virtues would be beautiful, whatever the colour of her hair. As for a dowry, that is unimportant. I have no need of it.'

'And have you found such a one?'

'No, which is why, once a month, I am disappointed.'

'You are teasing me again.'

'It amuses me.'

'Perhaps you do not come up to the ladies' expectations. Have you thought of that?'

'It is a possibility, I suppose,' he said, pretending to give it some thought. 'But as I have no wish to be married, I have never asked any of them what those expectations might be.'

'I surmise you have had many mistresses.'

'Well, you see,' he said with a deep sigh, 'they flock round me. I cannot seem to help it.'

She laughed. 'How vain you are.'

'No, simply truthful. Now are you going to tell me why you have no wish to marry? Have you had a surfeit of lovers, none of whom has lived up to your expectations?'

'Oh, of course,' she lied.

He knew she lied. She had been badly hurt in the past, he decided, and it had something to do with the colour of her hair. He could not believe anyone would be so unkind as to turn her down on those grounds. Why, he thought its richness was an asset and it certainly would not deter him, if he were ever to think of marriage, which of course he would not.

'What are those expectations, apart from liking the colour of your hair, I mean?'

It was impossible to be offended by him. They were, after all, simply enjoying a light-hearted exchange of views, a small flirtation, which, she guessed, was intended to take her mind off the problem of her cousin. 'He should be good-natured, generous, sympathetic to others, well read, able to converse without simpering,' she said, repeating his own words with a mischievous smile. 'And he must love me.'

'To distraction?'

'Oh, definitely to distraction.'

''Tis a pity that we have both eschewed marriage,' he said with another sigh. 'We might have made a match of it.' He paused to look at her. She was pensive, as if her mind had flown to some other place, some other time. 'But perhaps we can be friends.'

'Yes,' she said. 'Friendship is safer.' It was a strange thing to say, but he did not comment.

Instead he changed the subject abruptly. 'Your aunt will no doubt be upset to think of Ben in Norwich Castle, but we shall have him out of there tomorrow, I promise you. And as you are concerned that I shall roast him, I think you and your aunt should accompany me to Norwich to make sure I do not.'

'Both of us?'

'I think Mrs Whiteside might be glad of your presence. She seems a rather excitable lady and I am not skilled in dealing with distraught mothers.'

'Very well. We will put it to her.'

Augusta had been pacing the floor of the Windward House drawing room for hours, refusing to eat, drink or even sit down. As soon as she saw Pippa, she flung herself at her. 'There you are at last. Where is he? Where is my boy?'

'Calm yourself, Aunt,' Pippa said, leading her to a sofa and drawing her down beside her. 'Ben is to be let out tomorrow.'

'Tomorrow! Why not today? What have they done with him?'

Pippa looked up at Ash, who was standing looking down at them. 'Madam,' he said, coming to her rescue. 'Lord Borrowdale was concerned that the more reckless of the smugglers might attempt to free the prisoners by force and lives might be lost. He deemed it expedient to send them to Norwich gaol to await trial. I have been given a paper, signed by his lordship, consigning your son into my care, which I shall present at the castle tomorrow.'

Augusta raised a tear-streaked face. 'And they will let you have him?'

'Oh, undoubtedly. If you wish, you and Miss Kingslake may accompany me. We could do the return journey in a day if we set out early. But if we should be delayed, there are several good hotels that would serve for a night's lodging. I suggest we go prepared. And take something for your son to change into. He will undoubtedly be rather unkempt.' That was an understatement. From what he knew of Norwich gaol, the boy would have been confined in a filthy cell with dozens of others. Washing facilities and a change of clothes would certainly not be provided.

'Oh, thank you, thank you, sir. We will be ready whenever you say.'

'I will call for you at eight of the clock.' He bowed and left them without waiting for a servant to conduct him to the door.

'Oh, Philippa, you have no idea how my poor heart has been rent,' Augusta said. 'Every minute you have been gone has been torture and still Ben is not home. How the poor boy will survive another night in prison, I do not know. He is not strong… Wait until I see that brother of yours, I shall ring the loudest peal over him he has ever heard.'

'You mean Nat has not come home?'

'No. No one has seen hide nor hair of him, but when I asked Joe Sadler, he as good as admitted he had been with the smugglers.'

'He must be hiding up somewhere until the fuss has died down.'

'He could hide here as well as anywhere. If the Riding Officers didn't know he was involved, he would be safer acting normally and doing whatever he had planned to do today. Instead he chooses to disappear. I have no doubt he knows I am displeased with him and is too shamefaced to come home.'

'I wish you to be right, but I am truly worried he has come to some harm.'

'What does Sir Ashley say about it?'

'I have not told him. He is on the side of law and order and has no sympathy for the smugglers. I think he would like to see them all hanged or sent to the hulks.'

'But he went with you to obtain Ben's release…'

'Only because he believes Ben will tell him what he wants to know.'

'Ben knows nothing,' Augusta insisted.

'He must know what Nat was doing.'

'Oh, dear.' And she began to wail again. 'What are we to do? If I had known when I came to live in this godforsaken spot what it would lead to, I would never have come. We were snug and safe miles inland and that is where I wish we had stayed.'

This was something the good lady repeated almost daily and Pippa took no note of it, but she was very worried about Nat. Sir Ashley must not find out about him. But how could she warn her brother when she had no idea where he was?

Sir Felix was out when Ash returned to Narbeach Manor. 'He's rid off to the Customs House,' a stable boy told him when he followed his carriage and horses into the yard. Ash trusted his coachman, Tom Davies, to look after the horses, but it did no harm to let the other stable hands know how particular he was. 'There was a pitched battle goin' on there, an hour since. Had to call the militia in, they did.'

Ash decided to go and see what was happening for himself and asked for a horse to be saddled for him. He hurried indoors to change into a riding habit and buckle on his sword, then went back through the kitchen, grabbing a tart from the table and stuffing it into his mouth as he went. Once outside he sprang on the horse's back and cantered out of the yard and on to the lane in the direction of the quay.

It was obvious there had been a confrontation at the Customs House. Two men were sitting on the wayside nursing broken heads; a bale of tea had burst open and the leaves were scattered all over the road and a band of women were trying to scoop them up. The captain of the dragoons was talking to Sir Felix, both of them still mounted. There was blood on the captain's sword. Other soldiers had dismounted and were looking after their mounts. There was not a village man to be seen.

Ash rode up to the two riders. 'What happened?'

Sir Felix turned at the sound of his voice. 'Oh, you're back. Get the boy, did you?'

'No, he's to be released tomorrow. What happened here?'

'They stormed the Customs House and rescued the contraband.' He nodded towards the injured men. 'They battered those poor devils out of their senses.'

'You mean the smugglers?'

'Yes, who else?'

'Were any of them recognised?'

'No, so they say. The Captain here winged one of them, so we're making a search for an injured man, though no doubt his fellows will keep him well hid. As for the contraband, we'll search for that too, along with the rest that disappeared off the beach last night, though it's doubtful if we'll find anything.'

Ash was inclined to agree. Sir Felix did not seem in any great hurry to carry out the search. 'What can I do to help?'

'Nothing. You are too late.' He turned his horse towards home. Ash dismounted and led his horse over to the two Customs men, who were back on their feet. 'Is anyone looking after your injuries?'

'We'll go home,' one said. 'Our wives will see to them.'

'Did you know those who attacked you?'

'No, they wore scarves about their faces and hooded cloaks and it happened too quickly. We were eating our dinner when the door burst open and six men came in waving batons. They battered us about the head before we could even get to our feet. And though we shouted, no one came to our aid.'

'Well, they wouldn't, would they?' the other said. 'No doubt they took their share of the bounty for turning their backs.'

'What was it?' Ash asked. 'Tea? Brandy?'

'Some of it was. There was tobacco and silk, too. Now we've lost our prize. I said two was not enough to guard it and I were right, but Sir Felix would have it that it was enough. Why, I've known it take half an army to hold back the smugglers when their minds are made up to regain their goods.'

'I am sorry for you,' Ash said. 'Go home and have your injuries treated. If you remember anything else when you have had time to consider, I am staying with Sir Felix. Ask for me by name. Sir Ashley Saunders.' He gave them each a half guinea and returned to his horse.

Instead of riding straight back he chose to ride along the shoreline, looking for evidence. The tide had been in and out again since the landing and the sand was smooth. Where the tide did not reach the dunes were dry, held together with tough marram grass and weeds, but the wind had whipped away evidence of men's feet, horses' hooves and cart wheels. The smugglers had chosen a good night for their activities. He looked across at the marshes that ringed the western end of the village, but dared not venture on to them. A man who did not know his way could disappear without trace. So could the booty. If that was where it was hidden, it would have to be moved very soon. Goods needed to be taken inland to the markets to make a profit and the smuggling barons would not let it lie idle a moment longer than they had to. He resolved to come out that night and keep watch.

Pippa was sitting in the window of her bedroom, looking out at the sea. She could see Sir Ashley leading his horse along the beach. He was alone and looking at the ground.

She had been sitting there thinking ever since he left. The carriage ride and their conversation, which had appeared so light-hearted, had stirred up memories she thought she had managed to bury so deep they could never surface again. But she had been wrong. It wasn't that she still yearned for Edward as she had at the beginning; she had long ago convinced herself that if he could not love her as she was, red hair and all, he was not worth her anguish. But once that had been accomplished she was left with the humiliation, the whispers, the half-veiled hints that there must be something wrong with her. And everyone avoiding her.

She had learned to live with that, to accept her eccentricity and even exaggerate it, so that no one took any notice of the lone figure striding along the foreshore in fisherman's boots and a voluminous cloak that billowed out behind her, while the wind whipped her hair up into a fiery tangle. She could, of course, cut it off and wear a wig. Wigs were going out of fashion, but some still wore them. It was what Edward had wanted her to do.

Not only had he expected her to give up her writing, at which she had been successful enough to support her brother, aunt and cousin in comparative comfort since her parents had died and which she enjoyed, he had complained about the colour of her hair. He said his mother was superstitious and maintained red hair was the mark of the devil; if he married a red-haired woman, he would never prosper and a lot more nonsense that made her angrier and angrier, not only with his mother but with him for believing it. 'If the colour of someone's hair is so important,' she had stormed at him, 'then you had better find someone whose tresses you find more to your taste.'

She had expected him to pacify her and tell her it did not matter, that he loved her for what she was, but he had turned on his heel and left her. She had never seen him again and a little while later she heard he had left the country and his parents were blaming her.

Now Sir Ashley had brought it all back. He had said all the things she had hoped Edward would say, and he had said them in such a caring way, as if he knew she needed that reassurance. Were confirmed bachelors all so pleasant? Had they learned how to please without the need to propose marriage? Could they be friends as he had suggested?

It would be difficult if Ben really did know something about the smugglers or if Nat turned up and he was also involved. Her need to protect her brother and cousin would certainly come between any possible friendship. She would have to be especially careful when dealing with Sir Ashley. And that was a great pity because she liked him. He made her laugh and let her be herself. One day she might even tell him about Philip King. So deep in thought was she, she did not hear her aunt enter the room until she spoke.

'Philippa, Sir Felix has just sent round to ask us to supper.'

'I do not feel like going. I am tired and worried about Nat.'

'I know, dearest, but we must not let anyone see that and as Sir Felix and Sir Ashley have been so accommodating about Ben, I think it behoves us to make the effort. I could not bear it if they changed their minds because we snubbed them.'

Pippa sighed and got up. 'You are right. I will change my clothes.'

'Put on something attractive—that green silk with the quilted stomacher enhances your figure, you know. It is your best feature.' She pulled the gown out of the clothes press as she spoke and shook it out. 'And try to do something about your hair. I will send Babette in to help you when she has finished with me.'

'Yes, Aunt,' she said meekly, beginning to take off the blue wool. 'But if you think I will put up with Sir Felix mauling me, you are mistaken. He gives me the shivers. I cannot think what he sees in me.'

'Why, a very attractive young lady when she can put herself out to be so,' her aunt said. 'But I was not thinking of Sir Felix particularly.'

'Sir Ashley!' Pippa laughed. 'He is a lifelong bachelor, he told me so. We have decided to be friends.'

'That is something anyway. Usually you frighten men away with your top-lofty manner.'

'I am not top lofty. How can I be with a head like mine?'

'Very easily,' her aunt said. 'And I wish you would not adopt it. You do yourself no favours.'

'It would not work with Sir Ashley in any case. He would laugh at me.'

'That would be very uncivil of him and I am persuaded he is the epitome of good manners.'

'And all the more dangerous for that.'

'What do you mean, dangerous?'

'He is on the side of law and order. We must be

circumspect in what we tell him. If he thinks Ben or Nat are smugglers, he will feel he has to do his duty and hand them over to the law.'

'They are not. At least I am sure Ben is not. As for Nat, we might find out if he deigned to put in an appearance.'

'I am worried he might be hurt and unable to come home. I asked Joe to try to find out what has happened to him.'

'Nathaniel is a grown man. It is up to him what he does, but I wish he had not involved Ben.'

'You do not know that he did. Oh, Aunt, I wish there was an end to all this smuggling. It is ruining men's lives. Sir Ashley thinks so, which is why he is so against it. He would like to know who is at the back of it, the men who provide the money for the ships and the cargo. They are the real villains, not the poor inhabitants.'

'We all know that, but I am sure Ben does not know who they are and can tell Sir Ashley nothing. Now finish dressing. We must not be late. Sir Felix is a stickler for punctuality.' And with that she left to go to her own *toilette*.

Pippa dressed slowly. Her stomach was churning, partly on account of Sir Felix who repulsed her and had to be dealt with politely but firmly, and partly on account of Sir Ashley, who was far too perspicacious and far, far too attractive for her comfort.

Babette, her aunt's maid, arrived in time to help lace up her bodice over the stomacher and to brush her unruly hair into obedience. It took a great many pins, combs, ribbons and powder to achieve it, but she emerged a tall, elegant beauty with a long neck, a full bosom, decorously hidden beneath her corsage, and a small waist from which her full overskirt billowed out, embroidered with pale pink flowers. She rarely wore jewellery, but tonight she fetched out her mother's emeralds and fastened them about her neck where they lay on her throat, competing with her eyes in their greenness. Her aunt commented, 'You'll do', and led the way to their carriage.

Ash, who had returned late to the house, had only just managed to complete his *toilette* and go down to the drawing room to join his host before the ladies were announced. What he expected to see he was not at all sure, certainly not the vision of loveliness that quite took his breath away. Who would have believed the wild woman could be so tamed? She would turn heads in any drawing room. Politeness dictated he must acknowledge Mrs Whiteside first, which he did with admirable aplomb. Then he turned to Pippa and swept her the bow of a London courtier, putting his foot forwards and circling his arm before lowering it over his extended leg. 'Miss Kingslake, your obedient slave.'

'Hmph.' This from Sir Felix who certainly did not approve of this extravagance.

Pippa, her green eyes sparkling, returned this courtesy with a deep curtsy. 'Sir Ashley.' Then she turned and afforded the same to her host. 'Sir Felix, good evening.'

He bowed and seized her hand to kiss the back of it. 'Dear lady, you are in looks tonight. One would never guess that you had endured a carriage ride all the way to Wells and back today.'

'It took no endurance on my part,' she said, retrieving her hand. 'Sir Ashley's carriage is the last word in comfort.'

'And he has secured Ben's release,' Augusta added. 'We are to fetch him tomorrow, but no doubt Sir Ashley has told you that.'

'Yes, he has. I am indebted to him.' He indicated a sofa

with a wave of his hand. 'Please be seated. Supper will not be long. I ordered it for half past eight.'

Pippa, taking a seat alongside her aunt, glanced at the ormolu clock on the mantel. It wanted a minute to the half-hour. She sat silently counting the seconds.

'Supper is served, Sir Felix.' Even though she had been expecting it, the voice made Pippa jump, the footman had entered so silently.

Their host held out his hand to her and Pippa took it to rise and thus she went into the dining room on the arm of Sir Felix, leaving Ash to escort Mrs Whiteside.

The meal was superbly cooked and presented and the wines very fine, but Pippa hardly noticed what she was eating and drinking. She was acutely conscious of Sir Felix at the head of the table on her left and Sir Ashley on her right and the need to be circumspect. The atmosphere was fraught with tension. There was too much unspoken, too much that must not be spoken for normal conversation, though Sir Ashley did his best. He entertained them with stories of London gossip and what was going on at court and in Parliament, anything except what was most on their minds.

'We had some excitement while you were away today,' Sir Felix said in a pause in the conversation. 'The smugglers stormed the Customs House and rescued the contraband. Knocked the two guards clean out of their senses.'

'Oh, dear, I am sorry to hear that,' Pippa said. 'Did they recognise their assailants?'

'No, they do not seem able to remember anything about it, nor who was responsible. I do not suppose we shall ever trace the smuggled goods now.' It was said almost triumphantly.

'You think it has all been spirited away?' Ash asked him. 'They must surely wait until dark to do that.'

'My dear fellow, of course they must, but no one in his senses would attempt to stop them. They will have a hundred batmen escorting them, all armed with batons and muskets, ready to do battle with anyone attempting to interfere. It would take an army and we do not have an army. I have spoken to Captain Lovechild and he will not risk his dragoons on so unequal a fight. It is his opinion that it would be best to alert the people at the receiving end.'

'Do you know who they might be?' asked Pippa.

'No, but perhaps Sir Ashley does. He seems to be an authority on the trade.'

'I beg your pardon, Sir Felix,' Ash put in. 'I claim no such thing. I am as ignorant on the subject as you are', which was a statement that could mean something or nothing.. 'I am here to learn.'

To learn from poor Ben, Pippa thought, but said nothing. She would go with Sir Ashley and her aunt tomorrow and make sure her cousin did not implicate the local men, particularly Nat. Where was he? The longer he was away the more worried she became and her ambivalent feelings towards Sir Ashley were not helping. On the one hand she wished him and his probing away and on the other she knew he would be a staunch support in a crisis. Was there a crisis? She did not even know that.

When the lengthy meal ended the ladies repaired to the drawing room for tea, leaving the men to their port and cognac. 'I wonder if Sir Felix's brandy is duty-paid?' Pippa murmured, accepting a dish of tea from her aunt.

'I do not think he is at all enthusiastic about tackling the smuggling.'

'He is simply thinking of the danger to the dragoons if there is a pitched battle,' Augusta said. 'And perhaps he is trying to protect Nathaniel.'

'Protect his own supply, you mean.'

'Philippa!' her aunt protested. 'You must not say such things. He would be deeply offended. After all, he would be doing it for your sake.'

'Mine?'

'Do not be obtuse, my girl. It cannot have escaped your notice that he pays you very particular attention.'

'And I wish he would not. Short of telling him I find him repulsive, which would be cruel, I do not know how to put him off.'

'Why do you want to? Six and twenty you are, and unlikely to get another offer. If what you tell me is correct, Sir Ashley has already made it plain he is not interested. Who else will take you? Especially since you refuse to go to London in the Season.'

'I did that once and look what happened. No, Aunt, I am resigned to remaining single.'

Her aunt heaved a sigh. 'I have never met anyone as stubborn as you are.'

'It goes with my red hair,' Pippa said, trying to make a joke of it. 'Stubborn, fiery-tempered, not to be trusted...'

'Who said you were not to be trusted?'

'Lady Cadogan.'

'Oh, that.'

'Yes, that. Now, you will please me if you say no more on the subject.'

'Very well, though I do think—'

'No, Aunt,' Pippa stopped her. 'It is all behind me and that is how I would like it to stay.'

If Augusta was going to continue, she did not because the gentlemen joined them and she was kept busy dispensing tea to them at Sir Felix's request, and asking Ash about the latest London fashions on which he seemed more knowledgeable than Pippa would have expected for a bachelor. But then, she told herself, he had, on his own admission, had several mistresses. Was he a rake? Had his light flirtation with her in the coach been leading to a proposition? Why, oh, why had she told him she had had lovers? It must have given him quite the wrong impression.

Sir Felix settled down on the sofa next to Pippa, and though she edged away, he simply shifted closer. In the end she stood up and went over to a spinet that stood in the corner and began idly picking out notes with one hand.

'Do you play, Miss Kingslake?'

She turned to find Sir Ashley at her side. 'A little.'

'Then please do entertain us.' He regarded her quizzically with a slight smile. 'I think "Greensleeves" would be most appropriate? That is, if you know it.'

'Of course.' She pulled out the stool and sat down to play. He stood beside the instrument and began to sing, 'Alas, my love, you do me wrong to cast me off discourteously…' He had a mellifluous voice and sang effortlessly. She joined in and did not notice Sir Felix's scowl. Ash did and was amused by it. The man was as jealous as hell. He hoped, oh, he hoped that Miss Kingslake would not be so foolish as to accept the man's suit; he was far too old and set in his ways for someone as lively as Miss Kingslake. He smiled to himself as the song came to an end. He was being foolish; after all, what business was it of his whom the lady married?

The last dying notes and the flourishing bow Ash gave the pianist signalled the end of the evening and the ladies prepared to leave. Sir Felix gave orders for their carriage to be brought round to the front of the house.

'Ask my man to saddle a horse for me,' Ash told the footman who was being sent on this errand. 'I will ride beside the carriage.'

'It is very kind of you, Sir Ashley,' Pippa said. 'But not at all necessary. It is less than three miles…'

'I think it is,' he said. 'The smugglers might be abroad and I would see you safely home.'

'I think I should come, too,' Sir Felix said. 'One escort would not be enough to protect you against a mob. And I am a magistrate, after all. They will respect me.'

Ash doubted that. He suspected Sir Felix wanted to make sure he did not go out looking for smugglers after he left the ladies, which he had every intention of doing. It was a dark night, ideal for moving the contraband from wherever it was hidden and sending it on its way. He bowed in acquiescence, Sir Felix gave orders for his horse to be saddled, too, and thus the little cavalcade journeyed to Windward House without meeting a soul. All the village houses were in darkness, which could mean the occupants were in bed and keeping out of the way or they were gathering for the move.

When they arrived, the gentlemen saw the ladies safely into the house and the carriage driven round to the stables, then they returned to the Manor in silence. They had nothing to say to each other.

Chapter Three

Having had little or no sleep the night before, Pippa was dog-tired. She said goodnight to her aunt and went to her room, intending to go straight to bed. The maid had not drawn the curtains and she crossed the room do so; it was then she caught a glimpse of people moving about on the marshes. Her tiredness left her. Nat might be with them and she had to persuade him to come home before Sir Ashley found out what he was up to.

She hurried to her brother's room and fetched a pair of breeches, a shirt, a waistcoat, a coat and hat from his clothes press, which she took back to her own room.

Ten minutes later a red-haired young man crept from the house and made his way down to the marshes. There were crowds of men working there in almost total silence, some knee-deep in icy water, as they fetched kegs and oilskin-wrapped bundles from their hiding places among the creeks left by the receding tide and loaded them onto carts waiting on firmer ground.

Pippa joined them, trying to appear as though she belonged there, but all the time looking about for her brother. She knew most of the men, but dare not make herself known to them. If they thought she was spying on them, they would have no mercy.

'Nat Kingslake, what are you a-doin' here?' one of the men said, as she helped haul a keg into a cart. 'Thowt you'd a mind to mek yarself scarce.'

Pippa looked about her, expecting to see her brother until she realised the man was John Bristow, the blacksmith, and he was addressing her. She put on her gruffest voice. 'Why d'you say that? I'm one of the team, aren't I? I was on the beach when this lot came in.' She had only Joe's word that this statement was true.

'Yes, but I see yew jump into the boat and get rowed out to the *Sally Ann*. Do that mean the rest of the cargo hev bin landed some other place? That i'n't fair, that i'n't. That cargo were ours.'

Nat was not dead as she had feared he might be, but it was clear he was one of the smugglers. How to answer the blacksmith she did not know. If the smugglers thought Nat had betrayed them and kept a landing from them, they would be after his blood; on the other hand, if they realised who she was, they would be equally merciless. 'I didn't go on board,' she said, trying to sound like her brother. 'We waited until the coast was clear and the sailors rowed me back.'

'Why didn' yew go home then? Joe Sadler hev bin askin' all round after yew.'

'I couldn't. Sir Felix is there much of the time and he has a guest.'

'We know that. Yew'd do better goin' home and keepin'

an eye on the man for us. We want to know what he's up to.'

She could learn no more about Nat and the longer she stayed the greater the risk someone would penetrate her disguise, which hadn't been meant as a disguise but simply a convenience. 'Very well.' She nodded and turned to go home.

'We'll see yew in a day or two when yar've had time to find out more about that there guest,' he called after her.

The night was very dark and she had to pick her way carefully for fear of falling into one of the creeks or being sucked into the bog. It was not long before she realised she was being followed. Either they did not trust Nat or they had realised she was not her brother. She tried to hurry, but was hampered by the terrain.

'Oooh!' The cry was forced from her as she lost her footing and found herself slipping sideways into a water-filled creek. The coldness of it took her breath away and she floundered helplessly, trying to find her feet. The next minute she was grabbed about her waist from behind and hauled out. Her rescuer set her on her feet on firm ground, but he did not let go of her. She was shivering uncontrollably and it felt comfortingly warm against his broad chest.

'Little fool!' he murmured.

She knew the voice and twisted her head round to see Sir Ashley Saunders looking down at her. Had he recognised her? She had not seen him among the men, but that was not surprising; he was dressed in the rough clothes of a labourer. Spying, she presumed, but she could hardly condemn him for doing something she had been doing herself. 'I thank you for your timely rescue, sir,' she said, trying to sound masculine, but failing miserably on account of her chattering teeth.

If he was surprised to discover who it was he had rescued he gave no sign of it. 'My pleasure and privilege, Miss Kingslake,' he said, still holding her close, though she was soaking the front of his coat. She felt his warm breath on the back of her neck and it was enough to send trickles of heat down her spine, right down into her frozen toes. It did nothing to stop her shaking. Quite the opposite.

'You knew...'

'Of course. Slim young men do not usually have curves where you undoubtedly have them. And very delectable they are, too. But let us not waste time in idle chatter—you must go home and into the warm. Explanations can wait.' As he spoke he turned her round and slipping off his coat, put it round her shoulders, then he held it there, drawing her against his side while he guided her steps to higher ground. Neither spoke.

Pippa's shoes were full of water and her head full of questions. What was he doing out on the marshes when the land smugglers were busy? Why had he come alone instead of being supported by dragoons and Revenue men? And how could she explain away her own presence? Did she need to? Was it any of his business? And why, oh, why did the feel of his arms about her, have such a devastating effect on her body? It was not only the cold making her shake.

They reached Windward House and went round to the kitchen door, which she had left unbolted against her return. They stood on the step, facing each other. The air was fraught with tension, with unanswered questions and the realisation of the sheer absurdity of their situation. Knowing her aunt and everyone else were in their beds she could not invite him in and yet it seemed churlish to dismiss him out of hand. She took off his coat and handed it to him. 'Thank you for your escort, Sir Ashley. You had better put this on, you must be very cold.'

'Yes,' he agreed, smiling and slipping it on. 'And so must you. I suggest you go in and strip off those wet clothes before you catch your death of cold. I would not like to be held responsible for your demise. Go to bed. We have an early start in the morning.'

'You are still going to take us, then?'

'Of course. I do not go back on my word.'

'I will say goodnight, then.'

'Good morning would be more appropriate. It is past midnight.'

'Is it? How time flies.'

He laughed and, turning her about, opened the door with one hand and gave her a gentle push with the other. 'Much as I would like to prolong this delightful encounter, I must insist you go in and go to bed. I will return at eight o'clock and we shall see if you are well enough to go to Norwich.'

The next minute she was standing in the kitchen, lit only by the dying embers of the fire, and the door had been shut behind her. She heard his footsteps as he strode away and then she began to shiver so violently she could hardly light the candle she needed to see her to her bed. She needed something to warm her. She thrust a poker into the embers of the fire, filled a cup with wine and held the poker in it for several seconds. Then she drank the hot liquid down in one long gulp. She felt its warmth course its way down her throat and into her stomach and rather unsteadily climbed the stairs to her room, where she flung off Nat's clothes and climbed into bed. It took a little time, but the shivering ceased at last and she slept, her dreams filled with near-drownings and strong warm arms engulfing her.

* * *

It was her aunt's exclamation of dismay that woke her next morning. 'Philippa, whatever has happened? Has Nathaniel come home?'

Pippa opened one sleepy eye to see her aunt, fully dressed, surveying the heap of soaking wet clothes flung all over the floor. Reluctantly she sat up. 'No, I borrowed his clothes to go out looking for him.'

'Philippa!' Augusta was aghast. 'Is there no end to your foolishness? One of these days you will come to a bad end. Why are they so wet? I was not aware that it had rained.'

'It did not. I fell into a stream. Sir Ashley rescued me.'

'Sir Ashley,' her aunt repeated, as if unable to believe her ears. 'What was he doing out in the middle of the night? Did you arrange to meet him?'

'Certainly not. He was out spying on the smugglers. They were moving the cargo.'

The good lady sank onto the bed and stared at her niece in disbelief. 'What happened?'

'Nothing. He brought me home and I came to bed.'

'That's all?'

'Yes. What did you expect, that I would bring him in for a night of unbridled passion?'

'Do not be vulgar, Philippa. I meant if you were in Nathaniel's clothes, did he recognise you?'

'Of course he knew it was me. He wasn't fooled by my disguise for a moment.'

'Heaven help us! You will give him a disgust of you and he will cease to assist us over Ben. I wish you would think of the consequences when you do these hoydenish things.'

'On the contrary, I think it amused him. And he said he

would be here at eight o'clock, ready to go to Norwich, so if you will get off the bed, dear Aunt, I will dress.'

Augusta stood up. 'I am not sure you should come. You would do better to stay in bed today to get over your ordeal. I will make your excuses.'

'If you think you are going to leave me behind, you are mistaken, Aunt. I do not need to get over my ordeal because it was not an ordeal, but a slight mishap from which I have fully recovered. Now off with you. I shall be down directly.'

Her aunt sighed and left. Pippa scrambled into a padded petticoat and warm wool overskirt in a soft turquoise colour, and a red military style jacket. She tied her hair at the back of her neck with a narrow black ribbon and set a tiny turquoise hat on top of it. Slipping into her shoes, she made her way downstairs just as the knocker sounded and Teresa, the elder of their two maidservants, opened the door.

Pippa took a deep breath. That there were going to be repercussions from the night before, she did not doubt, but she had as much right to be out on the marshes at night as Sir Ashley had and if she was going to be quizzed, so was he. The trouble was she did not feel quite so courageous when face to face with him.

He stepped into the hall and swept her a bow, just as if they had not been soaking wet and in each other's arms barely hours earlier. He was looking incredibly handsome in a suit of heavy grey silk and a pale lemon waistcoat embroidered with tendrils of leaves in grey. His white cravat and stockings were pristine. What was more, unlike Pippa, he was bright-eyed and alert. She felt herself wilt under his steady gaze and it was an effort of will to pull herself together and answer him with a deep curtsy.

'Sir Ashley, good morning,' she said as her aunt joined her in the vestibule. 'As you see, we are ready.'

They each had a small portmanteau and Augusta had a change of clothes for Ben in another bag, which was stowed in the basket at the back of the vehicle. Then Sir Ashley helped them into their seats. The morning was cool and he had provided hot bricks and rugs, which he carefully arranged over their knees before ordering Tom Davies to proceed.

Pippa hoped nothing would be said about the night before, but in this she was thwarted because they had no sooner started to move than her aunt addressed their escort. 'Sir Ashley, I believe I owe you a debt of gratitude for looking after my niece last night when she was so unfortunate as to fall into a stream.'

Pippa's face turned scarlet.

'Mrs Whiteside, your gratitude is unnecessary,' he said, looking at Pippa with a faintly amused smile. 'I am sure Miss Kingslake would have extricated herself eventually. Besides, she has already thanked me.'

'She should never have gone out at night alone,' Augusta continued, adding to Pippa's mortification. 'There are dangers all around.'

'True,' he murmured. 'But I am persuaded Miss Kingslake takes no account of danger. She told me she often goes out alone.'

Augusta gave Pippa a reproachful look, while continuing to address Sir Ashley. 'I am afraid her parents brought her up far too liberally. They made no distinction between her and her brother and, as they had no other playmates, they did everything together.'

'Ah,' he said and to Pippa there seemed to be a deal of meaning in that little word. She wished her aunt had not mentioned Nat. 'I conclude Mr Kingslake takes no note of danger either.'

'They are as bad as each other. To give Philippa her due, after my dear brother and his wife died, she felt she must look out for Nathaniel and curb his mischief and to do that she must follow in his footsteps. It has given her a love of adventure that is not confined to books.'

'Aunt, I never told you that.' Pippa found her voice at last.

'But it is true, is it not? You have often taken the blame for a misdemeanour of Nathaniel's. Do not think I have not noticed.'

Ash turned to Philippa. She was looking decidedly uncomfortable and he began to feel a tiny bit sorry for her, but he was not going to let her off the hook just yet. 'And was that what you were doing last night, protecting your brother by impersonating him?'

'No,' she said. 'You said yourself I am nothing like a man.'

'So I did.' He smiled at the memory and she knew why he was smiling. She felt the colour flare in her cheeks.

'Then you have your answer.'

'I do not think so,' he said. 'Why were you there?'

'My aunt has told you. A love of adventure. Call it curiosity.'

'Curiosity, my dear Miss Kingslake, was the death of the cat.'

'That is a silly saying. And I am not a cat.'

'Ah, then I need not fear your claws.'

A 'hmph' from the other corner of the carriage reminded him that they were not alone and Mrs Whiteside did not appreciate his teasing. He stopped smiling and became serious. 'What did you hope to learn?'

'How it was done, how the cargo was dispersed. I had no idea it was such a huge enterprise. I thought it was simply a barrel here, a keg there, a few packets of tea to be distributed among the local population. Instead it is a whole caravan of carts, mules and men moving in the dark.'

He did not believe she had been so ignorant. An enterprise such as had taken place the previous night could not help but be known to everyone, including Sir Felix and the Revenue men. Pretending ignorance was much more comfortable, your conscience need not trouble you and, unless you were as foolish as Philippa Kingslake, you stayed indoors when the 'gentlemen' were about.

'And what did the men say to you when they saw you among them?' he asked.

She wondered if he had heard what John Bristow had told her. 'They did not speak,' she said. 'They needed their breath for the task in hand.'

'Pity. So you did not discover what happened to your brother?'

'My brother, sir, is from home. I believe I have already told you that.'

'So you did, but you did not say where he was.'

'He is at sea.'

'At sea?' he queried, one eyebrow raised.

'Why not?' she said, ignoring her aunt's startled gasp. 'We are a sea-faring family. My father was a naval captain before he retired on half-pay and my mother frequently went on voyages with him. And sometimes my brother and I went with them. Is it any wonder that Nat should want to follow in our father's footsteps?'

'You mean he is a naval man?'

'No, but he goes out with the fishermen and sometimes signs on to a merchantman.'

Augusta opened her mouth to speak but, catching Pippa's warning look, subsided into silence, much to Pippa's relief. She dare not look at Sir Ashley, who must surely detect her prevarication in her eyes. She was not used to being deceitful, hated it, especially now when Sir Ashley who was doing his best to help them. But it was necessary. He did not hold with smuggling and if he knew Nat was well and truly involved, he would have no hesitation in tracking him down and giving him over to the law along with the village men who acted as tub carriers and batmen. Each had a financial stake in the safe delivery of the cargo and it was more than they could earn legitimately in six months. Even though Nat was not among them this time, she did not want them caught because most of them had families who would be destitute without their bread winners. In one way she was glad she had fallen in the ditch because helping her had distracted Sir Ashley from following them.

Knowing he was watching her, she turned her head to look out at the countryside. There were meadows with cattle and horses grazing, but the animals were mostly sheep—thousands of them, with their young lambs frolicking about them. It always lifted Pippa's spirits to see them. They were usually a promise of summer and better times to come, but with the wheat flattened by hailstones and other fields still the dark brown of tilled earth, their crops barely visible, it did not look as if this year's harvest was going to be any better than the years before it. No wonder the men needed to smuggle.

The coachman pulled up at an inn in Fakenham to rest the horses. The ladies used the opportunity to refresh their *toilette* and sit over a cup of tea which Ash ordered for them before he left to speak to Tom about their onward journey.

'Philippa,' her aunt burst out, as soon as they were alone. 'Why did you tell Sir Ashley that Nathaniel was at sea? It would have been better to tell him the truth. He has been so very accommodating over Ben, I am sure he would help.'

'Aunt, it is the truth. John Bristow said he saw him jump into the longboat when the dragoons came onto the beach. He was rowed out to the smugglers' ship.'

'John Bristow spoke to you?'

'Not exactly. He thought he was talking to Nat and wondered how he had come ashore again. He wanted me—I mean Nat—to find out what Sir Ashley was up to in Narbeach…'

'Philippa, this is all becoming far too involved. Let us concentrate on fetching Ben home. If Nat has gone to sea, he will find his own way home eventually. And we will naturally not spy on Sir Ashley. That would be a poor way to repay his kindness.'

Pippa sighed. She had no intention of telling the blacksmith anything about Sir Ashley, even though she realised it would be a way of getting rid of him and his curiosity. His fate if she did that was too terrible to contemplate.

'We will go to Fairfields and change these horses for the bays,' Ashley was saying to Tom as he watched the horses drink from the leather buckets Tom had filled with water from the inn's trough. 'I have no wish to leave my prize cattle at a common inn. It is only a few miles out of our way and we will easily reach Norwich by the middle of the afternoon.'

'Will we return tonight, Sir Ashley? It will be a long journey for the ladies and will be full dark before we arrive back at Narbeach, even if you get your business done quickly.'

'I was thinking the same thing, Tom. I will suggest we come back as far as Fairfields and stay there tonight.' He gave a wry smile; it seemed even his coachman knew his errand and he supposed every inhabitant of Narbeach did too. He wondered idly if an attempt might be made to stop him fulfilling it. On the other hand, while he was going after one mischievous lad, they would be able to distribute their cargo without hindrance. He hadn't warned the Customs and Excise, as he should have done, because he did not want a battle in which the villagers might be killed or injured, if not arrested and hanged. It was not the villagers he was after. And there was another reason, which he was loath to admit and it had something to do with how deeply involved Miss Kingslake was and how much he wanted to save her from her own folly. 'If they agree, of course. Miss Kingslake may have other ideas.'

Miss Kingslake was a puzzle. That she was a hoyden, he did not doubt, but he was also sure there was more to it than that. He suspected she was trying to shield the smugglers. Was it only on account of her young cousin, who would be little help to him, or was her brother also involved? She was certainly reluctant to talk about him. Was he really at sea? If so, what was his business if it wasn't smuggling? The contraband had to be brought from France or Holland before it could be landed in England and Kingslake might be one of the crew or even the agent who bought the goods, trusted by the man with the money to strike a good bargain. Did Miss Kingslake know that or even suspect it? He hoped she did not.

He wanted to believe her innocent. He found her disturbingly attractive even when dressed in her brother's clothes.

Especially then. Shivering with cold and fright, she still had the spirit to stand up to him. There was between them, not sympathy, she would hate that, but a kind of empathy which he would never have believed possible a few days before. He had come to Narbeach in full control of himself and his mission, determined to do his duty and bring the smugglers to justice, and instead had found himself wavering between exasperation and tenderness. No woman had ever come close to disarming him like that before and yet she had done it in the space of forty-eight hours. The sooner the business of the smugglers was concluded, the sooner he could go back to London, hand in his report and go back to the life he was used to.

The horses were ready to go on and he went into the inn to fetch the ladies and a few minutes later they were on their way again. No one spoke—they seemed to have run out of things to say—and Augusta was snoring lightly with her hat tipped forwards over her eyes, and neither liked to waken her. But when the carriage turned off the main road onto a narrow track, Pippa became alarmed. 'Sir Ashley, where are you taking us? We have left the Norwich road.'

'A slight diversion, Miss Kingslake,' he said. 'The horses must be changed and as Fairfields, my home, is nearby, I wish to do it there. I prefer my own animals to those the inns provide. Besides, we have had no time to send on ahead for a change to be made ready. While it is being done, we shall have nuncheon. You do not object, do you?'

'No,' she said, doubtfully. 'But my aunt is very anxious on account of Ben, she will be impatient at any delay.'

'We will soon make up the time with fresh horses and your young cousin is safe enough for now.'

The carriage turned into a wide drive and Pippa caught

her first glimpse of his home. Surrounded by parkland, it was not as large as some country seats, but impressive for all that. It was a square three-storey building with a white-columned portico and a great double oak door in the centre of its facade. A crenulated balustrade almost hid its roof from which tall twisted chimneys rose against the sky. Ivy clung to its walls and framed its gothic windows, which gleamed in the spring sunshine. Before it was a wide carriage sweep in the middle of which was a statue of a soldier on a prancing horse.

'My grandfather, the Earl of Ashley,' he said, noticing her gaze upon it. 'I was named for him.'

'But you are not a peer?'

'No, my father was a younger son. I inherited this house from him, but not the title. My uncle has that along with a much larger country seat in Hertfordshire.'

'And your mother, is she still living?'

'No, she died giving me birth. I was raised by a succession of nurses and governesses, none of whom stayed very long. I no sooner grew to love them and depend on them than they were gone for one reason or another.'

'That must have been very upsetting for you,' she said, her heart going out to the lonely little boy.

'I soon got over it.'

'Who taught you about women?'

Understanding what she meant, he laughed. 'A chambermaid. I was fourteen at the time and she was several years older, but she was kind to an ignorant boy. She was sent away when my father found out what was going on.'

'Perhaps that is why you have had no lasting relationship with a woman,' she said thoughtfully. 'You cannot trust yourself to trust.'

'You may be right.'

They had come to a stop before the door and Augusta woke with a start. 'Where are we?' she asked, sitting upright and hastily adjusting her hat.

'We are at Fairfields, Sir Ashley's home,' Pippa explained. 'Sir Ashley is going to change the horses here.'

'I know you are in haste, dear lady,' Ash said, jumping down and turning to hand her out. 'But we shall make good time with a new set of horses and I am sure you will feel better for a little refreshment.'

He turned to help Pippa out, but she was already standing on the gravel gazing up at the impressive façade. The carriage was driven away and he offered each lady an arm to escort them inside.

The door opened before they reached it and a butler stood ready to welcome them. 'Sir Ashley, I heard the carriage arrive. I did not expect you...'

'I am sorry, Andrew, there was no time to warn you, but we are not here to stay. We are on the way to Norwich and stopped to change the horses. Will you ask Mrs Bellamy to find us something light to eat and then we must be on our way again. And send one of the maids to conduct the ladies upstairs to refresh themselves.'

Pippa looked about her. They were in a wide hallway. In front of her was an impressive carved oak staircase, which led to a gallery that ran round three sides of the hall. She tilted her head upwards. The ceiling, three storeys up, was a glass dome. Each section was a different colour and the sun shining through it cast intricate patterns on the tiled floor at her feet.

'You like it?' he asked with a smile.

'Oh, yes, it is beautiful.'

'Would you like to see the rest of the house while we are waiting?'

'Oh, yes, please. If we have time.'

A maid appeared with a jug of hot water and curtsied. 'Go with Betsy,' Ash said. 'She will show you where you can refresh yourselves. Come down when you are ready and we shall have a quick tour of the house before nuncheon.'

'Sir Ashley, I beg you to remember we are not paying a social call,' Augusta said. 'Any other time I would be charmed to see over your house, but today I am in ferment over my darling boy.'

'Dear lady, of course you are, but we shall soon make up the time and you cannot go all day without sustenance.'

There was nothing she could do but acquiesce and she followed the maid and Pippa up to one of the bedrooms where they were able to tidy themselves before returning downstairs. Their repast was not yet on the table and Ash made good his promise to show them round. Pippa would have loved to dawdle, to examine the furniture and draperies, the pictures and carvings, to admire the views from the windows, to ask innumerable questions, but, aware of her aunt's impatience, the tour was a swift one.

'You have a lovely home,' Pippa said when they were seated at the table, which was heaped with food, in the dining room. Sir Ashley's cook had worked wonders in the time available.

'Yes. I have a good and loyal staff who keep everything as I like it.'

'But no wife,' Augusta put in, attacking a cold chicken leg.

'No. I have no wife,' he admitted.

'Sir Ashley is a lifelong bachelor, Aunt,' Pippa told her.

Not for the world would she divulge what he had said to her in the coach. 'He is, I believe, too particular and no lady lives up to his ideals.'

'Is that so?' the good lady queried. 'But do you not miss the love and companionship a good wife can bring to a man?'

'He can get love and companionship without marrying,' Pippa said before he could answer. It sounded very much as if her aunt were matchmaking and it embarrassed her so much she said the first thing that came into her head and immediately regretted it.

'Philippa!' her aunt exclaimed.

'I beg your pardon, Sir Ashley,' she said. 'Sometimes I forget I am a lady.'

He turned to look at her. She was very fetching in her turquoise and red. He was especially coming to like her flaming hair and he certainly admired her wondrous green eyes. If he looked into them too long, he was sure he would be mesmerised out of his senses. 'Today, you look every inch the lady,' he said with a smile that told her he was remembering the time when she did not.

'Thank you, Sir Ashley.' She lowered her gaze to her plate and concentrated on the food on it: a cold chicken leg, a slice of ham, a wedge of game pie and a green salad, simple fare but superbly cooked and presented. She ate some of it, but her stomach was churning so much she found it difficult to swallow. Sir Ashley Saunders was making her behave like a schoolgirl, saying outrageous things and blushing like a turkey cock. For six years she had been cool, calm, practical, concentrating on her writing, putting all her energies into producing adventure stories. Now she was in the middle of an adventure herself and this time it was real. And what was worse, she had no idea how it would end. The control she liked to have over her plots had deserted her. Even her tongue was running away with her.

The meal came to an end, the carriage was brought to the door, this time drawn by a pair of bays, and they resumed their journey. Philippa sat in the corner of the roomy interior and tried to make herself as small as possible. Her determination not to be drawn into any more indiscreet utterances and her lack of sleep the night before had the effect of making her doze. Ash watched and smiled.

'She is exhausted, poor dear,' Augusta whispered. 'She takes everyone's burdens on her own shoulders. It is a wonder they don't break under the strain. When my husband died, she was such a comfort to me, coming to stay and helping to look after Ben when I truly could not face the world. And then when her own parents were so tragically drowned, she tried hard to manage on her own, looking after the house and being a second mother to her brother. I could see what a struggle it was for her and so I came to Narbeach to live. I try to curb her enthusiasms, but…' She shrugged.

'I am sure she appreciates your efforts.' He paused to glance in Pippa's direction. The even rise and fall of her chest told him she slept. 'I am surprised she has not married.'

'We hoped for it. There was a young man. I should perhaps not tell you this, but you have been so kind to us, I feel I can trust you.'

'Oh, indeed you may.'

'When she was nineteen I accompanied her to London for the Season. I felt I owed her that. She met a young gentleman who was eminently eligible. He escorted her out and about and even proposed. She was so happy. But he changed his mind before an announcement could be made. I think his parents may have had something to do with it.'

He found himself remembering their conversation about red hair. 'The man was a fool. What reason did he give?'

'If he gave one, she did not tell me what it was. We returned home and that was the end of that.'

'There must have been others.'

Augusta sighed. 'There might have been, but she would not venture to the capital again and became so eccentric she put the local young gentlemen off. And now there is Sir Felix.'

'She would not consider him, would she?' A faint stirring in the corner stopped him from going on. He should have felt guilty about discussing the young lady like that, but he did not. It helped him to understand her. He did not doubt her unconventional behaviour masked a deep hurt. How could anyone do that to a beautiful young girl in the throes of her first love?

'Here we are at the gates of Norwich,' he said, raising his voice above the whisper it had been. 'Not long now. I suggest we go to the Maid's Head, where I shall leave you and go to the castle alone. I am persuaded you would be overset to see your son in such a place. I will bring him to you there. Do you agree?'

Augusta took her cue from him and answered loudly, 'Thank you, Sir Ashley. Ben will be able to change into the clothes I have brought for him at the inn.'

Pippa was fully awake by the time they rattled through the gate and into the noise and bustle of England's second city. Carriages, carts, tumbrels and riders filled the roads and pedestrians hurried along the footways, pushing their way through the throng. The city was a hub of commerce from the quays where sailing ships anchored to discharge their cargos, the cloth-weaving sheds, the breweries and leather works, to the markets and shops selling everything a person could want or need. All three were familiar with it; it was where most of their important shopping was done, but today they were more concerned with reaching the castle, which dominated the town. Set on its own steep hill it was huge and dark and frightening, an awful warning to lawbreakers.

They pulled up into the yard of the Maid's Head and Sir Ashley escorted the ladies inside and bespoke a room for them. But Pippa was not inclined to be left behind while he went to the castle. The outside was perfectly familiar to her, but she had never been inside and wanted to see the conditions in which the prisoners were kept. If the smuggling hero of her book were to be captured, she needed to know how to describe it and how difficult it would be to escape. When he was leaving, she insisted on accompanying him.

'You will not like it,' Ash told her. 'And I do not want to have a swooning woman on my hands.'

'I have never swooned in my life,' she retorted. 'And I do not want to be shielded from life's unpleasantness.'

'Why not? Do you enjoy squalor?'

'Certainly not,' she said, walking beside him, trying to keep up with his brisk pace. 'But if we shut our eyes to these things, how can we remedy them?'

'You wish to remedy them?'

'Of course. Don't you?'

'I am a man.'

'Do you know, I never noticed that,' she said, laughing.

He chuckled. 'And for all your pretence at being different, you are all woman. Tell me how you propose to remedy the squalor in the prison?'

'By drawing people's attention to it,' she said promptly. 'The written word, Sir Ashley, repeated until someone takes notice.'

'Commendable,' he said. 'But first you need to know your words will be read and taken note of. People do not like being preached at.'

'I know that.' She stopped speaking to dodge a woman with a flower basket hurrying in the opposite direction. Ash threw a sixpence into the basket and picked up a posy of violets and primroses, which he presented to Pippa with a little bow.

'They will make the dungeons smell a little sweeter,' he said.

'Thank you.' She put the posy to her nose, half sad, half glad that the conversation had been brought to an end. Edward had decried her writing as unladylike and she wondered if Sir Ashley also thought that. After telling her she was all woman—whatever he had meant by that—she did not want him to change his mind. This man, this handsome, all-seeing man, was breaking down the walls she had built around herself. She knew that could be dangerous and lead to more heartbreak, but she could not seem to help herself.

They climbed the hill and entered the castle. Ash stated their business to the janitor and they were shown to the chief warder's room. A fire burned brightly and there were the remains of a meal on the table: a plate of crumbs, a jug of beer, a pewter pot, a clay pipe, a paper of tobacco. Of the warder there was no sign. 'Wait here,' their escort said before leaving them. 'He is doing his rounds. He'll be back direc'ly.'

'Shall we go and look for him?' Pippa asked after several minutes. She did not wait for a reply, but opened the door and went out into the corridor and Ash had perforce to follow. Assuming the cells were in the dungeons, she walked deeper into the castle until she found some stone steps leading downwards and from which issued a babble of noise: shouting, unintelligible singing, groans, raucous laughter. The sound was accompanied by the most appalling smell. Pippa put her posy to her nose and kept going.

'Miss Kingslake, there is no need for you to go down there,' Ash said, but she took no notice and he kept after her.

The farther down they went, the darker it became. At the bottom of the stairs was a corridor, lit by torches, and it was lined with cells, cells filled with humanity—some of them were stretching their arms out through the bars towards her. 'Ben!' she called out. 'Ben Whiteside, are you here?'

There was no answer except an echo caused by everyone who had heard her words repeating them in a cacophony of sound. She stepped farther into the foetid atmosphere and tried again.

'He is not here,' Ash said, appalled by what they were witnessing, and ashamed, too, to think that any human being could treat another like that. 'No doubt they are holding him in a sweeter place considering he has not yet been tried and convicted. Come away, please. You have surely seen enough.'

They turned and retraced their steps. At the top of the stairs they encountered a fat man with a huge bunch of keys on his belt and a lantern in his hand.

'Are you the Chief Warder?' Ash asked.

'I am, sir, I am. Want to look at the condemned prisoners, do you? It will cost you a shilling.'

'No.' Ash pulled Lord Borrowdale's letter from his pocket. 'I have papers here for the release of Benjamin Whiteside into my custody.'

'Benjamin Whiteside?' the man said, scratching his head. 'I never heard of one by that name, but that don' signify, use all sorts of names, they do.'

'He was sent here by Lord Borrowdale with six other smugglers,' Ash said. 'It was only yesterday.'

'Oh, that lot,' the man said. 'They got away. The wagon fell into an ambush in Bawdeswell Woods. The escorts came here, bleedin' like stuck pigs to report what happened. There's a price on their heads now, so if you come across that there Benjamin Whiteside, you turn him in.'

'Oh, no,' Pippa murmured, feeling herself sagging and doing her best to remain upright. 'Poor Aunt Augusta.'

Ash gave the man a shilling and, putting his arm about Pippa's shoulders, led her away. Once outside she stopped and took huge gulps of fresh air. He held her. His red-haired beauty was not as formidable as she thought she was; she was standing in his encircling arms, leaning into his chest, wanting comfort. All he could do was stand with her until she recovered her composure, while the business of the street went on around them. And he did not care how long it took.

At last she pulled herself away and he felt suddenly cold, as if an east wind swirled round them. The situation had become even trickier than it had been before and he was unsure how he could resolve it without hurting her and those she loved—it was strange how important that had become. He put his finger under her chin and lifted her face to his. 'Better now?'

'Yes, thank you.'

He could not help it, the tilt of her head, her emerald eyes searching his, her slightly parted lips were an invitation he could not resist. He bent his head and, oh, so gently rested his mouth on hers. It was featherlight, but not in the least tentative. It told her he was there for her, that he understood, that she need not fear him and that he would not walk away.

Chapter Four

The journey back to Fairfields was a silent one; even Augusta's sobbing had dwindled to an occasional sniff. Ash was trying one scheme after another in his head, but not deciding on any, and Pippa was savouring that kiss which she could still taste on her lips, so gentle, so caring, giving not taking. Edward had never kissed her like that. Edward had been clumsy and would have gone further if she had not stopped him. But was that simply the difference between Edward's immaturity and Ash's greater experience, that Ash knew how to rouse a woman and it really meant nothing at all? If she had been more experienced herself, she might have been able to tell, but here she was six years later still a spinster, dreaming of something she could not have. She would do better to think of poor Aunt Augusta and try to comfort her.

'Do not despair, Aunt,' she said, reaching for her aunt's hand. 'Why, we might even find him at home ahead of us.'

'But he cannot stay there,' Augusta cried. 'The Revenue

men will come and arrest him. We shall have to go into hiding.'

'That would put you beyond the law yourself, madam,' Ash said. 'I would not recommend it.' He paused because she looked as though she were about to burst into tears again and Miss Kingslake was looking at him as if she would like to thrust a dagger into his heart. 'But do not despair, it has not come to that yet,' he went on. 'If the boy was freed against his will and forced to go with the others, we may yet save him.' He had tried to explain this when he told her why Ben had not returned with them from the castle. She had spread Ben's clean clothes out on the bed, ready for him, and had been loath to leave, as if her boy would find her in Norwich, but they had persuaded her at last and she had reluctantly folded everything back into the bag and taken it out to the waiting carriage.

They arrived back at Fairfields in a very different mood from the one they had been experiencing when they left there that afternoon. Then there had been hope, now there was very little. Ash's cook was expecting them this time and had gone to great lengths to impress the ladies. And their bedchambers had been prepared with crisp sheets, warm blankets and plenty of hot water.

Pippa appreciated this and was at pains to express it, but there was little conversation over the meal. What there was centred round Ben's disappearance and what they could do to find him, and wondering who the other six might be. Pippa, who had only seen them in the dark, could not say. She wondered why Sir Ashley continued to help them; he must surely have given them up as a lost cause by now. Here they were, two foolish women in league with smugglers, and they were being entertained royally. She was grateful, but wondered what recompense he would demand and when it would be demanded. Information or something more personal? Had that kiss been a prelude to something else? If he began all his liaisons like that, gently and without pressure, was it any wonder the ladies flocked to accommodate him? Why did the prospect of that put her insides in such a turmoil?

When the meal came to an end, the ladies excused themselves and said they would retire early. Ash escorted them up to their rooms. Stopping outside Augusta's, he bowed and took her hand. 'Goodnight, Mrs Whiteside. Things will look brighter in the morning. If you think of that you will sleep.'

She thanked him, kissed Pippa and went into the room, shutting the door behind her.

'Poor thing,' Pippa said as they moved along the corridor. 'I do not know how to comfort her.'

'I am persuaded you are already a great comfort to her, Miss Kingslake, but who comforts you?'

She looked startled for a moment, remembering that fleeting kiss, and was tempted to say, 'You do', but decided that would be much too forward of her. 'I do not need it,' she said.

'Everyone does at some point in their lives,' he said quietly.

'My aunt has always been someone I can turn to,' she said. 'Now, when she needs me, I have failed her. If I had not filled Ben's head with adventure stories, if I had kept a better watch on him, I might have persuaded him not to go down to the beach.'

Was that why she had been hiding in the sand—she had been trying to rescue her cousin? Why had she not told him so? Did she not trust him? 'Ben is fifteen years old and no doubt he considers himself a man,' he said. 'You cannot hold yourself responsible for his mischief.'

'But I do. And how to put it right, I do not know.'

'We will think of something,' he said. Saving adventurous boys and stubborn women was not part of his remit, but he knew he had to try.

They had stopped outside her door. She turned to say goodnight. Instead of sweeping her a bow, he took her hand and raised it to his lips, looking into her face over their joined hands. 'You are a good woman, Miss Philippa Kingslake,' he said, releasing her. 'You deserve a good man.'

She did not know what to make of that and was still puzzling over it when she was in her room with the door shut between them.

Ash returned downstairs to sit alone in the book room with a glass of cognac. Never before had duty and desire clashed so clamorously as it was doing now. Until now, given the choice between his mistress of the day and his commitment to the Piccadilly Gentlemen, there had been no contest; the mistress had to put up with his frequent disappearances on society business and he always returned with a costly gift to compensate her. This was different. Miss Philippa Kingslake was a woman of undoubted charm, but she was not mistress material. And it was not only her charm that attracted him, but her selflessness, her essential goodness. She seemed incapable of seeing ill in anyone and yet her cousin—and, he did not doubt, her brother—were like to destroy her if she insisted on helping them. It behoved him to extricate her and then disappear from her life. He was not the good man she deserved, and it had been wrong of him to kiss her like that.

He went to his desk and wrote his daily report for the Gentlemen. It was untypically skeletal. Until he resolved his dilemma to the satisfaction of his conscience, he kept most of it back. Whether the others would read between the lines he did not know. Explanations would have to come later. He dusted the ink and sealed the paper before laying it on the table in the vestibule for one of the servants to take to the mail, and then he went up to bed.

They set out immediately after breakfast the next morning. Augusta was dry-eyed, but white as a ghost; Pippa did not look much better. When they reached the Bawdeswell crossroads, where the prisoners had been freed, Augusta insisted they stop. 'Sir Ashley, please make enquiries to see if anyone witnessed the incident and can say which direction the prisoners took after they were set free.'

He complied, asking the women grouped about the village well filling their containers and then at the inn, though he knew perfectly well that no one would dare tell him for fear of reprisals. He returned to the carriage none the wiser. 'They were all blind or looking the other way,' he told the ladies. 'Let us go on. Ben might already be at home waiting for you.' But he was not and Augusta's brief upturn in spirits plummeted again.

There were men missing from their homes, Pippa discovered, when she went into the village the following day. 'Gone to market,' she was told when she asked after them, or 'visiting relations in the shires'. Pippa assumed they had either been one of those arrested or were escorting the contraband inland. There was no sign of Ben. Or Nat. And there were posters fastened to trees and walls offering a reward for news of the whereabouts of the seven escapees. The Customs did not like losing prisoners.

To add to her problems Sir Ashley Saunders was still staying at the Manor. He muddled her head until she did not know what to think. Friend or foe? Her earlier decision that he was her foe teetered when she thought about his kindness and his kisses. Especially his kisses. Was she a fool to trust him?

As if to conjure him up, he came riding towards her on the mount he had borrowed from Sir Felix. Reaching her, he dismounted and led the horse towards her.

Her heart began to beat frantically and she had to take a firm hold of herself to face him. In a brown riding coat, cream breeches and shining leather boots, he filled her vision to the exclusion of all else. 'Miss Kingslake, your obedient.' He was looking at her almost as if he had heard her unspoken thoughts about him.

'Good morning, Sir Ashley.' She was surprised there was no detectable quiver in her voice. 'Have you any news of the escaped prisoners?'

'None, I am afraid. Have you?'

'No. I was on my way home. I do not like to leave my aunt too long. She is distraught and her head is full of dreadful images, the least of which is that Ben has gone abroad and she will never see him again.'

He turned to accompany her, throwing the horse's reins over his shoulder, so that it plodded along behind them. 'I think that unlikely. My own feeling is that the fugitives must have a safe house somewhere. If only we knew where it was.'

'If you did find out, what would you do?' she asked. 'Have them all re-arrested?'

'It is what a law-abiding citizen should do,' he said

slowly. He gave a short bark of a laugh. 'But it would undoubtedly make me very unpopular hereabouts.'

'I had not thought you would be bothered about popularity.'

'There is only one person, or perhaps two, whose good opinion I would have and keep,' he murmured.

She looked sharply at him, but did not comment. 'What shall we do now?' she asked.

'I think it would be wisest not to show too much curiosity. We may learn more by appearing indifferent. Your cousin, wherever he is, is undoubtedly being looked after. If we pry too closely, he might be put at risk.'

'I expect you are right,' she said with a sigh.

They arrived at Windward House and she invited him in for refreshment. He accepted and tethered his horse at the gate before following her inside.

'Have you news of Ben?' Augusta demanded as soon as the courtesies had been performed and he was seated on one of their sofas with a cup of tea in front of him.

'None, ma'am, I am afraid. But do not despair. He will turn up. I will leave no stone unturned to locate him.'

He had been talking to Sir Felix over breakfast, but that gentleman had been sanguine. 'Lord Borrowdale should have sent them by a more roundabout route and with a heavier guard,' he had said. 'I could have foretold what would happen. And now we have lost the boy and the good opinion of the ladies at Windward House.'

'And also six smugglers and the contraband from the Custom House,' Ash had reminded him because he seemed to have forgotten them.

'Those, too. Captain Lovechild and his dragoons are out searching for them, but I doubt they will be found. No one will inform on a smuggler.' It had been said with just a hint of satisfaction. Ash was more than ever convinced Sir Felix knew what was going on and condoned it, even if he was not actively involved. But in exposing the man, he ran the risk of endangering Ben and losing the good will of Mrs Whiteside and Miss Kingslake. He was in a cleft stick.

'Sir Felix tells me the dragoons are out combing the countryside for the fugitives,' he told the ladies.

'Oh, dear, I wish we could find Ben first.'

'I still have Lord Borrowdale's authorisation to take him into my custody,' he said. 'I shall make use of it if I can.'

'We are most grateful to you, Sir Ashley,' Augusta said. 'Are we not, Philippa?'

Pippa, who had been gazing out of the window across the yard, puzzled by what she saw, was brought back with a start. 'What? Oh, yes, we are in your debt, sir.'

He rose to take his leave and Pippa accompanied him to the gate, walking between him and the yard and keeping up a flow of conversation about the calmness of the sea, which had been so rough two nights before, and how the clouds were like ships in full sail, forcing him to look seawards. As he picked up the reins he turned to bid her good day and was puzzled when she suddenly skipped round him and he was forced to make a half-turn in order to face her.

'Good day to you, Sir Ashley,' she said as he prepared to mount. 'You will keep us informed of developments, won't you?'

'Naturally I will. I hope you will do the same.'

'Of course,' she said, wishing him gone.

He touched his hat and cantered away.

She watched him out of sight and then sped to the stables. Joe was just coming out, carrying a tray containing an empty tankard and a plate on which was the remains of a meal. Joe normally ate in the kitchen with the rest of the servants; there was no need to take food to his room. 'Joe,' she said, blocking his path. 'What have you got there?'

He looked sheepish. 'I were hungry,' he mumbled.

'Don't lie to me, Joseph Sadler, you had a good breakfast with everyone else. You're hiding Ben, aren't you? Where is he?'

He stood looking at the ground and said nothing.

'Joe, he may have sworn you to secrecy, but I am unswearing you. His mother is beside herself with grief and you are keeping his whereabouts from her. That is unkind.'

He jerked his head upwards without speaking. She ran to the ladder that led to his quarters and ran lightly up it. Flinging open the door, she marched over to the bed and stripped off the blankets to reveal her cousin curled up in the middle. 'There you are, Ben Whiteside,' she said angrily. 'Just what do you think you were about, frightening your poor mama as you have, getting arrested and then, to make matters worse, escaping and trying to hide?'

He was large for his age, almost full grown, but now he cowered like a frightened child. She curbed her inclination to hug him and continued her tirade until she ran out of breath.

'I didn't mean to,' he pleaded. 'I just wanted an adventure. Nothing ever happens in Narbeach and I was bored. When I heard Nat and Joe talking about going down to the beach, I thought I'd go too.'

'That much I guessed,' she said, her voice softening. 'But have you any idea of the trouble you have caused? And it's not over yet, for we have to decide what to do with you.'

'You'll never hand me in?' he queried, his blue eyes bright with alarm.

'It's what you deserve.'

'Oh, no, Pip, you wouldn't, would you?'

'You had better come into the house and see what your mother thinks about it. She has been so worried, I doubt she will scold you.'

'You have done enough for both,' he said, his cheeky grin returning. Nevertheless, he followed her down the ladder and into the house.

Augusta shrieked when she saw him, battered him about the head and body with her hands and then, breathless, hugged him until he called for mercy. Then she pulled him down onto the sofa beside her and demanded to know what had happened.

'I followed Nat and Joe down to the beach—'

'I knew it,' the good lady said. 'It is Nathaniel's fault.'

'No, Mama, it was not. When he realised I was there, he sent me home, very angry with me, he was. But then the dragoons came. We were marched off to the Customs House, but they decided we would not be safe there, so they sent us to Wells in a cart. We saw the beak there the next morning and he sent us to Norwich, shackled to each other. I didn't want to go. I kept saying I was no smuggler, but no one took any notice and when we reached Bawdeswell crossroads, a crowd attacked the escort. Very rough they were, too. We were led into the woods where our shackles were broken off. After that it was every man for himself and I came home.'

'Thank God,' Augusta said, hugging him again.

'That's all very well,' Pippa said. She had been standing looking down at them, only half-listening to the story, which bore out what she had already surmised. Her thoughts had gone to Sir Ashley Saunders and what to do about him. 'We cannot hide him for ever.'

'No, we will tell Sir Ashley he is found. He will do what he can.'

'You think he can be trusted?' she queried.

'Yes. Don't you?'

'Who is Sir Ashley?' Ben demanded, before Pippa could answer.

'Who is Sir Ashley?' Pippa repeated, wondering herself. 'He is a gentleman and he has been helping us to look for you, but he doesn't hold with smuggling, so if you ever meet him, you must be careful what you say to him. Do not mention Nat.'

'I will not, but I'd as soon you kept away from him. Nat would not like it.'

'Nathaniel is not here and we have to trust someone,' his mother put in. 'Besides, Sir Ashley has a paper for your release. We need that.'

'Do you know who finances the runs?' Pippa asked him. 'Or who pays the men's wages?'

'No, course not. Nat might.'

'You will not tell Sir Ashley that,' she said sharply. 'I wish Nat were here. It is too bad of him to leave us to deal with this alone.'

'We are not alone,' her aunt said. 'Go to Sir Ashley, Philippa.'

'I cannot go to the Manor and ask to see him. Sir Felix will not leave us alone and I cannot speak in front of him. I must find another way. In the meantime Ben must stay indoors.'

She had her son back so Augusta did not argue. She fussed round him and fed him to bursting point, while Pippa went up to her bedchamber where she could be quiet, contemplating the sea from her window and discarding one plan after another. Her worry over Ben and Nat was all mixed up with her feelings for Sir Ashley, which were beginning to take over every waking moment and some of her sleeping moments too. Her aunt wanted her to throw herself on his mercy and beg his assistance and that, deep in her heart, was what she wanted to do. But her head was telling her to beware, that he had hidden motives of his own which she had yet to learn.

She wished she understood men more, but, apart from Edward, she had little experience dealing with them. Edward was shallow, so shallow that he allowed his superstitious mother to dictate to him. Sir Ashley was not shallow, he was deep, deep as the sea, and just as mysterious.

The sea was calm today, only a few breakers rolled against the shore. The tide was out and the cockle gatherers were busy digging in the wet sand. There were fishing boats out beyond the sandbanks and a cutter was sailing slowly along the horizon parallel to the coast. As she watched its sails were furled and it dropped anchor. Suddenly the cocklers picked up their baskets and hurried back to dry land. Pippa ran to find her brother's spyglass and, bringing it back, trained it on the ship. It was the smugglers' cutter and was undoubtedly bringing in the remainder of the contraband they had not managed to unload before. It might also be bringing her brother back. She jumped up, eyes alight, a smile on her lips, joyfully anticipating their reunion, but that feeling suddenly left her. He was a smuggler wanted by the law and the law demanded that smugglers hang. He must be warned about Sir Ashley's presence in the village and sent away again.

* * *

Pippa was not the only one to see the vessel drop anchor; almost the whole population knew in no time at all that another run was imminent. Ash, riding round the village, apparently deep in thought, saw it too, but gave no sign he had. He assumed the Coast Watch was aware of it and the Revenue men and dragoons alerted. It would be folly to make a landing under the circumstances. He was surprised when he returned to the Manor for dinner to find his host was absent. 'Called away suddenly to his daughter's sick bed,' the butler told him. 'He begs to be excused and bids you make yourself at home. He has left orders for a meal and wine to be laid out for you.'

Ash thanked him. He did not doubt Sir Felix knew there was going to be a run and was making himself scarce. He ate the meal provided, but was sparing with the wine though the butler kept trying to refill his glass. Afterwards he changed into his rough working clothes and ventured out on foot.

It was a dark night with low cloud that obscured the moon and the sea was calm, a good night for a run, he decided, as he made his way to the Customs House. It was deserted. When he enquired of the only man on watch, he was told everyone had ridden off with the dragoons because there had been intelligence of a landing being attempted farther along the coast at Hunstanton. He had no doubt the information was false and wondered who had provided it as he turned and went down to the beach where the tide was nearly in. He could watch, but single-handed he could do nothing.

The beach was crowded with men and he blended in with them, as they hurried down to the water's edge to haul in the boats and land the contraband. He was not the only one who should not have been there. Miss Kingslake, dressed in her brother's clothes, was in the forefront with them. His disappointment with her was profound. She was not the innocent he had believed and wanted her to be, but an active participant. She had been using him, making him feel sorry for her, enough to dull his sense of duty, taking him off to Norwich so that the convoy could take the contraband inland. And here she was again, helping to unload the boats. What a fool he had been!

She turned and saw him watching her, making him smile grimly at her expression of shock. 'Ah, you did not expect to see me here,' he murmured, standing very close to her so that the others could not hear. 'No doubt you thought I was safely at the Manor enjoying Sir Felix's hospitality.'

'I did not think about you at all, sir,' she said, also in a low voice, though if she had shouted it, the others on the beach would have made sure he would do no more spying. She could not condemn him to that. Unless, of course, he was a smuggler himself; that would account for his presence, not only tonight but on previous nights. 'But I am not surprised. You seem to be able to change your coat whenever it suits you. Upholder of the law one day, smuggler the next.'

He did not answer that. Instead he said, 'And I wonder how it is that whenever there is mischief afoot, you are in the thick of it, Miss Kingslake.'

'Nat, don't stand there like a post, catch hold of this.' John Bristow tossed an oilskin-wrapped bundle at her. Its weight was nothing to a man as big and powerful as he was, but she could not hold it and it bowled her backwards into Ash and they both went over into the wet sand. The blacksmith laughed and turned away, expecting them to get to their feet and retrieve it.

'Are you hurt?' Even in anger Ash managed to sound concerned.

She was almost sitting in his lap, with her head against his chest. It reminded her of the time he had hauled her out of the stream. She could still feel the prickling in the back of her neck. 'No,' she said breathlessly. 'Just winded. It caught me in the chest.'

He looked down at her heaving bosom. How could that dolt of a blacksmith not see that she was not her brother? He scrambled to his feet and, bending, took hold of her arm to haul her to her feet. 'I think we had better get you home before you are really hurt,' he said.

'No.' She stood beside him trying to brush the wet sand from her breeches.

'I insist. As soon as the Revenue men realise they have been sent on a wild goose chase, they will be back here, rounding everyone up. You cannot expect to escape a second time.'

'Who sent them on a wild goose chase? Was it you?'

'Now why would I do that?' He had his hand firmly under her elbow and was leading her away as he spoke. She tried turning back to look at the crowd on the beach, but she could not see her brother among them.

'Perhaps because you are one of the smugglers, the one with the biggest stake in the enterprise, I shouldn't wonder. It is the men with the money who are responsible for ordinary working men and boys like Ben being led astray.'

'Yesterday, you were blaming yourself, as I recall,' he countered. 'You said you had filled his head with adventure stories. The trouble with those is that they do not reflect real life.'

'I know that,' she snapped.

'Come, my dear,' he said placatingly. 'Do let us stop bickering. I am exactly who I said I was. As for you, there is no sense in going about dressed like that. No one could be deceived for long. And if you were to be arrested with the others you would be a laughing stock.'

'So, you would save me from myself.' She gave a dry laugh. 'I am left wondering why you bother.'

'Do you know,' he said, pretending to consider it, 'I have no idea, except that to see a lady mocked would affront my sensibilities.' They were approaching Windward House. 'Ah, I see there are lights showing. Your aunt must still be about. Does she know you go out like that or must you creep in unobserved?'

'I do not need to creep into my own home, Sir Ashley.'

As they approached the door, it was opened by her aunt. 'There you are, Philippa. You have been gone an age. Goodness, child, you have never gone out in those clothes again. You will give Sir Ashley a disgust of you.'

Pippa took that to mean that Ben was out of sight and it was safe for Sir Ashley to enter. She smiled. 'It is easier to walk about like this, Aunt. And as you see, I have brought Sir Ashley back with me.'

Augusta turned to Ash and bobbed her knee. 'Good evening, sir. I hoped you would come. I was just enjoying a cup of tea.' She stood aside for them both to enter. 'You will join me?'

He doffed his hat and followed her into the back parlour where she habitually sat of an evening when they did not have guests. It was cheaper to keep that room warm than the larger drawing room. She had not been alone; there was a young lad sitting in the rocking chair by the hearth. 'Heaven forfend, Pip,' he said, seeing Pippa. 'You are wearing Nat's clothes.'

She did not answer and Ash smiled. 'Mr Benjamin Whiteside, I presume.'

'Yes, yes,' Augusta said. 'He has come home. Ben, make your bow to Sir Ashley.'

The boy did as he was bid, but Ash saw the wary look in his eyes and smiled. 'Young man,' he said in mock severity, 'you have led us a devil of a dance. What have you to say for yourself?'

'Tell him,' his mother urged her son as she sat at the table on which the tea things were set out. 'Tell him what you told us. Do sit down Sir Ashley.' She indicated the sofa where Pippa had already seated herself.

He put his hat on the table and folded himself down beside her. 'Yes, I am anxious to hear your tale,' he said, addressing Ben.

Pippa gave her cousin a warning look as he launched into his account of why he had gone down to the beach and been arrested and why he was obliged to escape with the others when the wagon was attacked. Ash listened without interrupting. At the end, he said, 'You realise that you have put yourself outside the law?'

'I did not mean to. It was an adventure. Pippa's heroes are always having adventures and falling into scrapes, but they always win out in the end.'

'Pippa's heroes?' Ash murmured.

'Yes, you must have read some of her books,' Ben went on, ignoring Pippa's frantic shaking of her head. 'She is famous for them.'

'Ben!' Pippa warned.

'But you are,' the boy protested. 'Though perhaps Sir Ashley don't know they are yours.'

'I am intrigued,' Ash said, looking at Pippa.

She declined to reply, but Ben was not to be held back. 'Pippa is Philip King. Surely you have heard of him?'

'Philip King,' Ash repeated. 'I certainly have. The last volume, *Honour Redeemed,* I believe it was called, caused a stir in literary circles in London. I read it myself. You are to be congratulated, Miss Kingslake. A great story and the military research was well done.'

The colour flared in Pippa's face. Now he would have another reason to disapprove of her. 'Thank you, sir.'

'It is how she has supported us all,' Ben went on. 'Without Pippa we should be in dire straits.'

This was all a revelation to Ash and it explained a great deal. His admiration for her, already high, increased until he knew he would do anything to help her out of the coil into which she had unwittingly led her young cousin. 'Am I to conclude the next book is to be about smuggling?' he asked her.

'That was the idea,' she admitted. 'But I am finding the research a little complicated. Real life keeps getting in the way, which is not nearly so romantic.' She paused. 'However, we were not talking about me, sir, but what is to be done about Ben.'

'Ah, yes. I am afraid, young man, that you will have to turn yourself in.'

'No!' Augusta cried. 'I thought you would help us.'

'So I will, dear lady, but I cannot do it while Ben is a fugitive. Give yourself up, lad. Your mama and cousin know I have a letter from Lord Borrowdale giving you into my custody.'

'What then?'

Ash had been thinking while they had been talking and had come to a conclusion that meant more involvement, not less, but he could see no help for it. He believed the boy had only been curious and understood now why Miss Kingslake blamed herself. 'I will confine you at Fairfields, my home, until your innocence or otherwise is established,' he answered. 'That may take some time, so you will be expected to work while you are there as one of my outdoor staff. Is that agreeable to you?'

Ben looked from him to his mother. 'You must go with Sir Ashley, son. You cannot stay here, for sooner or later someone will see you and the Customs men will hear of it and come for you.' She turned to Ash. 'I shall hate being parted from him, but it is better than seeing him in prison or condemned to death. If you can prevent that, Sir Ashley…'

'I will do my utmost. And if you wish, you and Miss Kingslake are welcome to come to Fairfields as my guests. I shall not always be there, but my servants will take good care of you.'

'Oh, thank you, thank you, sir.' Augusta jumped up and seized Ash's hand. 'You are our saviour. Philippa, is that not so?'

'Yes,' she agreed, but she was wondering what Sir Ash would do when Nat turned up. Would he be so ready to help them then? 'But I shall stay here and put it about that you and Ben have gone to stay with Aunt Martha. It will look less suspicious that way.'

Ash looked sideways at her. She appeared somewhat discomfited, fiddling with the neckerchief she wore as if it were strangling her. What was she plotting now? And then he remembered the blacksmith twice mistaking her for her brother, which must surely prove Nathaniel was one of the smugglers. But where was he? Was he hiding about the building as Ben had been doing? If he was, would he have remained hidden when his sister went down to the beach in his clothes? But why had she? Surely not to further her research? Oh, how he wished she would confide in him!

'I expect you to come with me now,' he told Ben. 'The longer we delay the worse for you. We will go to the Manor and you will give yourself up to Sir Felix, who will formally hand you over to me. As soon as it becomes light enough we will go to Fairfields.' He stood up and retrieved his hat. 'Mrs Whiteside, I will come with the carriage in the morning, if you will be so good as to be ready.' He bowed to her and then turned to Pippa, who was on her feet beside him. 'Miss Kingslake, your obedient. I trust you will do no more research until I return.'

'You mean to return?'

'Oh, do not doubt it. There is something about Narbeach that draws me hither—the wild coastline, the hospitality of the people, the adventures I keep having here. And I would discuss your next book with you. I have never met a lady author before and the plot intrigues me. So, you see, you will not be rid of me so easily.'

She smiled wanly at what was meant to be a joke, but there was in his dark eyes something she could not fathom. He seemed to be able to see through the masculine garments she wore to the softly feminine woman she really was, a woman who craved tenderness and love, something he had demonstrated he was capable of giving when he kissed her. Love! Oh, no, she had eschewed that and he must never be allowed to weaken that resolve. She was a source of amusement to him, a nuisance, always into scrapes from which he was obliged to rescue her. Never again, she told herself, never again. She curtsied. 'Goodnight, Sir Ashley.'

* * *

Ash strode to the Manor with Ben beside him. The village was in darkness as it had been when the smugglers had landed three nights before and there was now no one on the beach. When the Revenue men arrived, they would be too late; the contraband would be hidden and the villagers all in their beds. He smiled ruefully to himself; once again Miss Kingslake had thwarted his investigation.

'I am sorry to be a trouble to you, sir,' Ben said.

'You will be a lot sorrier if you do not do as I bid.'

'I will, sir, I will. Anything you say.'

'You must be thankful that Sir Felix is inclined to be well disposed towards you. Any other magistrate might be less accommodating.'

'That's on account of him hoping to marry Pippa.'

He ought not to quiz the boy about her, but he could not help allowing his curiosity to get the better of him. 'And will she accept him, do you think?'

'Might—she's not likely to get another offer at her age, so Mama says. But I hope she don't.'

Ash silently agreed. 'Why not?''

'Don't like him. He's too pompous. And I heard he wasn't kind to his previous wives. They both died young.'

'Good enough reasons, I suppose. But I believe there was someone once who caught her eye.'

'Edward Cadogan, yes, but that didn't come to anything. She said they would not suit, though I reckon there was more to it than that. Miserable she was, snapping at everyone.'

'Edward Cadogan?' Ash repeated, shocked. 'You mean heir to Lord Cadogan of Holbeach?'

'That's the one. Do you know him?'

Ash's only answer was a grunt. Edward Cadogan was

his cousin on his mother's side. Aunt Gertrude, Teddy's mother, had said he had been disappointed in love and had asked Ash to help him come out of it. 'Take him to London,' she had said. 'Introduce him to some suitable young ladies.' Ash had done his best, but the trouble was that Edward, once out from under his mother's thumb, was quite capable of behaving rashly. He had been bored and had soon discovered the ladies of the night, who were suitable only for amusement and satisfying a man's physical needs, not what his aunt had in mind at all. When she found out, she had come up to London, rung a peal over Ash, as if it were all his fault, and taken her son back home. A little while after that Edward had gone to India.

Had Edward really decried Pippa's red hair and used it as an excuse not to marry her? How could he? He was not a cruel man; in fact, he was on the soft side, allowing his mother to dictate to him. She was a strange woman, extremely superstitious, so she might have said something about red hair being the mark of the devil. Had that really been enough to put Edward off? He found it hard to believe, but if that was really what had happened, it was no wonder Pippa had become hard and mannish and why she had assumed no one would marry a red-haired woman. He found himself wishing he could put it right, persuade her that not all men were so unchivalrous.

'You won't tell Pippa I told you that, will you?' Ben said. 'She will be very angry and Pippa in a temper is not something you want to see, I can promise you.'

'No, I will not tell her.'

But it had given him food for thought.

Sir Ashley, Augusta, Babette and Ben set off early the following morning and as soon as they were out of sight,

Pippa set about looking for Nat. She searched every nook and cranny of the house and the outbuildings and quizzed Joe mercilessly, to no avail; her brother was nowhere to be found. She poked about in the church and the inn, pretending to have lost a shawl. She asked in the village, phrasing her question carefully, but no one had seen him, except John Bristow, who told her Nat had been on the beach the previous night and related with glee how he had bowled him over. She felt obliged to tell him the truth, which made him laugh so much the tears ran down his face.

'And what have you discovered about the guest at the Manor?' he asked, when he had finished laughing.

'Nothing. As far as I can tell he is a gentleman amusing himself travelling about the country. And he has gone now.'

'Good. We don' want strangers poking their noses into our business, do we?'

'What am I to do about Nat?' she asked, refusing to be drawn on what Sir Ashley was up to.

'I'll ask some of the others if they know what's happened to him, but I'll swear he got into that longboat.'

'If he did go on board the *Sally Ann*, why did he not come back when the rest of the contraband was landed yesterday?'

'I dunno, do I?' He was clearly not concerned.

Pippa had returned home and tried to settle down to write, but, for the first time in her life, the words would not flow. There was nothing swashbuckling in the real-life smugglers, especially as she was so closely involved. As were Nat and Ben and Sir Ashley. Sir Ashley was the problem. She kept stopping, her pen idle in her hand, because he would not leave her head and, while it was filled with thoughts of him, she could not concentrate on anything else.

She could not make him out. If it were not for his interest in smugglers, she would have been wildly attracted to him. No, there was no 'would have' about it, she *was* attracted to him. He drew her towards him with his gentleness, his humour, his apparent understanding and acceptance of who and what she was, his sheer physical presence. And yet, on his own admission, he had had many mistresses and preferred those to having a wife. That should have repelled her, but it did not. Considering what he had told her about his childhood, it did not surprise her. The women in his life had never lasted. She supposed he had come to mistrust the whole of her sex.

Her reverie was interrupted when Teresa came in and announced Sir Felix. He was the last person she wanted to see and she was tempted to say she was not at home, but he was already in the doorway, coming towards her, both hands outstretched. 'My dear, Miss Kingslake, forgive my intrusion, but I simply had to come and see how you did,' he said, grabbing one of her hands in both of his. 'Such good news about your young cousin, is it not?' He stopped in full flow to give her a belated bow.

She curtsied, indicating to Teresa she should stay in the room. 'Sir Felix, good morning. Do sit down.' She waved him to a chair as far from the sofa as she dared. 'I am afraid my aunt is not at home.'

'I know that,' he said, lifting up his coat skirts and making himself comfortable in the chair. She was not going to be easily rid of him. 'Sir Ashley has acquainted me with his plans. It is to be hoped that nothing goes awry with them or you might be wishing I had dealt with your cousin. I could easily have acquitted him and am distressed to think you did not trust me enough.'

'We did not wish to embarrass you, Sir Felix,' she said, thinking quickly. 'We felt it might make others think you too soft or showing favouritism. After all, is that not why you agreed to Sir Ashley going to Wells on your behalf? Once he had become involved, it would have been discourteous to turn down his offer of help.'

'True,' he said. 'But are you quite sure you can trust Sir Ashley? We none of us know him well and we do not know the real reason he came to Narbeach, do we?'

'I felt sure you knew, Sir Felix. Did he not tell you?'

'Oh, he gave me some cock-and-bull tale about tracking down some smugglers.'

'Do you not believe him?'

He shrugged. 'Who knows? He certainly seems interested in your young cousin. Will Benjamin tell him what he wants to know, do you think?' He paused to look closely at her.

'If Sir Ashley hopes for information from Ben, he will be disappointed. Ben knows nothing, not even who the other men were, though one may assume they are men from about this area.'

She was not sure, but she thought he seemed relieved. 'That is not the reason I called,' he said quickly. 'The vicar has decided to give a little supper party. He wanted to invite Sir Ashley and though I told him the gentleman was away, he has decided to go ahead without him. He has invited me and bade me give you this.' He brought his hand from his pocket and flourished a folded paper.

She took it from him and opened it. The note was written in the vicar's untidy scrawl, inviting her to supper the next evening. 'Oh, I am not sure,' she said, dubiously.

'Pray, do say you will come. I will fetch you in my carriage and bring you safely home afterwards. There can be nothing said against that, surely? And you will disappoint the vicar and Mrs Fearson if you do not go.'

She still hesitated; Sir Felix was becoming more and more of a nuisance and she would have loved to give him a set down, but while Nat was missing she dare not risk his anger. He might shut his eyes to the smuggling, might even accept smuggled goods, but he was, after all, a magistrate and he could make life very difficult for her family if he chose. 'Very well,' she said.

'Oh, I am delighted,' he said, springing to his feet for all his corpulence and rushing to kiss her hand. 'I will fetch you at half past seven.'

As soon as he had gone, Pippa turned to the maid. 'You will come too, Teresa. If Sir Felix thinks I will travel even three miles alone in his company, he is mistaken. An unmarried lady needs a chaperone.'

She was ready when he arrived; if he was annoyed to find Teresa dressed ready to accompany her mistress, he did not show it. He escorted them both to his carriage and got in beside them and they set off at a spanking trot. Pippa noticed the village was deserted and the shutters of the houses were closed. There was no noise coming from the Cross Keys either. This silence could mean only one thing: later that evening, when everyone who could put a stop to it were safely in the Reverend Fearson's dining room, last night's contraband would be fetched from its many hiding places and taken inland under guard. And once again, Sir Ashley was elsewhere at the crucial time. She wondered if it were deliberate or simply coincidence.

As they passed the church she thought she saw movement

in the porch. It was no more than a fleeting shadow of a man dressed in dark clothes, but it made her wonder if the church was being used to hide some of the contraband and if the vicar knew about it. Was the whole village in collusion? Even Sir Felix? Was she the only one left out? Was tonight's supper party intended to keep her away from the action? Whose idea had that been?

She had no answers and, as they were drawing up at the vicarage door, was obliged to put her questions to one side, to be sociable for the rest of the evening.

The Reverend Mr Fearson had been the incumbent at All Saints for many years and Pippa was on good terms with him and especially with his wife. They often worked together to ameliorate the plight of the poor in the village. She was made heartily welcome while Teresa was ensconced in the kitchen quarters to have supper with the servants after the party had been served.

'We are but a small gathering,' the reverend said, as he led the way into the drawing room where a servant dispensed sherry wine. Doctor Witherspoon and his wife were there and Captain Lovechild of the dragoons with his wife. They rose and exchanged greetings.

'Do sit down, everyone,' the vicar said. 'I am sorry Sir Ashley is not with us. My wife was looking forward to hearing the London gossip and news of the latest fashions. Sir Felix tells us he is an authority on the subject.'

'I believe he is knowledgeable on many subjects,' Pippa said, accepting a glass of wine.

'I hear you visited his home,' Mrs Fearson put in.

'Yes, very briefly on the way to and from Norwich. It is very fine.'

'I am agog to hear all about it. Do describe it to us.'

Pippa obliged, keeping her description of Fairfields

strictly factual: the number and size of the rooms, the hangings, furniture and decorations, all of which was lapped up by her listeners. By the time she had finished, a servant announced supper and they lined up to go into the dining room.

They all knew each other well and there was no shortage of discourse during the excellent meal, but Pippa could feel a tension in the air, a feeling that the conversation covered something else, as if they were waiting and listening for something to happen, that if there was a sudden explosion, none of them would be surprised. There was no explosion and no undue noise, except the chatter in the room and the clatter of plates and when the meal finished the ladies retired to the withdrawing room for tea, leaving the men to their brandy. Pippa noted, with amusement, there was no shortage of either commodity. On reflection she realised the same could be said of the Manor. Those who were supposed to be examples of rectitude saw nothing wrong in dealing with smugglers even if they did not take part in the activity. Her smile was rueful; knowing Nat was a smuggler, she had little doubt their own tea had not had duty paid on it. The pot could not call the kettle black.

The men joined them after a short while and they entertained each other with poetry and song and the evening came to an end. It had been a pleasant diversion and had taken Pippa's mind off her problems temporarily, but another cropped up when they were on their way home. Sir Felix instructed his coachman to take them to the Manor.

'Sir Felix, it is much too late for calling,' Pippa protested when she realised where they were heading.

'Not too late for a nightcap, surely?' he said. 'There is something I want particularly to ask you.'

'Can it not wait until tomorrow?'

'It could, but we are here now and I have been looking forward to it all evening.'

The carriage had stopped and he got out to hand her down. 'Wait there for your mistress,' he commanded Teresa, who was preparing to get out.

Pippa's heart sank. She had an idea what was coming and was not looking forward to having to turn him down. She did not think he would react well.

He ushered her into the drawing room where both were taken by surprise, one with ill-concealed delight, the other with a scowl. Sir Ashley was lounging on a sofa, reading a newspaper.

Chapter Five

Ash put the paper down and stood up to bow to her. 'Miss Kingslake, your obedient. Sir Felix, good evening.'

'Evening,' Sir Felix said. 'I did not expect you back so soon.'

'I could not stay away. Narbeach is such an interesting place, it draws me back—'

'My aunt and cousin,' Pippa put in. 'Are they well?'

'Happily ensconced, ma'am. Ben has given me his word he will not attempt to leave, while his case is pending, so I felt free to return. There are other matters to attend to.'

'Then do not let us keep you from them,' Sir Felix said.

Ash looked at Pippa, who was standing behind Sir Felix and slowly shaking her head. He smiled. 'They can wait until tomorrow. How did the party go? I am sorry I could not be there.'

'It went the way of most supper parties,' Sir Felix said grumpily. 'Food not bad, wine better…'

'And the conversation?'

'Inconsequential.'

'So you did not discuss the smugglers?'

'Why should we discuss them? The ladies are nervous enough without bringing those gentlemen's antics to the supper table.'

'I do not think Miss Kingslake is of a nervous disposition,' Ash said, smiling at her and noting the colour rising in her cheeks. 'Heart of a lion, she has. Take care you do not come within range of her claws.'

'I think it is time I went home,' she said hurriedly. 'If you will excuse me, gentlemen.'

'But you have not had the nightcap I promised you,' Sir Felix complained.

'I think I have had enough wine for one night,' she said, moving towards the door.

'Then I will accompany you and bring the carriage back.'

Ash, pretending to go back to his newspaper, saw her look back towards him as Sir Felix followed her out, but he gave no sign of it.

He waited until they had gone and then hastily left the room to go after them. By crossing the headland at a run, he was at Windward House as the carriage drew up. From the shelter of the stable door, he watched as Sir Felix handed Pippa out, ready to intervene if he became troublesome. But then a maid also emerged from the coach and the two women went into the house and left Sir Felix to return to his carriage and drive away. Ash chuckled to himself; Miss Kingslake was no fool.

He walked back more slowly, still smiling. His amusement was with himself as much as anyone. He was behaving like a lovesick calf, imagining Miss Kingslake needed or appreciated his concern for her or that she needed his protection against Sir Felix. But she had looked prodigiously relieved to see him back and she *had* been shaking her head. He had done what he could for her cousin, but then her cousin was a naive boy. Would she be so happy to see him if he was instrumental in having her brother arrested? How could he resolve that dilemma without incurring her fury? It was extraordinary how much he wanted to keep her good opinion of him.

Pippa was not surprised when he called on her the following afternoon. She had managed to write a few pages, but the work was not going well and she was glad of the interruption. Bidding him be seated, she sent for refreshments, and on this occasion she did not ask Teresa to stay in the room.

'Sir Ashley, please tell me how my aunt goes on,' she said, when they were both seated with a cup of tea in their hands.

'She is in the best of spirits and insisting on helping the cook and housekeeper—to pay for bed and board, she says. It is not at all necessary, but I have told them to humour her if it makes her happy.'

'And Ben?'

'Ben has been put to work in the stables and I have told my head groom not to spare him. He needs a spell of hard work to knock the notion that smugglers are romantic, gentlemanly vagabonds out of his system.'

Pippa smiled. 'You do not hold with romance, sir?'

'In the right place, given the right circumstances, it can be a thing of wonder and beauty, but when it deceives, there is nothing worse in the world.'

'And you, I collect, are an authority on the subject,' she said. 'You fall in love at least once a month.'

He laughed. 'I deserved that.'

'Have none of your loves lasted longer?'

'One or two have been with me half a year.'

'You, sir, are a rake.'

'I know it,' he said, with a sigh.

'When you parted from them, who deceived whom in the end?' she queried. 'I ask out of professional curiosity, you understand.'

'Is that what you do? Put your lovers in a book, I mean.'

'But you are not my lover,' she said, setting her cup and saucer down on the table at her side to give her hands something to do, careful not to let it rattle and betray her nervousness.

'Alas, no, but tell me, if I were, would you put me in your book?'

This conversation was bizarre, Pippa thought, and becoming stranger by the minute. It was as if they were talking in code. Later, perhaps, she might be able to untangle it. At the moment, she was more concerned with not allowing him to put her to the blush and to succeed in that, she must trade repartee with him. It was a kind of contest. 'I might.'

'Hero or villain?'

'Now that would depend on the plot and whether you are a true gentleman or a rake.'

'Ah, we are back to that.'

'I meant in my story, of course.'

He glanced over to her desk where her writing things were scattered: sheets of paper, a pot of ink, several quills and a small knife. 'And this one is about smugglers?'

'Yes, that is the idea.'

'But it is also a romance?'

'Of course. You said yourself—where would we be without it?'

'I should not like to be the villain,' he said softly. 'Is it possible for a rake to reform, do you suppose?'

She had a feeling they were no longer talking about the book, but he had to be answered, if she were not to lose the contest. 'He could,' she said, pretending to think about it. 'But it would depend on how sincere he was. If he was only pretending to reform in order to lull the heroine into trusting him, then he would have to end up being the villain.'

'But supposing he has a very good reason for doing what he does?'

'Can you give me one?'

'Honour, perhaps. A secret he must keep because it is not his to divulge.'

'He does not trust the heroine?' she suggested.

'Perhaps he is not sure of her allegiance.'

She laughed, taking his empty cup from him and putting it down beside her own. 'I think, Sir Ashley, you had better write my book for me, you are so full of ideas.'

'Oh, no, Miss Kingslake, I do not have your talent. I look forward to reading it when it is published.'

'It never will be at this rate,' she said. 'I have hardly had more than an hour or two at my desk in the last four days.'

'Yes, but think of all the material you have gathered in that time.'

'Material I cannot use. It is too close to home.'

She knew, as soon as the words were uttered, that she had made a mistake. She saw a light in his eyes which could only be triumph and this was borne out when he spoke. 'Because of your brother's involvement?'

'My brother, sir?' she snapped, angry with herself.

'Yes. You were not on the beach doing research four nights ago, nor, I suspect, looking out for your cousin. You were searching for your brother.'

'No, sir, I was not,' she said with perfect truth. At the time of the first landing she had not known Nat was missing. 'My brother is a man full grown and I am not his keeper.'

'But he has disappeared and you do worry about him. Is that not true?'

She stood up, angry with him, but more annoyed with herself for falling so easily into his snare. 'You are despicable, sir. That was a foul trick to play.'

Because she had risen, he was obliged to stand himself. 'I never intended to trick you, Miss Kingslake. You debate so prettily and I was simply enjoying the cut and thrust of it.'

Tall as she was, he was several inches taller and she found herself having to tilt her head up to look at his face, but if she did not, he would think she was cowed and she was certainly not that. 'Yes, you did. You lulled me into thinking we were talking about books, when all the time…' She could not finish. She knew she had lost that particular contest and betrayed her weakness into the bargain. How stupid she had been!

'But I *was* talking about books. It was you who diverted the subject.'

'You trapped me into it!'

He reached out and took her shoulders in his hands. 'Be easy, Pippa, I would be your friend, believe me. I want to help you. Have I not proved it?'

She ignored his use of her pet name. 'Yes, but now you have spoiled it.'

'And for that I am heartily sorry.' He still had hold of her shoulders; though she seemed to be calmer, he did not release her. 'Please say you forgive me.' It was said so penitently she could only nod.

He led her to the sofa and pulled her down beside him. 'Now let us talk about your brother in a spirit of trust and friendship. I can see you are very worried about him, there is no use denying it, and I might be able to help.'

Her aunt had been more worried about Ben than Nat's disappearance and there was no one else in whom she could confide. The weight of anxiety and fear was dragging her down, sapping her energy, making her tense, ready to flare up at the least little thing and unable to work. It would be a relief to unburden herself. And so she did, telling him why she had been on the beach, not knowing her brother was also there. 'I do not know if he went on board the cutter or not,' she said. 'But if he did, why did he not come home when it came a second time?'

'There could be a number of reasons,' he said slowly. 'Do you know the name of the ship?'

'I believe it was the *Sally Ann*. Why?'

'The *Sally Ann* might have had a legal cargo as well as the contraband, in which case we should be able to find out who owns her and who is her master. We might learn where she picks up her cargoes and the ports at which she calls.'

'You mean Nat might have a legitimate reason for being on board?' There was a note of hope in her voice, which he did not have the heart to crush.

'It is possible,' he said. 'It is worth making enquiries. For instance, did she sail back to home port after the landing was interrupted four nights ago? Did she put in somewhere else? Did she simply stand off until the captain received the signal that it was safe to come in again? If the cutter put in somewhere, your brother may have disembarked....'

'Then he would surely have come home.'

'Unless he was on foreign soil when that would not be so easy.'

'I cannot imagine why he would go ashore in any other country.'

'I could endeavour to find out for you.'

'And have him arrested the minute he shows his face?'

'I do not have the authority to arrest anyone, Miss Kingslake.'

'But you took Ben into custody.'

'He surrendered himself, and that is what I would encourage any smuggler to do. It is easier to defend such a one if he voluntarily gives himself up and publicly regrets his lawbreaking.' He paused. 'Do you think your brother is guilty of smuggling?'

'No.' She was emphatic. She had to be. 'I am sure he only meant to fetch Ben home.' She prayed that when Nat was found, he could convince everyone that was the case. With Sir Ashley on their side, they might win. 'Do you think you can find out where he is? If he is in Norfolk, I am sure he would have come home or at least found a way of letting us know he is safe.'

'I can but try. I have to go to London on business, but while I am there I shall find out all I can about the *Sally Ann*.'

Her shoulders began to relax as the burden was lifted from them, and though it had not completely disappeared, she found herself breathing more easily. Sir Ashley, for all his insistence on staying within the law, was her liberator.

She prayed he could liberate Ben and Nat too. Why he should want to was a mystery. 'I will come too.'

'No, my dear, much as I should enjoy your delightful company, you must be here in case your brother returns.'

'I suppose you are right,' she conceded, plainly reluctant.

He smiled. 'You will not do anything foolish while I am away, will you? I do not want to hear you have gone off tracking the tub carriers to their destination. They will have no mercy if you are discovered and it matters not if you are dressed as a man or a woman.'

'I won't. I am sure Nat is not with them.'

'Nor do I wish to hear you have agreed to marry Sir Felix.'

She laughed. 'You need have no fear of that, sir.'

'Be especially careful not to let him lure you into a compromising situation as he very nearly did last night.'

'I had no idea when we left the vicarage that he would take me to the Manor. I was shocked and so glad to see you…'

'Because I saved you from a fate worse than death, or would you have been pleased to see me without that?' He did not seem able to stay serious for long.

'You are roasting me again, sir. And I will not answer.'

He smiled. 'Then I will take my leave.'

They both stood up, so close to each other it was easy for him to reach forwards and take her face in his hands and tilt it up to his. 'Goodbye, my muse, take care of yourself until I come again.' He studied her face for what seemed a long minute, then lowered his mouth to hers.

It was the same gentle, undemanding kiss as before, but it was enough to set her body on fire with longing. She could feel the warmth spreading right inside her, down into the very core of her, where all her desires were hidden. But they were not hidden now, for she did not want it to stop and she did not care if he knew it. Her arms came up and then dropped again as she surrendered. He took his hands from her face and put his arms about her, holding her against him from shoulder to thigh. She put her arms about his waist so that she could pull him closer. Closer. Tighter.

This was becoming dangerous. He lifted his head and leaned back to look at her, smiling crookedly. 'How is it that you manage to make me forget I am a gentleman?' he murmured, taking her arms from around him and putting them by her sides.

'Were you ever one?' She was pink and breathless.

'I thought I was.' He reached forwards and took a wild red curl in his finger and tucked it behind her ear. She shivered. 'Now I must go before I disgrace myself entirely,' he said. 'Remember what I have said. I will return.'

It was only after he had gone, after the last echo of his horse's hooves had faded from her hearing, that she sat down in a kind of trance, trying to make sense of her own feelings, wondering what that kiss had meant to him. It had meant all the world to her. She could still taste his lips, still feel his hands cupping her cheeks, his body crushed against hers, and she squirmed with sensuous pleasure.

It took some time for her to come down from the clouds, but when she did and began to think rationally again, she remembered he was a rake, he had had any number of mistresses and he certainly knew how to seduce. She had come within a whisker of giving in to him. He had known that, of course he had. But he had been the one to draw away. Was that how he operated? Giving just enough to make his paramour beg for more and then holding back? But she was not his paramour and she had learned her lesson. Put it down to experience, she told herself, but, oh, how impossible that was!

She returned to her writing, but it was dead; there was no life to it. She put it on one side and went out for a brisk walk along the shore line, hoping for inspiration. There were a few fishermen mending nets and farther out the cockle-pickers had returned and were filling their baskets. It was so peaceful it was almost impossible to believe it had been the scene of two smugglers' landings when the beach had been littered with contraband. Every single ounce of tea, every drop of cognac, every pinch of tobacco, every yard of silk and teaspoon of spice had gone from it and the sand was clean, washed once more by the tides.

Some of it must surely be stacked in local houses for the occupants' use, but most had been sent on, she knew not where, bought and paid for, and the tub carriers and batman compensated. It was they who took the greatest risk and it enabled them to earn prodigious sums of money, which she found hard to begrudge them. Perhaps she ought to forget about using smugglers in her story and find another theme; a book which sympathised with the lawbreakers would find no favours with the upholders of law and order. It might even be banned. The trouble was that Robert Dodsley, her publisher, was expecting a book about smuggling; they had talked about it at some length.

By the time she had returned home, her mind was almost made up. She would go to London and visit Mr Dodsley and maybe, just maybe, she could join Ash in his enquiries about the *Sally Ann*. She refused to examine her motives any closer than that. She was sure her mother's cousin,

Eleanor, would welcome her for a visit of a few days. Eleanor, who was the wife of Lord Trentham, had a fine house in Piccadilly. They had been out of the country during that disastrous Season when she and Edward were courting, so they were unlikely to have heard the gossip. Even six years later, she was still sensitive about that.

There was no one to dissuade her, no aunt, no Nat, her resolve was doubly strengthened when Sir Felix called late that afternoon and, after a lengthy preamble about his own needs and eligibility and the hopelessness of her ever attracting a better offer, proposed marriage.

'I am persuaded you will find the arrangement to your liking,' he said. 'I have much to offer. The Manor is not my only home. I have another property between Norwich and Yarmouth and an interest in shipping. You would have all the new clothes, jewels and trifles you want, and you would not need to work at your books again.'

'I enjoy writing them,' she said, wondering who had told him about them. Sir Ashley or her aunt, or even Ben. It was most likely to have been Ben when explaining why he went to watch the smugglers.

'Naturally, I have nothing against you continuing your hobby, when you are not occupied with wifely duties, that is.'

She was tempted to laugh and would have done if the subject had not been so serious. She had been keeping Windward House and all its occupants in a fair degree of comfort for the last eight years and he called it a hobby! 'Sir Felix, you honour me,' she said, forcing herself to be polite. 'But I fear the answer is no.'

'Do not be in such a hurry to reject me,' he said, apparently unperturbed. 'Give it more thought. I can make sure your brother and cousin are freed of all charges.'

'They have not been charged with anything.'

'Oh, but they will be, you may be sure of it,' he said.

It was a scarcely veiled threat. She wondered if he would have made it if Sir Ashley had been present. Sir Ashley had said he would help her and he had not asked for payment. Yet. 'Very well, Sir Felix, I will give your kind offer due consideration,' she said.

'Good,' he said, bowing his way out. 'I shall expect your answer by the end of the week.'

As soon as he had gone, she sat down and contemplated a future as Lady Markham and shuddered with horror. Yet, if she refused, Nat, and even Ben, might die at the end of a rope. Both prospects were insupportable. But if she were in London, she would not be in Narbeach when he required his answer. It would only postpone it, but it might give her a little more time to locate Nat. She summoned Teresa. 'Pack,' she told her. 'We are going to London.'

'We?' Teresa squeaked. 'You mean me, too?'

'Yes, I cannot travel without a maid and companion. We shall only be gone a few days so we do not need to take more than one trunk and a portmanteau. And then alert Joe that I shall need the carriage tomorrow morning immediately after breakfast to take us as far as Fakenham. We can go by stage the rest of the way.'

The next day, accompanied by an excited Teresa, they set off with a reluctant Joe driving. He was quite sure, he muttered, that Mr Nathaniel would not countenance the trip if he were at home. She ignored him and in Fakenham she and Teresa boarded a stagecoach for Norwich, leaving him to return to Narbeach with instructions to look out for Nat and tell him all that had happened.

The stage travelled along the same road they had used when Sir Ashley had taken her and her aunt to Norwich and would be passing close to Fairfields. She could break her journey to visit Aunt Augusta and Ben, but decided her aunt would only try to persuade her not to go and it was better not to give her the opportunity. Once in London, she would write and tell them where she was.

The journey took a great deal longer than it had when travelling in Sir Ashley's luxurious carriage and it was late when they arrived in Norwich where she intended to change on to the London stage. She had perforce to take a room in the Maid's Head for the night. Luckily the proprietor remembered her coming with Sir Ashley and that was enough to secure them excellent accommodation.

Pippa had no idea how Sir Ashley was travelling but had no doubt he was a long way ahead of her. She did not mind that; meeting him on the way would almost certainly end in him insisting on taking her back and that would delay their investigation. It was desperately important to locate Nat before the week was up and she had to give Sir Felix her answer.

Ash had taken his carriage as far as Norwich. Sending it back to Fairfields, he had boarded the London stage a whole day ahead of Pippa. The coach was unsprung and thoroughly uncomfortable, but he hardly noticed. He was immersed in thoughts of Pippa and memories of that kiss. She had wanted it, had as good as invited it and, cur that he was, he had succumbed. She pretended to be a hoyden, went about dressed in strange garb, but at that moment she had been sweetly feminine. Her eyes, when he had released her, had been shining like two emeralds, except that emeralds were hard and her eyes had been softly unfocused, her cheeks a rosy pink. As for her mouth… It had taken all his resolve not to kiss her again. He could still taste her lips, could still feel the warmth of her lovely body against his. He was in mortal danger of falling in love, really in love… Had he run mad?

Sir Ashley Saunders, dilettante and rake, was how he was known. It did not detract from his popularity and, when in town, he was invited everywhere. He had cultivated the image; it was surprising how much he could learn from the ladies whose pillows he shared and it was all grist to the mill of his investigations as one of the Piccadilly Gentlemen. It was not all duty, he was obliged to admit, because he enjoyed their company. But Miss Philippa Kingslake was altogether a different matter. This time the recipient of his kisses was a true lady, not a Cyprian who obliged for payment and presents. He must not let it happen again because in the end she would be the one to be hurt and he would do anything to avoid that.

London, when he arrived the following day, was its usual bustling self. The streets were wet and muddy after the rain and he hired a chair to take him to his London home, halfway down Pall Mall. The houses at the western end of the street, particularly those on the south side, were the residences of the upper echelons of society, Ash among them. He had moved there after the lease of his apartment in Lincoln's Inn Fields expired and he needed something more befitting his status. Mortimer, his valet, had been left behind when he went to Norfolk, much to that gentleman's annoyance; now he clicked his tongue at his master's dishevelled appearance, as he helped him out of his travelling clothes and into a bath. 'It is hoped no one saw you arriving,' he said, bundling up the discarded clothes. 'Your reputation would be in ruins.'

'Yours, you mean.' Ash grinned. 'Rest easy, I saw no one I knew.' He stood up and took the towel Mortimer offered him. 'Now fetch out the dove-grey coat and breeches. And the yellow waistcoat.'

Once attired in the grey suit, pristine white shirt, lace neckcloth and canary yellow waistcoat, gold-clocked hose and buckled shoes, he left the house and made his way to Piccadilly and Lord Trentham's house for the regular meeting of the Society for the Discovery and Apprehending of Criminals.

He was the last to arrive. James, Jonathan, Harry, Alexander and Sam Roker were already seated at the table: James soberly dressed in slate grey, Jonathan very elegant in cream and blue, Harry, the fop, in pink and brown with an outrageous pink-spotted waistcoat. Alex was dressed in the dark blue affected by naval officers. Ash bowed to them all. 'I beg your pardon for my tardiness,' he said, taking his seat. 'I only arrived back from Norfolk this morning.'

'Then let us get down to work,' James said. 'Reports first. Jonathan, we will begin with you.'

Jonathan had been investigating a case of fraudulent share dealing; Harry was chasing up a couple of highwaymen who had escaped from Newgate with the help of one of the warders; Alexander was searching for a young lady who had apparently been abducted, though, in his opinion, she had gone willingly. James had been tied up with Lord Trentham over the effect the constant smuggling was having on the nation's finances and how best to combat this with troops returning from the war with France. This led to Ash's own investigation.

Reluctant as he was, it was his duty to report everything, but he made as little as possible over Ben's involvement and he said nothing at all about Pippa and Nat. 'The business is dragging in the whole population of the village,' he said, 'whether they want to be part of it or not. They are too frightened to refuse.'

'Frightened of their neighbours?' James asked.

'More likely of Sir Felix Markham, who holds the living of most of them in his hands.'

'And is Sir Felix the brains behind the enterprise?'

'I cannot be sure. He certainly deals in contraband goods. I was able to look round his cellars while I was there and there was a considerable amount of free-trade brandy stored behind the legitimate casks. Most of it was gone the following night.'

'Do you know where it was taken?'

'No, I was otherwise occupied when it was shifted.'

Jonathan grinned. 'Was she beautiful?'

Ash ignored him. 'I plan to make enquiries about the *Sally Ann*, which brought the goods in. She is a fast cutter. I am sure she was built for smuggling and, in that case, her owner is probably the kingpin of the operation.'

'How do you propose to begin?' James asked.

'I thought if the *Sally Ann* also had a legitimate cargo it would be listed at Lloyds.'

'And even if she didn't,' Alex said, 'some of the underwriters do not question the business of the ships, only the risk.'

Recently retired on half-pay, though still a young man, Captain Alexander Carstairs was a comparatively new member of the Piccadilly Gentlemen's Club.

'The risk for a smuggling ship must surely be high.'

'The premium likewise. And many of them are armed

to the teeth. It takes a determined Revenue cutter to take them on at sea. That is why the Customs prefer to grab the free traders when they are unloading. Less risk to the underwriters.'

'Yes, I can see you are probably right,' Ash conceded.

'Then I suggest you find its owner and quiz him,' James said. 'Could it be this Sir Felix you spoke of?'

'That's what I intend to discover, my lord. I will go to Lloyds coffee house tomorrow morning to see what I can discover.'

'I can help you there,' Alex offered. 'I am acquainted with some of the underwriters and will make you known to them. They will no doubt furnish you with an introduction to others. Is that agreeable to you, my lord?' he added, addressing James.

'Certainly. Keep Lord Trentham informed of your progress.' James paused and looked round the table. 'Has anyone anything else to report?'

None had and the meeting broke up. 'I hear you are to be wed, Ash,' Harry Portman said, as they gathered together their papers.

'Good Lord! Where did you hear that?'

'Rosamund heard it from someone who heard it from the lady herself.'

'How strange,' Ash said laconically. 'Do you know, I cannot recall making anyone an offer? Surely I have not forgot?'

'Then it is not true?'

'Certainly it is not true.'

'I thought it must be a whisker.'

'Tell me,' Ash said, 'who is the lady in question?'

'Mrs Thornley, who else?'

Ash was furious, not with Harry who was only warning

him, but with Arabella. Did she suppose she could force his hand? 'If you hear anyone else repeating that,' he said, 'you will oblige me by telling them how mistaken they are.' He dismissed the subject and, tucking his notes in his capacious coat pocket, made for the door. 'I am hungry. I have not stopped for a meal since I arrived back, so I am for dinner at Almack's. Would anyone like to join me?

Alex said he would and they set off for the eating house in Pall Mall, where they could wine and dine and listen to the latest gossip, which he hoped would not contain news of his coming nuptials. Something must be done about Arabella, but at the moment he was more concerned with finding the *Sally Ann* and Nathaniel Kingslake.

'Tell me more about your investigation,' Alex said, once they had been served with a huge helping of a succulent meat pie. 'There is more to this than meets the eye.'

Ash was startled. 'Why do you say that?'

Alex laughed. 'I am used to dealing with men and have learned to read between the lines of a report.'

Ash was chagrined to think he had not been as clever as he thought. On the other hand Alex had been a sea captain and his experience of ships and shipping might help, so he obliged him with a little more detail than his official account had given. 'A company of dragoons interrupted the landing and the *Sally Ann* went off without completing it. It came back two days later. Where do you suppose it went in that time?'

Alex shrugged. 'Could have gone anywhere. Does it matter?'

'Yes.'

'Why?'

Ash hesitated. 'It carried off one of the villagers and he hasn't been seen since.'

'And that is important?'

'Yes.' How important he was not prepared to divulge. He was not sure himself.

'Smugglers have been known to do that if they think the man might betray them. They land him in some remote place and leave him to find his own way home.' He chuckled. 'They have even taken captured Revenue men and dragoons to France and left them there. Was your man such a one?'

'No. But he might have been innocently caught up in the landing and when the dragoons arrived jumped into the longboat rather than be taken up.'

'To discover what happened to him, you need to speak to one of the crew prepared to talk.'

'Except I do not know who they are.'

'Then we must find the *Sally Ann*,' Alex said.

'We?' Ash queried.

'Yes. When it comes to sea and ships, I am your man. I have not had enough to do for the Piccadilly Gentlemen lately and my latest investigation has come to a dead end. I believe the young lady's parents were simply using me to bring an errant daughter home. It will be a pleasure to be useful.'

There was nothing more either of them could usefully say or do that evening and so they joined a game of cards in which Ash, to his delight, won a considerable sum. He forgot all about Arabella.

After the bracing air of the Norfolk coast, Pippa found the atmosphere of London dirty, smoky and noxious, even worse than Norwich with its tanneries and breweries. She had to put a scented handkerchief to her nose and mouth the minute she stepped down from the coach. There was a row of sedan chairs waiting along the road and she hired two to take her and Teresa to Piccadilly and a boy with a handcart to transport the luggage.

The footman at Trentham House, once Pippa had explained her connection to the family, made no bones about finding out if her ladyship was at home, but ushered her straight to the drawing room and announced her to an astonished Lady Trentham.

'Pippa!' Eleanor exclaimed, rushing forwards to take both Pippa's hands in her own and kiss her cheek. She was an amiable, plump woman of forty-three, whose dark hair was arranged in innumerable corkscrew curls. 'What brings you here? How did you get here? Why did you not warn me?'

Pippa laughed at the stream of questions. 'It was a sudden decision and we came by the stage.'

'The stage! Oh, my dear, it must have been a really important matter for you to risk that. And where is your Aunt Augusta?'

'She is still in Norfolk. I have a maid with me. You will give us house room for a day or two, won't you?'

'Of course. You do not have to ask.' She clapped her hands to summon a maid and gave orders for rooms to be prepared, hot water for washing and an additional place set for dinner. 'Now,' she said when that was done and Teresa had been sent with the maid to unpack and they had a cup of tea in front of them, 'sit down beside me and tell me all your news. Something momentous must have happened, I am sure. You would not leave your beloved Norfolk for the smoke else.'

Pippa hesitated. She could easily say she had come to visit Robert Dodsley and nothing more need be said, but Eleanor was a dear friend as well as a cousin and she could not dissemble. 'Momentous, yes, and worrying. Smugglers came to Narbeach and I am afraid Nat and Ben have become entangled with them and Sir Felix Markham is trying to blackmail me.'

'You are talking about one of your novels, of course.'

'No, this is all too real.'

'Then you had better tell me the whole and leave nothing out. William might be able to help—'

'No, Eleanor, you must say nothing to William. He is a member of the government, responsible for law and order. It will compromise him dreadfully. Promise not to tell a soul or I cannot go on.'

'You cannot stop now, Pippa, when I am all agog.'

'Then give me your word.'

'Very well, I promise.'

'It all began a few nights ago, when I went to the beach to watch the smugglers bringing in the contraband—'

'You never did!'

'Please do not interrupt or I shall be bound to leave out something important.'

Eleanor smiled and put her finger to her lips and remained silent while Pippa told her story. But when Pippa mentioned Sir Ashley, she could no longer remain quiet. 'Sir Ashley Saunders!' she burst out. 'What was he doing in Narbeach?'

'I am not at all sure. I think he was looking for smugglers.'

'Smugglers! That does not sound like the Sir Ashley I know. Are you sure?'

'No, I am not sure. How do you know him?'

'Why, my dear Pippa, everyone in town knows Sir Ashley. He is a notorious rake, but well liked in certain circles. I hope you have not become romantically involved with him.'

'No, of course not,' Pippa said, but her heightened colour gave her away. 'I have only known him a few days and he has been kindness itself. Aunt Augusta and Ben are staying at his country estate. Ben is more or less in his custody.'

'My dear, you astound me. Please go on.'

Pippa finished her story and explained about how Sir Ashley had come to London to find out about the smugglers' ship and how Sir Felix had accompanied his proposal with veiled threats, which she had no doubt he was capable of carrying out. 'I have to find out about the *Sally Ann* and where Nat is before he demands his answer,' she said. 'I am convinced Nat is not in Norfolk. He would have come home or at least made contact if he were. He might even be abroad. According to Sir Ashley, the first step is to find the *Sally Ann* and her owners.'

'How do you propose to do that?'

'I mean to go with Sir Ashley when he makes his enquiries.'

'My dear Pippa,' Eleanor said, shocked. 'You cannot be seen about town with Sir Ashley without an escort. Your reputation would be ruined in an instant.'

'Is he as bad as that?'

'Yes. He leaves a trail of broken hearts behind him, though Mrs Thornley seems to think she has his measure. She is putting it about that they are to be wed.'

Pippa's spirits plummeted. 'Who is Mrs Thornley?'

'Arabella Thornley is Sir Ashley's latest light o' love. She is a widow of a respectable man of business, on the fringes of society, though she would not thank me for telling you that. She thinks she is *ton*. She is hoping, if Sir Ashley marries her, her reputation will soar.'

'What is that to the point?' Pippa said, bravely fighting her sudden dejection. 'I still need to know where Nat is and if Sir Ashley is the only one who can help me...' She paused and sighed. 'Though why he should I do not know.'

'Pippa, I beg you not to consider that course of action,' Eleanor said. 'I know you do not care for London customs, but it is not to be thought of. Let me tell William.'

'No, you promised.'

As she spoke, Lord Trentham entered the room. He was considerably older than his wife. He had once been a tall man, but now was a little stooped, and, because he had once been an Admiral of the Fleet, habitually wore blue. His clothes were every shade of blue, from his pale aquamarine breeches to his sky blue waistcoat and navy velvet coat. Only his hose and neckcloth were white. 'Philippa, my dear,' he said, bowing to her. 'The footman said you were here. You are welcome, of course, but why did you not write ahead? Is something wrong at home?'

'No, everyone is well,' Pippa said, ignoring Eleanor's meaningful look. 'I came to visit my publisher to discuss my latest project. I hoped I might be given a bed for a day or two.'

'That you shall have and most welcome,' his lordship said, sitting on the sofa beside his wife, facing Pippa. 'Tell me all your news.'

Pippa hesitated. The news of the Narbeach landings was bound to have reached London, she decided, and it would seem strange if she did not to mention them. 'We had some excitement in the village,' she said, smiling. 'There was a smugglers' run and the beach was covered in contraband. The dragoons came and you never saw so many barrels, boxes and bundles disappear so fast. They only captured a tiny portion of it and even that was taken from the Customs House the next day in broad daylight.'

'You saw all this?' he queried in surprise.

'From my window,' she said hastily.

'Smuggling is a very serious matter,' he went on. 'It is become a contagion, spreading everywhere, and is like to ruin the economy of the kingdom. We must take firm steps to bring it to an end. I hope you told what you saw to the proper authorities.'

'Indeed, yes, but I saw very little,' she said, realising how right she had been to swear Eleanor to secrecy. She did not think Lord Trentham would have any sympathy for Nat.

'Guess what?' his wife said. 'She met Ash there. Is it not strange?'

'Not strange at all,' he said. 'Ash has an estate in Norfolk, as you know. He is a good man, none better.'

'You would say that,' his wife put in. 'All men together, but you know he has a reputation...'

'Whatever else he is known for, he has a reputation for honest dealing,' her husband said. 'I would trust him with my life.'

That was some small comfort to Pippa, but that was more than offset by the news that Ash was contemplating marriage. It looked as though falling in love once a month was a thing of the past. Was that how a rake reformed?

Having no idea how to find Ash and worried by what Eleanor had told her, Pippa decided not to seek him out. She was on her own and must try to find Nat herself. But as she had told William she had come to town to visit her publisher, it behoved her to do so first.

Next morning, after another sleepless night, she found her way to Pall Mall where Robert Dodsley, founder of

The Annual Register and publisher of Defoe, Johnson and Pope, had his premises.

Without telling him why the work was not going well, she suggested abandoning the idea of smugglers for something else. He would not agree. Instead he went over the book's plot and how the adventure and romantic element could be combined and bade her stick at it. 'Your duty is to your reading public,' he said, patting her hand in avuncular fashion. 'They are expecting a new Philip King book this year and if you start again, it will be late arriving. We cannot have that, can we?'

'No, you are right.' She paused. 'Mr Dodsley, how would one go about finding a ship, if one only knows her name?'

'One could go to Lloyds coffee house or to the docks, but I hope you would not go there alone, dear lady.'

'No,' she hastily reassured him. 'I was asking in the name of research.'

She did not know if he believed her, but took her leave to return to Trentham House. She was so deep in cogitating on what Mr Dodsley had said that she bumped into someone turning to go up the steps of the house. Her folder of notes flew from her hand. The man begged her pardon and stooped to retrieve the scattered papers and it was only as he straightened up and bowed to return them to her, she realised who he was and for a moment was speechless. She had come to London to find him, had been warned against him and here he was, apparently going into Trentham House.

'Miss Kingslake! What in heaven's name are you doing here?'

Last time they had met, he had kissed her and called

her Pippa; now, it seemed, they were back to being formal. 'Good morning, Sir Ashley,' she said primly.

'Oh, yes, good morning,' he corrected himself. 'But dash it, what *are* you doing here?'

'I am staying with Lord Trentham and his wife.'

'I did not know you were known to them.'

'There is much you do not know about me, Sir Ashley, but I can tell you Lady Trentham is my mother's cousin.'

'Good heavens!' He gave a crooked smile. 'So you have told them all.'

Remembering his kisses, she managed a chuckle, intended to convey light-heartedness. 'Not quite all, Sir Ashley.'

The door opened behind them and they both turned almost guiltily to find Lord Trentham on the step, dressed to go out. 'Don't stand on the step,' he said. 'Come in, both of you.'

They went inside and were ushered into the parlour where Eleanor was seated with some embroidery. 'Look who was standing on the front step, my dear,' Lord Trentham said jovially, apparently abandoning his original errand. 'Philippa and Sir Ashley Saunders.'

'We met on the step,' Ash said, bowing to Eleanor. 'My lady, your obedient.'

Eleanor, for all her condemnation of the gentleman as a rake, smiled a welcome and bade him be seated, then ordered refreshments to be brought. 'I am told you met Miss Kingslake in Narbeach,' she said. 'It is surely an out-of-the-way place for such as you.'

'I am very fond of Norfolk,' he said. 'I have an estate there and often travel around the coast.'

'Looking for smugglers?' She persisted in her questioning, much to the discomfort of Pippa, who was afraid she was about to let the cat out of the bag to William; as Ash did not know William was being kept in ignorance, the conversation could become tricky. 'I collect there was a landing there a few nights ago.'

'Indeed there was,' he said, looking at Pippa, who had taken a seat a little way off and was trying to convey a warning with her eyes. 'It caused not a little excitement, especially when the dragoons arrived, but as usual all but a handful escaped.'

'I have told my cousins how I saw it from my window,' Pippa put in quickly.

'Ah, yes, it would be unsafe to be abroad at such a time' he said and Pippa breathed a sigh of relief that he had understood.

'Hmph,' his lordship grunted. 'Sir Ashley, I believe you came on purpose to speak to me.'

'I did, my lord.'

'Then let us go into the library. Ladies, will you excuse us a moment?'

Eleanor nodded and Ash followed his lordship from the room.

'My goodness, he becomes handsomer every time I see him,' Eleanor said. 'And you had him to yourself in Narbeach when everyone in town was wondering what had become of him.'

'I thought you disapproved on him.'

'I do in a way, but it does not stop me admiring him. Such deportment, such sangfroid, such good manners—a woman would need to be made of stone to be indifferent to all that. Not to mention he is hugely wealthy.'

'Eleanor! It is as well William cannot hear you.'

'Oh, he does not mind me. We are content with each other. Besides, I may admire the gentleman, but I would not be seen out with him except in the best of company.' She sighed. 'I suppose if he were to marry Arabella Thornley we might be obliged to receive her.'

Pippa did not want to hear about the lady; it gave her a wretched feeling in her stomach even to hear her name. 'What do you suppose they are talking about?' she asked.

'I really cannot say. Gentlemen like to have their little secrets, my dear.'

'Yes, but if Sir Ash mentions Nat's disappearance, it will look ill for me keeping it from William. You know how he feels about smugglers.'

'I am sure Sir Ashley will be discreet and not betray you. Now tell me, how did you get on with Mr Dodsley this morning?'

'The government has charged me with putting an end to the rampant smuggling, as Lord Drymore must have told you,' Lord Trentham was saying. 'I believe that is why you went to Narbeach.'

'It was, my lord. He bade me report to you.'

'Then tell me what you have discovered.'

Ash repeated the account he had given to the Piccadilly Gentlemen the day before, once again omitting mention of Nathaniel Kingslake. 'Today I went with Captain Carstairs to Lloyds to make enquiries about the *Sally Ann*,' he said. 'The cutter is registered in London, but it has a consortium of owners and appears to be legitimate.'

'Is Sir Felix one of the owners?'

'Yes, but that proves nothing.'

'Even though you found smuggled goods in his cellar?'

'He would undoubtedly swear he did not know they were

there, just as the parson could swear he did not know there was an anker or two of brandy under his pulpit.'

'Where is the *Sally Ann* now?'

'At sea. She normally plies between London and Amsterdam when on legal business and according to my information is due back in London two days' hence. If she is laden with contraband, she could put in somewhere else first, although I doubt her master will use Narbeach again so soon. Short of knowing where that might be, I shall wait for her to arrive in London and question the crew.'

'Good. Good.'

'The trouble is that Miss Kingslake is writing a novel about smugglers and has fixed on learning all she can about them in the name of research. I fear she is determined to find the *Sally Ann* herself.'

'Good God, man! She must not be allowed to interfere. Nor must she write a book glorifying smuggling. It is the last thing we need.'

'I do not see how she can be prevented. This is a free country.'

'You are supposed to be adroit with the ladies. Put her off, use your wiles. I will ask my lady to amuse her, take her out and about in society. She could do with a little diversion, she is too serious by far. It comes from having to grow up too quickly after her parents died, I think.'

Ash smiled crookedly. It was all very well for Lord Trentham to tell him to use his wiles, but he was far from impervious to the lady's own wiles and he could end up hoist on his own petard. What an ignominious end for a rake!

They returned to the ladies, where they spent several minutes in polite but meaningless conversation, which ended with Lord Trentham suggesting Pippa might like to accompany him and Eleanor to Lady Portman's musical soirée the following night. 'I believe you go, Sir Ashley,' he said, almost as an afterthought. 'Perhaps you will make up a four.'

'It will be my pleasure.' Though he smiled at all three, Ash's eyes were on Pippa. He must make her understand that her involvement in his investigation was both unwelcome and dangerous, but he was half-afraid that telling her not to do something was tantamount to an open invitation. 'I look forward to seeing you there, Miss Kingslake.'

He was aware, as he strode home along Pall Mall, that he had displeased Pippa. She had hardly said a word to him, as if it were his fault Lord Trentham had taken him off for a private conversation. If his lordship did not see fit to tell her what had passed between them, it was not for him to enlighten her. Why, oh, why had she taken it into her head to come to London? And why was he so inordinately pleased to see her in spite of that? With the solid, but odorous pavement beneath his feet, he felt as though he were walking along the edge of a precipice and might topple over at any moment.

And there was Arabella; she was becoming an embarrassment and he was seriously displeased to think she might have been putting the word about that he had proposed to her. He must see her and put an end to their liaison; it would be as well to have the customary costly present to give her when he did. He changed direction so suddenly he sent a little urchin flying. Picking him up and dusting him down, he gave him a sixpence and hurried away in search of a jeweller.

Chapter Six

Mrs Arabella Thornley had a small house in the Haymarket, where Ash had installed her six months before. Because of his wealth and consequence, she had an exaggerated notion of her own importance and liked to queen it over others of her ilk who inhabited neighbouring properties. She had furnished it extravagantly, but he did not mind that; he had never been other than generous to his light o' loves. She had a maid and a housekeeper and the use of a phaeton whenever she wanted to go out. And for that she was expected to keep herself exclusively for him. That in no way gave her rights over what he did or how often he visited. Besides his work for the Piccadilly Gentlemen, he had a busy social life and had to maintain his character as a rake or everyone would be wondering what had happened to reform him, but he had always been faithful to his current mistress while she lasted.

Arabella knew all this; he had made no secret of it when he first met her and she had laughingly agreed, telling him they should both consider themselves free as air. But she had changed, become possessive and jealous and constantly hinted that he ought to make an honest woman of her. Until Jonathan saw fit to warn him, he had had no idea she had been telling everyone he intended to do just that. He had to put a stop to it. He went up the steps of Bella's house and let himself in.

Arabella was lying languidly on a sofa, dressed in a diaphanous undress robe which left little to the imagination. She was not alone. Ash paused in the doorway of the salon, considering whether to turn round and go out again without speaking, but decided not to. He bowed to her and then to the young exquisite who was sitting on a stool at her feet, feeding her sweetmeats. It stiffened his resolve to end his affair with her.

'Ash!' She almost choked on the sticky sweet as she scrambled into a sitting position. 'I did not expect you.'

'That much I can tell, my dear,' he said. 'Pray, do present me to your friend.'

'Antony Kirbey. Sir Ashley Saunders,' she said, waving a plump arm at each of them.

'How do 'ee do?' Kirbey said, rising from the stool to bow.

'I do very well,' Ash said. 'And shall do a great deal better for your absence.'

'Just leaving, sir, just leaving.' He grabbed his hat and cane from a chair and scuttled away.

Ash watched him go and then turned back to Arabella, who was looking mulish. 'Do not be angry with me, sweetheart,' she said. 'I was bored, you have been gone so long and he was so persistent.'

'I have been gone a week, no more. If you cannot stand a week's separation, then there is no sense in pursuing our arrangement. You knew the conditions...'

'I am sorry. It won't happen again.' She stood up and attempted to wind her arms about his neck. 'You know it is only you I love. Tony is only a boy and means nothing to me.'

'Then you should not tease him,' he said, disengaging her arms and standing back from her. Her perfume was overwhelming. He was quite sure he had not bought it for her; he had better taste.

'Oh, he doesn't mind it. I shall give him his *congé*.'

'Please do not stop seeing him on my account,' Ash told her. 'I shall not be coming here again.'

'Ash,' she wailed. 'You do not mean it. Not for one silly mistake.'

'It is more than that. You have taken too much for granted, assumed things you should not have assumed and that I will not endure.'

'What do you mean?' She was looking worried.

'You have been telling people we are to be married.'

'I never said that, not in those words. I only hinted that we were very close. I cannot help it if people jump to conclusions…'

'Then you had better set them right. We have had our good times, I grant you, but it is time to move on. There is no sense in dragging it out.'

'You have found someone else!' she said suddenly. 'You are using poor Tony as an excuse to be rid of me.'

'No, there is no one,' he said firmly, though he was aware that there was more than a grain of truth in what she said. 'I shall continue to pay your household bills for the next three months. I am sure by that time you will have found a new protector. I doubt Mr Antony Kirbey can afford you.' And with that he turned and left her. He could hear her stamping her feet and using the most unladylike language as he went down the stairs.

'You will be sorry for this, Ashley Saunders,' she shouted. 'I have not finished with you yet.'

Poor Arabella! He did not think for one minute he had broken her heart, but they had been together in harmony for six months, rather longer than usual, and he had enjoyed her at first. Perhaps he had been a little too hard on her. He would not go back, but he could still send her the pretty ruby-and-diamond brooch he had bought her, which was still in his pocket.

Pippa, walking up the stairs of Lord Portman's mansion between William and Eleanor, never felt less like going to a soirée; she was too wound up about Nat and wondering how much Sir Ashley had told William. It was all very well to swear Eleanor to secrecy, but supposing Sir Ashley had revealed all? After all, why should he protect her? And why should she be in such a fluster over meeting him at a social gathering? Had Eleanor been right, that he was known as a rake and yet accepted in society? It was one rule for the men and another for the ladies. This Arabella Thornley, for instance—did he love her? According to the gentleman himself, he did. And would she say they were to be wed, if they were not? Surely no woman would invent something like that. She wondered how to behave towards him. Could she be cool and distant when her heart was clamouring in her breast at the mere thought of seeing him? Traitorous, traitorous heart.

They reached the top of the stairs where Lord Portman and his wife, Rosamund, waited to receive them. William presented her. She curtsied.

'You are very welcome, Miss Kingslake,' her ladyship

said. 'Eleanor, it is very remiss of you. You did not tell me you had so handsome a cousin or we would have asked to be made known to her long before now.'

'I live in Norfolk and do not often come to town,' Pippa said, pleased by the compliment. Eleanor had insisted on giving her one of her gowns, since she had not brought a suitable gown with her, and they had spent most of the previous day altering it to fit. Made of figured cream silk over a wide padded underskirt, it had an echelle stomacher with rows of satin bows from the square neckline to the pointed waist which showed off the curves of her bosom and narrow waist to advantage. Only her fiery hair refused to be entirely tamed; Teresa was not as adept at arranging it as Babette.

'Now you are here we must see more of you. Do join the others. We shall be with you when we have greeted everyone.'

They strolled into the crowded room. Pippa looked about her, searching out a particular tall figure, but she could not see him even though she was sure he would stand out in any crowd. Perhaps he had decided not to come. Her disappointment was profound, but she was not allowed to brood on it, because Eleanor guided her round the room, introducing her to everyone.

She was standing talking to Viscount Leinster and his lovely wife, Louise, when she sensed someone behind her. She twisted round. 'Oh, Sir Ashley, you startled me.'

He was magnificent in black and white: his long coat was of black velvet, his waistcoat white figured brocade, his breeches and stockings white, tied at the knee with black ribbons. Unlike many of the guests who sported a variety of wigs, he wore his own hair, tied back in a queue with a narrow black ribbon. The ensemble made him seem taller and more powerful than ever.

'I am sorry,' he said, sweeping her an extravagant bow. 'You were so engrossed in your conversation with Lady Leinster, I did not wish to interrupt.'

'We were only speaking of the great crush,' Louise said, looking from one to the other. 'I can see you already know Miss Kingslake.'

'Yes, indeed. We met in Norfolk.'

'Ah, yes, I collect you have a country seat there. Is that where you have been hiding yourself this past week?'

'I have not been hiding, my lady. On the contrary, I have been here, there and everywhere.'

'We met in Narbeach,' Pippa put in. 'It is where I live.'

'Narbeach! But isn't that where—?' She stopped suddenly and looked up at Ash.

'Yes,' he put in. 'It has been in the news of late on account of a smugglers' landing.'

'Did you see anything of it, Miss Kingslake?' Louise asked.

'One could not fail to be aware of it,' she answered carefully. 'There were so many there and when the dragoons arrived, a great deal of noise.'

'The smugglers are becoming too bold,' Jonathan said. 'People go in fear of their lives when they are about. Only last week—' He stopped. 'No, it is not a subject for the drawing room.'

'You are too bad,' his wife said. 'Giving out hints and then not telling us. It is not fair.'

'The tale is too gruesome for ladies' ears,' he said.

'I agree,' Ash said. 'We will speak no more of it. Suffice to say the perpetrators will be found and dealt with.'

They were joined by Lord and Lady Portman. His lordship was a jovial, good-natured man and they were all soon laughing at his repartee, in which Ash joined with consummate ease. It was only Pippa who felt the strain of trying to be bright and cheerful when she was so worried about Nat. Had something dreadful happened to him? Did Sir Ashley know? She glanced across at him, in the middle of telling some monstrous tale about a mad marquis, which was holding his audience in thrall. She was unlikely to have any private conversation with him on this occasion and trying to engineer it would most certainly cause comment.

There was to be music and supper later and chairs had been grouped about a harp and a spinet in an adjoining room, but before they all trooped in to listen to it, the ladies went to a room set aside for them to repair their *toilettes.*

'Are you enjoying your evening?' Eleanor asked Pippa, patting her wig, which was flawless.

'Yes, or I would be if I were not so worried about Nat. When Lord Leinster spoke of some dreadful deed and would not tell the rest, I was afraid it might have been Nat.'

'Goodness, why should that be?'

'I do not know. And the way Sir Ashley said whoever did it would be punished, made me think he had the power to do it, though he told me he had no authority to arrest anyone.'

'Nor has he. But he is a member the Piccadilly Gentlemen's Club.'

'What is that to the point? There are gentlemen's clubs everywhere.'

'Not like this one. Its proper name is the Society for the Discovery and Apprehending of Criminals.'

Pippa gasped. 'They are thieftakers!'

'You could say that, but unlike some, they are honest and they take no money. They meet regularly in our house and report to William if it is something concerning national security.'

'And I told Sir Ashley all about Nat!' She was reeling from the shock of realising how easily she had been duped. 'No doubt he has told William. Oh, how stupid I have been.' She gave a hollow laugh. 'And I swore you to secrecy. How unnecessary that was. Why didn't you tell me this before? Is it a secret society?'

'Not secret, but they do not boast of what they do. William says it is easier to do their work if they are not well known. But I do not think you need worry, I am sure William would have told me if Sir Ashley had said anything to him about Nathaniel.' Eleanor paused. 'But, you know, if Nathaniel is mixed up in something bad and Ash does not report it, he will be compromising his integrity as a member of the club.'

'I did not know that, did I?' Pippa said in anguish. 'He encouraged me to tell him, made me feel I could trust him…'

'So you can.' Eleanor smiled. 'With anything but your heart.'

Pippa looked sharply at her. 'What do you mean by that?'

'Oh, Pippa, I have seen the way you look at him, as if you would like to swallow him whole. You could be badly hurt. He is vastly handsome and superior and all the young ladies swoon over him at some time or other, all thinking they can cure him of his rakish ways, but he is impervious…' She turned to Viscountess Leinster who had just entered the room. 'Louise, do you know how Sir Ashley got his reputation as a rake?'

'No, but in my opinion it is undeserved. He only has one mistress at a time and he certainly never dallies with single ladies. You are quite safe, Miss Kingslake.' Which was not what Pippa wanted to hear.

The ladies finished tidying themselves and went back to the music room, where the gentlemen had saved seats for them. Pippa found herself sitting between Ash and William.

'You have been gone an unconscionable time,' Ash whispered, as the musicians prepared to play. 'I was beginning to fear you had walked out on me.'

'I was talking to Eleanor,' she whispered back. 'It was a very enlightening conversation.'

'How so?'

'Shh,' she said, as the music began and those who had been chatting fell silent.

Pippa was as silent as everyone else, but she hardly heard what was being played. She was acutely aware of Ash beside her, his knee with its black ribbons, brushing against her skirt, his arm touching hers, his head tilted to one side in a listening gesture. How could a man be so attractive, so gallant, so utterly desirable and be so duplicitous? What had Eleanor said? *Trust him with anything but your heart.* The terrible truth was that she had done just that.

The concert came to an end and everyone gravitated back to the drawing room for a last gossip before wending their way homewards. Ash took Pippa's arm to hold her back and they strolled slowly side by side behind everyone else. 'You did not answer my question,' he said.

'What question?' she asked evasively.

'What Lady Portman said that was so enlightening.'

'Oh, it was nothing, simply town gossip.' She would not humiliate herself by showing an interest in his amorous affairs. 'Have you discovered where my brother is?'

'No, I am afraid not.'

'You would tell me if you had? Good news or bad?'

'Yes, I would tell you.'

They had caught up with William and Eleanor; though her head was full of questions, Pippa could not voice them. It was neither the time, nor the place. He escorted her out to the carriage behind her cousin, bent over her hand to kiss it and saw her safely seated. 'Goodnight, my lady,' he said to Eleanor. 'My lord. Miss Kingslake.' The door was shut and they were on their way, leaving him standing in the road staring after them.

'An enjoyable evening, do you not think so, Philippa?' William said.

'Yes, thank you for taking me,' Pippa said. 'Lord Portman and his wife are very agreeable and I found Viscount and Lady Leinster charming. Have you known them long?'

'Many years,' William said. 'Almost as long as I have known Sir Ashley.'

'We have been wondering how Sir Ashley came to have his reputation,' Eleanor said. 'Do you know, William?'

'Oh, you make too much of that,' he told his wife. 'He is no worse than thousands of men, almost the whole *haut monde* if one were to delve into their private lives, which of course I would not dream of doing.'

Pippa felt she had spent the best part of the evening talking about Sir Ashley and very little of it talking to him, which is what she most wanted to do: talk and be kissed and reassured, but that was asking for the moon. It did not help her pressing need to find her brother.

* * *

After a sleepless night, Pippa rose to a new day and a new determination. She would find the *Sally Ann* herself because that was where the answer to Nat's disappearance lay. She was glad that William had affairs of state to occupy him and Eleanor had a previous engagement she could not break and Pippa was left to amuse herself. 'Do not concern yourself,' she told Eleanor. 'I shall spend the time going over the notes I made at the publisher's.'

As soon as they had left the house, she sped upstairs and rooted Nat's clothes out of her trunk. Miss Kingslake could not walk about town alone, but Philip King could and she was glad she had had the foresight to think of it. Sir Ashley had commented on her curves the last time she had donned the clothes, so on this occasion she had Teresa help her to bind her breasts, much to that young lady's horror. 'Miss Philippa, you will not be able to breathe,' she said, when Pippa told her to make the binding tighter.

'Yes, I will. Now you are to stay here, I shall not be long, but if Lord or Lady Trentham come back before I do, you are to tell them I have gone to see the publisher to check something we said. Do you understand?'

'Yes, miss, but I wish you wouldn't. It can't be safe, not with all them thieves and cut-throats about. Let me come with you.'

Pippa laughed. 'Then who would be protecting whom, the man or the maid?' She crammed her riotous curls under Nat's hat, picked up a cane and sallied forth.

There had been rain in the night, as she well knew, having listened to it beating on the window pane when she could not sleep. The roads were awash with it and she had to pick her way carefully over the heaps of sodden rubbish. At least the air was marginally sweeter. Finding a hackney for hire she climbed in and directed the driver to take her to the docks.

The first person she saw on stepping down on the quayside was Sir Ashley Saunders. He was wearing a snuff-coloured suit of broadcloth, brown stockings and a brown wig, but even in that plain garb he stood out as someone to be reckoned with. As soon as he saw her he excused himself from his companions and strolled over to her. Instead of giving her a sweeping bow which he would have done to a lady, he simply inclined his head, then stood surveying her. 'Am I addressing Mr Nathaniel Kingslake?' he asked, trying to keep a straight face.

'You know very well you are not.'

'Then pray introduce yourself.'

'I am Philip King.'

'Ah, the renowned author.' He bowed. 'I am very pleased to make your acquaintance, sir.'

'Don't be ridiculous.'

'What is ridiculous about it? Would you have me sweep you up into my arms and kiss you until you were breathless? That would be a fine thing for a full-blooded man to do to another gentleman, don't you think? My reputation as a rake would be gone for ever.'

The idea of him kissing her until she was breathless was making her squirm, but she took a firm hold on herself to reply. 'And that might be no great loss.'

He laughed. 'What am I to do with you?'

'It depends on what you are doing here.'

'I am here at your behest to discover what has become of your brother. Am I to assume that is also your intention?'

'Yes. Take me with you.'

'Out of the question.'

'Why? I will not be a trouble to you.'

'My dear Pippa—I must call you Pippa because I cannot call you Miss Kingslake, can I? And Mr King sits uncomfortably on my tongue—you are nothing *but* trouble. Sailors, dock workers and warehousemen are a rough-and-ready lot and they will soon have the measure of you.'

'As a woman?'

'Perhaps, but certainly as a green boy, trying to ape a man. You would give them hours of amusement.'

'All the more reason to take me under your wing.'

'Oh, I am a mother hen now, am I?'

'You may think it clever to roast me,' she said, valiantly fighting back tears. Philip King would certainly not cry, and as for the heroes she invented so easily, they would never resort to tears. 'But I am worried to death about Nat and must find him and establish his innocence before—' She stopped suddenly.

'Before what?'

'Before he finds himself being investigated by the Piccadilly Gentlemen.'

'Who told you about them?'

'Eleanor. She said it would compromise your integrity as a member if you helped me find him.'

'So you thought to find him yourself. I am flattered that you should be concerned about my integrity, but what about your reputation? Did you not think of that?'

'Yes, of course I did. Why do you think I am wearing these clothes?'

'It is but a thin disguise,' he said, smiling and tilting his head on one side to appraise her from head to foot. 'Is it any use trying to persuade you to return to Trentham House?'

'None whatsoever.'

'I could take you by force and carry you there myself.'

'That would be a waste of precious time.'

'True, true.' He heaved a melodramatic sigh. 'Very well, we will proceed together, but I beg of you, stay in my shadow and do not speak unless you have to. And display no feminine distaste at bad smells and bad language. And do not expect to be helped up steps or into carriages. You are my assistant. Not,' he added, looking balefully at her, 'that I shall expect you to do any assisting. Is that understood?'

'Perfectly.'

'Then we will proceed to the dock where I believe the *Sally Ann* is moored.'

She trotted along beside him, trying and failing to match her stride with his. 'Do you have to walk so fast?' she demanded.

'I walk no faster than a normal man.'

'Yes, you do. You are so tall your stride is half as long again.'

'You would have me mince like a fop?'

'No, but you could just stroll.'

'I thought you were in a hurry.'

'I do believe you are being perverse and hoping I will give up.'

'No, for then I should have to escort you back to Piccadilly and, as you so rightly pointed out, we have no time for that.'

'You could simply abandon me.'

'That, my dear Pippa, I will never do.'

She was considerably heartened by this, especially as he slowed his pace and they were able to walk side by side.

The river was the great artery of the city. Almost everything the great metropolis could need or want was conveyed along it and across it. A forest of spars indicated merchant ships waiting to come into dock, wherries, barges laden with goods and passengers, pleasure craft with sails billowing in the breeze and rowing boats ferrying passengers from one side to the other—all seemed able to find their way between and around each other. The water was almost invisible, which was just as well—it was filthy and stinking. Detritus of all kinds floated in it and slapped against the sides of the quay. The quayside was crowded with sailors, dockers, ferrymen and businessmen, some standing in groups talking and gesticulating, some hurrying hither and thither, some wheeling barrows, some hefting bundles on their shoulders as if they were feathers and carrying them into the warehouses. There were a few women and one or two children, looking forlorn, come to say farewell to sailor husbands and fathers or awaiting their turn to board as passengers.

Pippa was glad Sir Ashley was with her; she would have been lost and bewildered on her own. 'That's her,' she said, pointing at a cutter moored to the quayside, and hurried forwards, anxious to be reunited with Nat.

Ash put a hand on her arm and held her back. 'Softly, softly,' he murmured. 'Remember what I said. Stay in my shadow, give no one a reason to look closely at you.'

The ship was high in the water; its sails were furled and there seemed to be no one on deck. 'It is deserted,' she said.

'There will be someone on watch.' He put his foot on the narrow board that bridged the water between quay and deck and was the only means of boarding. It had no handrail. 'Will you wait here?'

'No, I am coming too.'

'On your own head be it. But you had better precede

me.' He stood aside to let her go first. 'Whatever you do, do not look down.'

She had to summon all her courage to step onto the board, which juddered alarmingly as it took her weight. 'Go on,' he said. 'I am right behind you.'

What he would do if she fell in, she had no idea, but there was no going back. Remembering his advice not to look down, she concentrated on the ship's rail above her head and put one foot firmly in front of the other. At the top at last she jumped onto the deck and seconds later he sprang down beside her. 'Well done,' he murmured.

A sailor appeared from nowhere. 'Where d'you think you're a goin'?' he demanded.

'I have come to speak to the captain of this vessel,' Ash said. 'I have business with him.'

'He ain't on board. The mate's below decks. Will 'e do?'

'He might. Lead on.'

There were more steep steps to negotiate and the ship was far from still; it lifted and fell on the swell of the current. This time Pippa followed the men; if she fell Ash would break her fall. She had a momentary vision of landing in a tangled heap with him on the deck below and quickly put it from her mind.

At the bottom they were conducted along a narrow corridor and into a cabin. It was small and smelled of the sea and fish and stale bodies. An officer was sitting at a table writing.

'You've got visitors, sir,' the sailor said and motioned Ash and Pippa into the cabin.

The mate laid aside his quill and stood up. 'Who are you? What can I do for you?'

'My name is Thomas Smith,' Ash said. 'I am here on

business in connection with Sir Felix Markham. You do know him?'

'Certainly I know him. We do business with him.'

'I thought you might. You were at Narbeach recently.'

'What's it to you?'

'I also have business with Sir Felix. A little matter of a few barrels of spirits and several stones of tea and tobacco. I have paid for it, but have seen neither hide not hair of it.'

'You will have to speak to Sir Felix about that. We landed all that was ordered. Could have been delayed bein' taken inland on account of the Revenue men bein' tipped off.'

'You were there?'

'Course I were there. Didn't set foot on land, though.'

'I heard the run was interrupted.'

'So it was. But we went in ag'in later to finish the job. If you didn' get your goods, it's no affair of mine.'

'When you left, you had a passenger. Nathaniel Kingslake.'

'So, what if we did?'

'He is my servant. I'll have his hide when I catch up with him. He was supposed to be looking after my interests. Instead of that he disappeared and my goods with him.'

Pippa held her breath, astonished at the confident way Ash lied, but she was worried too. If Nat was known to the crew and they knew he was no one's servant, Ash would be challenged, and then what? Was Nat on board? Would they fetch him? He would surely deny all knowledge of Sir Ashley and when he saw her he would not be able to keep silent. She braced herself for trouble.

'You should ha' come yesterday,' the mate said. 'He was gone the minute we docked.'

'Oh.' Pippa could not stifle the little sound of dismay

that escaped her. The sailor looked at her for the first time. 'You look uncommon like Nat,' he said.

'Philip is his young brother,' Ash put in before Pippa could gather her wits. 'He is also in my employ. Do you know where Kingslake might have gone?'

The man shrugged. 'No, he never said.'

Ash prepared to leave. 'Thank you for your time, sir. If he should come back, I would be obliged if you would tell him we were asking for him. I am staying with Sir Ashley Saunders in Pall Mall. He will find me there. Anyone will direct him.'

Pippa followed him from the cabin and up on deck. It seemed impossible that the air could be better up there, but it was. Now she had to negotiate that awful plank again and she had a feeling it would be more terrifying in a downward direction.

Ash went first and she concentrated on his back, though if she stumbled and grabbed him to save herself they might both end up crushed between the ship and the quay. She had almost reached the bottom, one more step would have her on *terra firma* again, but it was that last step that was her undoing. Overanxious, she tried to hurry and her foot slipped from under her, making her cry out. Ash moved like lightning, turning to grab her at the same time pulling her to safety. He stood holding her, then laughed and pretended to dust her down.

'It is not funny,' she protested. 'I nearly went in.'

'I know, but we must not behave like a man and a maid, must we? There are others watching. As your employer, I would save you if I could, but I would have no sympathy for you.'

'I'm sorry.' She was still shaking. 'You saved my life and for that I thank you.'

'Come,' he said more kindly. 'Let's get out of here.'

He walked away and she followed half a pace behind him, carefully avoiding the mud and the noxious piles of rubbish in her path. 'Where are we going?'

'Home.'

'But we have not found Nat.'

'No, but have you any idea where to look?'

'No. He might have gone home.'

'He might. If he was going overland, he would have to take a stage. On the other hand, if the *Sally Ann* was sailing round the coast, he might return to her and travel that way. That is if he intended to go home in the first place.'

'Why wouldn't he? And you are walking too fast again.'

He slowed down. 'Who knows what is in his mind? I shall find a hackney and take you back to Piccadilly. When I have seen you safely indoors, I shall make further enquiries.'

'Without me?'

'Certainly without you.'

'But you said I was your assistant.'

He laughed. 'I have given you the bag.'

'That's not fair. I have done nothing to deserve dismissal.'

'The Piccadilly Gentlemen, Pippa, are *gentlemen*. There is no place for a woman among them.'

'Why not? There must be times and places when a woman is more use than a man.'

'Not you.'

'Why not me?'

'Because…' He stopped walking to turn and look at her and she almost cannoned into him. 'Because you are a lady, nurtured in gentility, or so I have been led to understand, but looking at you now, I begin to wonder...'

'There you are, then!' she said triumphantly.

'Miss Kingslake, no! I beg you not to try my patience. It is not infinite, you know.'

Pippa had been so engrossed in talking to him, she had hardly been aware of her surroundings, but they had been walking down a mean alley with tumbledown dwellings on one side and the high walls of warehouses on the other. It smelled of fish and wet rope. 'Where are you taking me?'

'Back where you belong. There is a hackney-carriage stand on the next street. I am sorry I had to bring you through this, but if I had left you on the quay while I fetched it, I could not be sure you would still be there when I returned.'

She laughed. 'You do not trust me.'

'Oh, yes, I trust you to find trouble and I cannot be for ever rescuing you. Now here's a fairly clean-looking vehicle.' He pointed to a hackney standing by the side of the road, its driver half-asleep on the box. He opened the door, handed her in, ordered the driver to take them to Piccadilly and got in beside her.

They were silent for a few moments, but her head was so full of questions, she had to voice them. 'How will you go about making your enquiries?'

He turned to smile at her. 'Do you never give up?'

'I am interested. Nat is my brother, after all, but in any case, knowledge like that can be very useful to Philip King.'

'What made you start writing novels?'

He was parrying one question with another, but she let it go. 'It is an acceptable occupation for a lady when so many others are closed to her and when Mama and Papa died, I had to look after Nat.'

'I thought your Aunt Augusta filled that role.'

'She felt it was her duty to come and look after us both, but she is a widow with a son of her own and though she had enough money for the two of them to live on, it did not stretch to keeping us all at Windward House. I had always been good at telling stories to Nat so I thought I'd try my hand at a novel. It went on from there.'

'I see. But why adventure stories? Why not something more ladylike?'

'I told the stories in the first place to amuse Nat. He would not have listened to anything about housekeeping or pressing flowers, would he? And books like that make very little money. My novels sell.'

'And because you write about adventures, you want to have them in real life.'

'Sir Ashley,' she said, suddenly serious, 'this is not an adventure for me. I am in deadly earnest to find my brother. He would not deliberately stay away from home, I know he would not.'

'But he is not being held against his will. You heard the mate say he had left the ship as soon as they docked.'

'The man could have been lying.'

'That I intend to discover.'

'Without me.'

'Most decidedly without you. Matters may become violent and I might need to move swiftly.'

'Oh, dear, I would not wish you to put yourself in danger on my behalf. I should feel dreadful if anything happened to you.'

'Would you, my dear?' he queried softly.

She felt the colour rising in her cheeks. It annoyed her

to think that Philip King, supposedly a man, could blush so easily. 'Of course. I should feel guilty.'

'That, my dear, is why a lady could not possibly do the work of a Piccadilly Gentleman. Sensibilities do not enter into their work.'

She did not immediately answer. He was doing the work of the Society and if that ran counter to her needs, then she knew which way he would go. He was on the side of law and order. But then she had thought Sir Felix was too. Until Sir Ashley mentioned him to the *Sally Ann*'s mate, she had almost forgotten about that proposal. No wonder he said he could get the charges against Ben and Nat dropped.

'I would never have believed it of Sir Felix,' she said suddenly. 'He is a magistrate.'

'That does not seem to be a barrier. He is not the only one. Gentry, parsons, magistrates, pillars of society—all indulge in a little free trading, but it is the big fish we are after.'

'You think Sir Felix might be such a one?'

'Yes.'

'Did you know what he was up to before today?'

'I suspected, but I had no proof. I still have no proof. I need to find someone to testify against him.'

'I do not think any of the villagers would dare.'

'No. Nor the sailors.'

She laughed suddenly. 'That's where a woman might come in useful. I could try to get Sir Felix to let down his guard and confess all.'

'Do not be so cork-brained, Pippa. He will swallow you whole.'

'No, for he has set his heart on marrying me. I could pretend to agree—'

'No!' He turned and grabbed her arm. 'You will not do anything of the sort, do you hear me?'

'Why not?'

'Because I say so.'

Her spirits, so low a few minutes before, shot skywards and then came down again with a thump. Sir Ashley was not for her either. 'And who are you to say whom I should marry?' she demanded, pulling herself from his grasp. 'You overreach yourself, sir.'

'I beg you pardon. You are quite right. But you see, in the last few days I have come to look upon myself as your guardian, since no one else seems to be looking out for you.'

Guardian! Was that why he called her his dear Pippa? He fancied himself *in loco parentis*, and he not more than seven or eight years older than she was. Well, she wasn't having that! 'I look out for myself,' she said. 'I have been doing it for nine years now and have come to no harm.'

'But you haven't been mixed up with smugglers before, have you? They are not the romantic heroes of your novels.' He paused and smiled. 'Did you go sailing with pirates for your last book?'

'No, of course not. But this is different. My brother has been taken in by the smugglers and must be rescued before he is in deeper trouble.'

'I understand.' His bantering abrasive tone was gone and he spoke softly, as if he genuinely did understand.

She did not know how to handle him when his moods changed so lightning fast: one minute teasing, one gently concerned, another almost distant, as if they were strangers. Would he find Nat? And would he help him or have him thrown into gaol? Was he friend or foe? She still did not know the answer to that. She had been so engrossed in their conversation, she had not noticed that they were back in the more salubrious neighbourhood of the west end of town and would soon be drawing up at Trentham House. And nothing had been achieved.

'Tell me where will you continue your investigation?' she said.

'So that you can follow me?'

'Would you have me, if I did?'

'No, I damned well would not!'

'Then I won't try to come, but please, for my peace of mind, tell me what you intend to do.' She hated herself for begging, especially as it made him smile.

'First I shall go back to the docks and track down any members of the crew I can find. At least one of them should answer to the lure of a fat purse. If your brother is no longer with them, I shall go to the coaching inns and ask if he has boarded a coach for Norwich or Peterborough or anywhere where he can pick up a lift to Narbeach.'

'If he had money, he might hire a chaise.'

'That would cost him dear. Are his pockets deep enough for that?'

'I do not know. He might have acquired some.'

'I hope he has not,' he said thoughtfully. 'It would mean he had been paid generously for his services and that might make it even more difficult to defend him.'

'Would you defend him?' she asked in surprise.

'I would defend any man I believed to be innocent.'

'He is,' she said firmly.

'I hope you may be right,' he said, as the hackney came to a stop outside Trentham House. He looked down at her male garb. 'Are you going in the front door dressed like that?'

'No, ask the driver to take us round to the mews. I'll

walk in the back way from there and hope I do not meet William or Eleanor.'

He gave the order and they trotted off again. 'Do you think Nat is still in London?' she asked.

'Do you?' There he was, answering one question with another again.

'I cannot think why he would stay in town. He must surely be anxious to go home to Narbeach. He must know how worried I am about him.' She paused. 'I think, if we do not find him in London soon, I shall go home,' she said. She had sworn, when Edward had rejected her, that she would not allow herself to be hurt again, but she knew if she stayed close to Sir Ashley Saunders, she would be hurt. She had to regain the independence she valued so highly.

'Once I have exhausted all possibilities in the Capital I will go back there myself, to continue my enquiries, you understand. It will be my pleasure to escort you.'

'There is no need. I can go the way I came.' To admit she wanted his company would be admitting defeat. And if Nat were at home and not as innocent as she claimed… Oh, what a dreadful muddle it all was.

When they stopped again, he insisted on walking to the house with her, telling her that if they should come across Lord or Lady Trentham, his presence might mitigate their dismay at seeing her dressed as she was. But his theory was not put to the test because they met no one and she was able to bid him goodbye and slip in a side door and up the back stairs to her room where Teresa waited. The maid had not dared leave the room in case someone asked her where her mistress was and she was in fever of anxiety. Pippa soothed her and stripped off Nat's clothes and dressed again in her own feminine garments. Then she went down to the parlour to join her cousin, just as if she had been working in her room all afternoon.

But her complexion was pink and her eyes bright and she was bubbling up inside with what had happened. She was realist enough to know that without Sir Ashley she would have achieved nothing and might even have come to harm. They had learned very little, but he seemed undaunted and meant to continue his quest for her brother. She prayed, oh, how she prayed that Nat was as innocent as Ben. Only then could she think of Sir Ashley as friend and not foe. And she would be able to reject Sir Felix, waiting in Narbeach for her answer. She dare not think any further ahead than that.

Chapter Seven

Ash strode home to Pall Mall deep in thought. Nathaniel Kingslake must be found and questioned. Of all the people he wanted to speak to, he was the most important. The young man could possibly point the finger at Sir Felix and give him the proof he needed. But what of Pippa? His feelings for her were in turmoil. Was she as innocent as she seemed? Had she come to London to meet her brother and been on her way to a rendezvous with him at the docks? If that were the case, she had retrieved the situation like a true Piccadilly Gentleman when he had come face to face with her.

He smiled to himself at the thought of a lady belonging to that elite band. There was no doubt she had courage—too much, perhaps; that part of London, down by the docks, was a dangerous place for anyone not used to being there. Young man or single lady, she could have ended up in the river, simply for her clothes and the money she carried. How glad he was he had been there, even if it did delay his questioning of the *Sally Ann*'s crew. He hoped fervently she would not go there again. He might not be on hand a second time. His concern for her did battle with his sense of duty and left him muddled and out of sorts with himself.

He was in no mood to act the exquisite and go visiting, but a summons from his uncle, Lord Cadogan, was not to be ignored, if only for the reason that his lordship hardly ever communicated with him. The abrupt instruction to visit him at home that evening was unprecedented. 'When did this arrive?' he asked Mortimer, pointing to the letter he had just read and put down on the table in his dressing room.

'This afternoon, Sir Ashley. A footman brought it round and said it was urgent. I had no idea how late you would be returning home so I could give no assurances except that I would see it was put into your hand the minute you arrived.'

'I had better change and go round at once, though I cannot, for the life of me, think what he wants.'

He stripped off the brown coat and breeches and handed them to Mortimer, who handled them as if they were alive and threw them in a corner. 'I shall need them again,' Ash warned him. 'Put them away neatly.'

'When I have you properly dressed, sir. What will you wear?'

'The plum velvet and the pink waistcoat,' he said after due consideration. 'Everything else in white. And I had better wear a wig and all the other paraphernalia. My uncle is a stickler for dress.'

'I am glad someone is,' the valet muttered as he went to fetch the clothes, the wig, the quizzing glass, the fob watch and the lace handkerchief to be tucked ostentatiously in his master's sleeve.

Ash wondered what Pippa would make of the vision

that faced him in the mirror when he was at last ready to go out. And thinking of Pippa, which, to his chagrin, he found himself doing more and more often, he was reminded that Edward Cadogan had offered her marriage and then reneged. A dastardly thing to do, if true. Could he learn anything about that on his visit?

The chair he had hired deposited him in Hanover Square a few minutes later. He stood outside the railings and looked up at the house. There were black ribbons attached to the door and the curtains were drawn. Someone had died. It could not be Uncle Henry because he had written the letter. Surely not Aunt Gertrude? And here he was in plum and pink, too late to go back and change again. He took a deep breath, went up the steps and knocked.

He was admitted by a footman and conducted to the drawing room, expecting the worst, but was relieved to find both his uncle and aunt sitting there. His aunt, a tiny woman hardly bigger than a child, was in deep mourning, and his uncle, as fat as his wife was tiny, wore black bands round the sleeves of his dark coat. Ash bowed. 'Uncle Henry, Aunt Gertrude, I am sorry to find you in mourning.'

'You have heard, then?'

'No, I have not. What has happened?'

His aunt began to weep and could not speak. His lordship looked at her and sighed. 'She has not stopped crying since she heard.'

Aunt Gertrude had always been a sensitive woman, given to fancies about ghosts and spirits and omens, but even she would not weep so copiously unless… 'I am sorry, but what have you heard?' He fancied he knew the answer.

'Edward is dead,' his uncle said flatly, while his aunt's sobs became louder. 'He died of a fever in India. We have only today heard and he has been dead and buried these two months.'

'Oh, I am so very sorry,' Ash said, sitting beside his aunt on the sofa and taking her hand.

'I wish he had never gone out there,' she said between sobs, taking the handkerchief Ash offered her. 'Pestilential place.'

'You sent him there,' her husband said irritably. 'If you'd left well alone, he would have tired of her and there would have been no need. He would have been safe and well here.'

Ash, in the middle of digesting the news and concern for his relatives, registered the fact that his uncle had referred to 'her' which he took to mean Pippa. 'I do not understand,' he said to his aunt. 'You sent Edward away?'

'He had formed an unacceptable attachment,' his uncle told him. 'The woman was a nobody, had nothing, no money, no pedigree and was eccentric, to boot. Earned her living by writing, would you believe? Your aunt was convinced she would ruin Edward and required me to do something about it.'

'Edward cannot have been all that attached to her if he allowed himself to be so easily separated from her,' Ash suggested.

Henry shrugged. 'It was made very plain to him what would happen if he married her. He would lose his inheritance. On the other hand, reneging on an offer of marriage was bound to cause a scandal, but if he went to India for a short time, he would be given an allowance generous enough to live well while there and in due course, when society had forgotten the circumstances, he would be allowed to return home. He was accustomed to the best of everything and the thought of living in a garret and having to earn a living for himself and a wife was not to be borne, so he agreed.'

'He was going to come home later this year,' Gertrude put in. 'Now, I shall never see him again.' And she began to sob louder than ever. Ash sat beside her in silence, longing to ask if the lady had red hair, but not daring to, since no one else had mentioned it.

Henry looked at her in exasperation. 'We have business matters to discuss,' he said to Ash. 'Ring the bell for your aunt's maid to look after her and we can go to the book room and talk in peace.'

This was done and the two men went to the library where Henry poured them both a large glass of cognac. 'Sit down, boy,' he said, indicating a chair and lowering himself heavily into another. 'A bad business all round.'

'I am sorry for you,' Ash said. He did not like being addressed as boy, but he supposed that was how his uncle, who was seventy if he was a day, thought of him.

'You realise, of course, that you are now my heir?'

'Good Lord, I never thought of it. I certainly never wished it.'

'Well, you are, and there are certain matters I must point out to you.' He paused, but when Ash did not answer, he went on. 'You know I have never approved of your way of living, made no secret of it, but while you were simply my sister's son and no closer to me, I did not feel it right to interfere.' He paused to take a mouthful of cognac, while Ash irreverently wondered if he had paid duty on it, then went on. 'As my heir, you must mend your ways.'

Ash was not sure how to answer this. He hated to be dictated to, but at the same time it coincided with his own sudden desire to live a more conventional life. 'How do you suggest I do that, my lord?' he asked, pretending puzzlement.

'You could start by ridding yourself of that woman.'

His thoughts went immediately to Pippa. Surely, his uncle did not know that he even knew her? 'What woman?' he asked, cagily.

'What's her name? Mrs Thorn something or other. She is telling everyone you are going to wed her.'

Ash breathed again. 'I certainly am not.'

'But you did make her an offer?'

'I did not. That is a fabrication.'

'Glad to hear it. But it is time you were married and starting a family. How old are you? Thirty-four?' Ash nodded and he went on. 'As my heir I expect you to carry on the line. Find someone suitable, someone of breeding, someone like Lady Jane Ponsonby. I had been talking to her father with a view to matching her with Edward when he came home, but now...' He shrugged. 'You take her.'

Lady Jane was the daughter of an earl, and though pretty enough, she was brainless and her conversation did not stretch beyond fashion and gossip. 'She would have made a good match for Edward,' Ash said slowly. 'But I beg to point out, Uncle, I am not your son and I think I am old enough and wise enough to choose a bride for myself. Lady Jane is not to my liking.'

'Pity. She has a prodigious dowry.'

'That would not influence me. I am wealthy enough not to have to take a dowry into consideration, if my affections are engaged.'

'Affections?' His uncle sounded astonished. 'You would marry for love?'

'Yes, I would.' For the second time he surprised himself. The first was when he had spoken to Pippa on the subject.

'A recipe for disaster that would be.' Henry shook his head. 'Wives who think their husbands are in thrall to them tend to make impossible demands on a man's purse and time. You are as bad as Edward. He thought himself in love until he realised what it would mean for his daily comfort and then love quickly flew out of the window.'

'Then he could not have been in love in the first place,' Ash said firmly. 'I would not allow anyone to dictate to me whom I should marry and, unlike Edward, the threat of losing an inheritance will have no effect on me at all.'

'You have someone in mind?'

'No,' he said quickly, too quickly to be convincing. 'But it will certainly not be Arabella Thornley or Jane Ponsonby.'

'Then make haste and look about you for someone else who will do. I should like to see the next heir before I leave this earth.'

'You are not ill, are you?'

'No, but I am old. I married too late and your aunt was almost past childbearing, which is why we only ever had Edward. Do not let that happen to you, my boy. I have always regretted it.'

'Tell me,' Ash said mildly. 'What happened to the young lady Edward was enamoured of?'

'I believe she went to live in the country. Norfolk, I think. I have heard nothing of her since. Why do you ask?'

'I wondered how she had taken Edward's rejection of her.'

'I have no idea. I only met her once. Gertrude disliked her on sight.'

'Why? Was she ugly? Ill mannered? Top lofty?'

'Not exactly ugly, no, but she had the brightest and wildest red hair I have ever seen on anyone. Gertrude said she had been kissed by the devil and no good would come of marrying her.'

'Did she say that to Edward?'

'I cannot recall. It was not important.' Henry rose ponderously to his feet and even that small effort made him breathless.

Ash stood up. He was head and shoulders taller than his uncle. 'It might have been important to the lady herself, had she heard it.'

'No reason why she should. There were sufficient reasons to reject her without mentioning that. I told you what they were.'

'Yes,' Ash murmured. 'No breeding and no dowry.'

Ash went to bid farewell to his aunt and then walked slowly homeward, ignoring the chairmen calling out for him to hire them. He needed to think.

Edward and Pippa. It was an unlikely match. Edward was a conventional soul, thoroughly spoiled by his doting mother and used to his comforts. No wonder he did not like the idea of living in straitened circumstances. Had he hoped Pippa would move into his family home after they were married? He smiled wryly; he could just imagine what she would have said about that. And there was her brother and her aunt and cousin, all of whom depended on the money she earned—his uncle would not have taken them on as well. The red hair was a minor issue. Except that he was sure she had been hurt by it. Poor Pippa. But she wasn't poor, she was infuriatingly independent. Anyone who married her would have his hands full. Life with Pippa would never be dull. And then he laughed aloud, making several passers-by look at him as if he were mad. What would his aunt and uncle say if he told them he was going to marry Miss Philippa Kingslake? They would have a fit. Not that he would do it, of course.

He stopped laughing suddenly. It could never be Pippa Kingslake. She was a real lady of gentle birth and he was well aware of his reputation, as was she. Real lady she might be but she did not behave like one. She was too independent, too fond of adventure and getting into scrapes, too mettlesome to be called ladylike. But wasn't that exactly what attracted him? And now he was expected to persuade her to be otherwise, to keep her lovely nose out of national affairs. How could he do that and at the same time, keep her at arm's length, her good name unsullied?

Was his uncle right? Was it time he settled down to marriage? He liked the idea of becoming a father. He had a sudden vision of a wife and children at Fairfields, scampering about on the lawn, their happy voices rising to the sky, or riding ponies or learning their lessons in the schoolroom, not used since he had been a child himself, and in his mind's eye, every one of them had red hair.

Pippa wanted to go home. She wanted everything to be back to what it was, when her only problem was how to get her hero and heroine out of the muddle they were in and bring about a happy ending. She could manipulate events in a story, could have her readers on the edge of their seats, knowing, even as they turned the pages, it would come out all right in the end. Why could she not manipulate real life like that? If she went home, could she make it happen? She lay on her bed in her shift, waiting for Teresa to bring her hot water to wash and dress for supper and mentally set out the real life plot so far, hoping for inspiration.

There was Nat, who was goodness knows where, and Aunt Augusta and Ben staying at Sir Ashley's country house, more or less under house arrest. There was Sir Ashley himself, ubiquitous, self-assured and unbelievably attractive, and there was that ridiculous band of thief-takers. How could half a dozen men imagine they could make a difference to the lawlessness of the country? But that was where Sir Ashley's first loyalty lay. And for some even more ridiculous reason that hurt. She had no call to be hurt, she told herself angrily, she had no claim on him at all. Why then did her heart thump so uncontrollably whenever he was near? Why did she feel weak and boneless when he kissed her? She was being a traitor to Nat feeling like that.

And there was Sir Felix. He was almost certainly in league with the smugglers, was perhaps the kingpin of the Narbeach operation. The sailor on board the *Sally Ann* had implied as much and Sir Ashley had not seemed at all surprised. Sir Felix might know where Nat was. Dare she ask him? But then he would want an answer to his proposal. If she turned him down again, what then? Would it seal Nat's fate? She did not know and had no time to try and think of a way out, because Teresa came in with the hot water and she scrambled off the bed to dress.

William and Eleanor were having a little supper party. 'Nothing elaborate,' Eleanor had said. 'And afterwards a few hands of cards and a little music.'

Pippa went downstairs, dressed simply in a blue-and-white striped taffeta open gown over a quilted petticoat in a paler blue embroidered with pale yellow rosebuds, a matching quilted stomacher and her hair partially tamed by judicious use of combs, to find the guests already congregating. Eleanor had misled her; they were all splendidly attired in silks, satins, brocades and velvets in every hue of the rainbow, embroidered, ruched, pleated, covered with gold or silver embroidery, the men no less than the ladies. And standing head and shoulders above them was Sir Ashley Saunders, in plum-coloured velvet.

There were other guests she did not know, milling about, all talking at once. She hesitated, wondering whether to flee back to her bedchamber, but Eleanor saw her and, taking her arm, led her into the room to be presented to those she did not know. When her cousin left her for other hostess duties, Pippa found herself standing next to Viscount and Lady Leinster and Lord and Lady Portman, with whom she was already acquainted. They introduced her to Lord Drymore and his wife, Amy, and Captain Alexander Carstairs. All the men, she realised, were members of the Piccadilly Gentlemen's Club, all determined to promote law and order and see every wrongdoer in custody. It made her feel uncomfortable.

It was not long before Ash excused himself from the couple he was talking to and drifted over to them. He bowed to the ladies and had a compliment for each, before stationing himself beside Pippa so that when the meal was announced they went into the dining room together.

Eleanor's idea of nothing elaborate was a seven-course meal with everything from soup, pork, broiled pigeons, crayfish, stewed carp, pheasant, peas, broccoli and cucumber with mock turtle as a centrepiece. After that came buttered apple pie, tarts with every conceivable filling and a pudding covered in a cobweb of spun sugar. When all that was removed there was still candied and preserved fruits. No one commented on the vast quantities, but attacked everything as if they were starving.

Pippa, with no appetite, looked round at the company

close to her. She and Ash were surrounded by the Piccadilly Gentlemen and their wives.

'I collect you have but lately arrived in London,' Amy Drymore said to Pippa.

'Yes, last week. It is a short visit with my cousin, Lady Trentham. I am from Norfolk.'

'What a coincidence,' Amy said. 'My home is on the border of Cambridgeshire and Norfolk. Blackfen Manor, Highbeck—do you know it?'

'I believe I have passed through Highbeck, but I do not know it.'

'Miss Kingslake's home is in Narbeach,' Louise informed Amy. 'It is where Ash met her.'

'That is not far from Highbeck,' Amy said. 'Barely half a day's journey. You must come and visit us, Miss Kingslake.' She turned to her husband. 'Do you not say so, James?'

'You will be most welcome,' James said. 'My wife is infrequently in town. She prefers the country and the company of our four children. But she loves entertaining.'

'You will love Blackfen Manor,' Louise put in. 'It is so peaceful and Amy's children are delightful.'

'I should certainly like to pay a visit,' Pippa said slowly. 'When my commitments allow.'

'Then Sir Ashley must bring you.' This from Amy.

Pippa was taken aback by this. Had they taken for granted that she was destined to become Ash's next mistress? She felt her face turning scarlet and wished she did not blush so readily. 'Sir Ashley is a very busy man,' she said. 'I am sure he is…' She stopped in confusion.

'I am never too busy to visit Blackfen Manor,' Ash said, rescuing her with a smile. 'But Miss Kingslake is also very industrious.'

'Are you?' Louise asked her. 'In what way are you industrious?'

Pippa looked round at them, all waiting for her answer. 'Oh, this and that,' she said.

'Miss Kingslake, you do yourself a disservice,' Ash said. 'I am sure the ladies would like to hear what occupies you.'

At the moment what occupied her to the exclusion of almost everything else was how to find her brother. Did he mean that or was he referring to her authorship? She smiled. 'I write.'

'Write,' Amy repeated. 'You mean letters and poetry?'

'No, novels.'

'Novels!' they exclaimed almost in one breath. 'How clever of you!'

'What about?' Louise demanded.

Pippa, who had never made much of what she did, preferring to hide behind her *nom de plume*, felt embarrassed and murmured, 'Oh, simple adventure stories.'

'Have you ever heard of Philip King?' Ash asked them.

'I should think I have!' Amy said. 'My sons, John and William, love his stories.' She turned to Pippa. 'Do you mean to say you are he, Miss Kingslake?'

She nodded, hating to be the centre of attention.

'Annabelle loves them too,' Rosamund said. 'Goodness me, she will be overcome to think I have met you.'

'Then you must all come to Highbeck and bring your children to meet the famous author,' Amy said. 'We shall have a house party, especially for the children.' She laughed at Ash. 'You have no children, but that does not mean you cannot come. It will be practice for when you do.'

'I do not think Sir Ashley needs practice,' Rosamund

said. 'He is very good with Annabelle. Is that not so, Harry?'

'It is indeed,' her husband confirmed. 'I have been telling him this age that he ought to marry and set up his own nursery.'

'Oh, not you too,' Ash laughed. 'I have had enough of that from—' He stopped. He had been going to say his uncle Cadogan, but suddenly remembered that mentioning that name might upset Pippa, especially when she realised there was a family connection between him and Edward. One day he would tell her, but not in public. 'My housekeeper, Mrs Bellamy,' he finished somewhat lamely. 'She has known me since I was born and thinks she can say what she likes to me.'

'Do you have siblings, Miss Kingslake?' James asked her.

Pippa had supposed she would be asked that question sooner or later and was prepared to answer. 'I have a younger brother, Nathaniel. Our aunt and her son, Benjamin, have lived with us for many years and it was for the boys I began to pen the stories. They are grown up now, but I continue to write them and will do so while others enjoy reading them.'

Ash leaned towards her to whisper, 'Well, done, my dear.' It seemed he was not about to expose her for concealing her brother's smuggling and for that she was thankful.

'We must make the most of your stay in the capital, Miss Kingslake,' Rosamund said. 'Why do we not make up a party to go and watch the military review in Hyde Park tomorrow? I am told it is to be a prodigious grand affair, a stirring memory for Miss Kingslake to take back to the country with her. She might even write a tale around it.'

Louise, the youngest of the three women, clapped her hands. 'Oh, do let us all go. Say you will come, Miss Kingslake.'

Ash looked at Pippa and smiled, one eyebrow raised in the idiosyncratic way he had. 'Will you be free to accompany us?'

Pippa understood he was asking her, as clearly as if he had said the words, if she intended to pursue her search for Nat, which in his opinion was best left to him. 'If Lady Trentham can spare me, I should like to come,' she said, giving him the answer he hoped for. It did not mean she would not find other opportunities to look for Nat. She might even see him among the crowds, but if that proved abortive, she would go home the following day and confront Sir Felix.

'The gentlemen will undoubtedly be looking about them for thieves and pickpockets and passers of counterfeit coins,' Rosamund said. 'They do not seem to be able to help themselves. We might even have a little excitement if they catch one.'

'Do you always occupy yourselves so assiduously with society matters?' Pippa asked, looking from one to the other of the gentlemen, picturing them chasing after criminals and her brother in particular. Oh, how humiliating that would be.

'We do what has to be done to the best of our ability,' James said.

'Do your wives work for the Society, too?' Pippa asked.

'Work for the Society?' Rosamund asked, puzzled.

'Miss Kingslake thinks a woman might be an asset in certain situations,' Ash put in.

'A lady member of the Piccadilly Gentlemen,' Louise laughed. 'What an extraordinary idea!'

'And yet every one of you has been involved in the Society's work one way and another,' Ash put in quietly, rescuing Pippa yet again. 'Not one of you met your husbands in a conventional way.'

'That is true,' Amy said, nodding her head in agreement and making the feather on her turban dance. 'Did you know, Miss Kingslake, that there is a tradition that the Piccadilly Gentlemen find their marriage partners through the Society? James and me, Jonathan and Louise, Harry and Rosamund, even our servant, Sam Roker. Ash and Alex have yet to succumb, but I am persuaded they will in the end.'

'Ash does not subscribe to marriage as an institution,' Alex said, laughing.

'Oh, you do not have to believe that,' Rosamund said. 'It is simply that he has not yet found his match.'

Pippa felt more uncomfortable than ever. There were matchmakers among them who were intent on marrying Sir Ashley off, and she had become their target. She wondered if they did that with every new female acquaintance or were simply trying to disentangle him from Mrs Thornley. He might be willing, in his good-natured way, to be the butt of their jokes, but she did not like the idea of being used in that way, especially as the Piccadilly Gentlemen were all for law and order and punishing the wrongdoer, whereas she was on the wrong side of the law/lawless divide. It put them on opposite sides of a wide abyss. The sooner she sorted out her own problems the better.

'I wish you ladies would not try to decide my fate for me,' Ash said, pretending to be aggrieved. 'I am perfectly capable of doing that for myself.'

'Then you are being an unconscionable long time about it,' Amy said. 'I fear you are too particular.'

'No doubt I am,' he said.

This put an end to that particular strand of the conversation, much to Pippa's relief, and they began making plans for the following day. These had been concluded to everyone's satisfaction when the meal ended and they went to listen to music provided by a string quartet and afterwards played a few hands of whist. Unaccountably, Ash, the most successful gambler they knew, lost for once and Amy was heard to laugh and say, 'Unlucky at cards, lucky in love', to which he refused to reply.

Soon after that the party broke up and Pippa escaped to her own room, to ruminate on what she had learned about the Piccadilly Gentlemen's Club. They appeared light-hearted about it, but she suspected that covered a serious intent which did not bode well for Nat. Or her.

As soon as he arrived back at his home, Ash changed into his rough brown clothes, covered his head with a scratch wig and a tricorne hat, and set off for the docks again. Here he made a tour of the taverns, looking for any crew of the *Sally Ann* who, with money in their pockets, were roistering until the ship sailed again. He was glad he had a strong stomach because he was obliged to buy ale in them all and there were more of those than he cared to count. He had to be careful not to appear too affluent or the customers of these establishments would have his purse and clothes off him in the twinkling of an eye.

He slouched, rather than strode, and appeared a little half-seas over, as he took his mug of ale over to the noisiest group in each tavern. 'May I join you, gentlemen?' he asked, swaying on his feet.

They shifted up to make room for him. 'Where you from?' one of them asked.

'Off the *Merry Matilda*,' he said, naming a lugger he knew had docked late that afternoon. 'Where are you from?'

They named several ships, not one the *Sally Ann*. He stayed with them for several minutes, then moved on. It was the same with every drinking place he entered. It seemed the *Sally Ann* crew had gone to ground. Unless they were all back on board, ready to sail again. He took himself off to her berth. It was still anchored, but there were one or two seamen making their way up the plank to the deck. They were most of them drunk and he wondered how they managed to negotiate it without falling in. There was a man coming along the quay towards him who seemed a little less foxed than the others. He approached him cautiously.

'Are you from the *Sally Ann*?' he asked.

'What do you want to know for?'

He repeated the tale he had told the first mate and was met with gales of laughter.

'I am glad you find it amusing,' he said, pretending to be affronted, though he realised he had made a serious mistake. The man was laughing because he must know Nat Kingslake was no servant. It was imperative he retrieve the situation.

The man stopped laughing. 'And supposin' you tell me what you really want with Nat Kingslake, Mr Whatever your name is, for I do not believe it is Thomas Smith.'

Ash did not think it wise to supply his real name. 'When are you due on board? Have you time to join me in a quart of ale? It might be to our mutual advantage.'

'I ha' got half an hour, then I've to get aboard. We sail on the tide.' He pointed to a dingy-looking building tacked on the side of a warehouse. 'I'll take a sup with you there.'

Most taverns in the area were dirty, ill lit and stinking, but this was worse than usual. Trying not to breathe the fumes or show his distaste, he followed the man into its smoke-filled interior and they sat down in a corner. Ash called the tavern keeper over to them and ordered ale.

'Tell me what you know about Nathaniel Kingslake,' he said, when they had the pots in front of them. 'I'll make it worth your while.'

'First, you tell me why you want to know. You ain't his guv'nor, I do know that.'

'So you do know him?'

'I didn't say that. You gotta give me chapter an' verse afore I say a word. For all I know you could be from the Revenue.'

'I give you my troth, I'm not.' He paused and decided the truth would do. 'Fact is, he disappeared from his home at Narbeach a week ago and his family are worried sick about him. We heard he'd boarded the *Sally Ann*.'

The man took a long pull at his ale. He was still suspicious. 'Wha's it to you?'

'I am betrothed to his sister and she's blaming me for his disappearance. I've got to put her mind at rest or the wedding's off.'

The man laughed again and drained his pot. 'Gentry mort, is she?'

'You've met Nat, so you know the answer to that. She is a gentlewoman.' He signalled to the tavern keeper to bring more ale, though he had only pretended to drink from his own tankard. It was too dirty to put to his mouth.

'What's her name?' his companion demanded. 'Her given name, I mean.'

Ash did not hesitate. If Nat had talked about his sister, he would probably have named her. 'Philippa, but she's known as Pippa or Pip to family and friends.'

'Hmm. You could be on the level…'

'I am. Do you know where Nat is?'

'No, but I can give 'im a message if I was to see 'im.

'In other words, when he reports back on board. Unless he's already aboard.'

'You want to know too much, you do. I'll give 'im a message, but tha's all I'll do *if'n* I see 'im and *if'n* you make it worth my while, o' course.'

Ash produce a guinea from his capacious pocket and slid it across the table towards the sailor, though he kept his finger on it. 'Tell him his sister is worried to death about him and wishes he would come home. His cousin, Ben, has been arrested and she needs him to help extricate the boy. Sir Felix can't keep the judiciary off him much longer. He won't try either if he doesn't get his next cargo safe and sound.' This last statement was a shot in the dark; he had no idea when the next consignment of contraband was due in Narbeach or whether the mention of Sir Felix would have any effect. Surprisingly, it seemed to make the man more talkative, or perhaps it was the ale loosening his tongue.

'Sir Felix!' He spat on the floor, already ingrained with filth. 'He can whistle. He ain't paid the crew for the last voyage. He said we'd get it when he was paid for it, but we ain't seen 'ide nor 'air on it, nor of 'im. If Nat hadn't give us somethin' on account, we'd ha' refused to sail ag'in.'

'Nat paid you?' Ash asked, surprised. 'Where did he get the money to do that?'

'I dunno, do I? I reckon it were what Sir Felix give 'im to buy cognac and tobacco in Calais.'

'He is Sir Felix's go-between?'

'Some o' the time.' He struck his forehead with the heel of his thumb. 'But, I just recollected he said Sir Felix aimed to marry his sister.'

'Sir Felix may aim to do what he pleases. The lady has chosen me.' He had said he was betrothed to Pippa in order to give credence to his story and justify his questions and no doubt he would pass that on to Nat if he saw him. What would the young man make of it? he wondered. Deny it or rush home to ascertain the truth? And what would Pippa say when she heard it? No doubt she would be furious. And would it reach the ears of Sir Felix?

The man laughed. 'Good on 'er. But that could be a dangerous move. Sir Felix don't like bein' thwarted.'

'I can manage that gentleman, so long as you get that message to Nat.' He took his finger off the guinea. 'My future felicity depends on it.' He was aware as he spoke how near the truth that was.

The seaman laughed again, pocketed the coin and stood up. 'I'll be goin' on board now. We sail on the morning tide.'

'Where to?'

He shrugged. 'The Cap'n don't confide in the likes o' me, mister. But I reckon as we're to take on wool when we get down the river, it'll be the Netherlands.'

Ash nodded and watched him go. Then he set off back home, striding along the noisome streets, picking his way over the rubbish and keeping a careful watch out for thieves and cut-throats.

He was in a devil of a fix. Nathaniel Kingslake was a smuggler, he did not doubt it. He thought he had had problems enough before—now they were a hundred times worse. Should he tell Pippa what he had learned? While there was a chance that Nat had been taken against his will and was innocent of smuggling, he could hope to keep her good opinion of him, but that seemed unlikely now. She knew he was one of the Piccadilly Gentlemen and committed to maintaining law and order, she would see him as her brother's enemy and by that token hers, too, however innocent she herself was. On the other hand, if Nat went home of his own accord with some tale about being taken prisoner, could he, in all conscience, let it go, pretend to believe him? That was not the way of the Society for the Discovery and Apprehending of Criminals to which he had sworn loyalty. And it would not help to apprehend Sir Felix who, if cornered, would undoubtedly betray Nat.

He had reached Pall Mall while he was musing, a good half-hour walk and yet he had not even noticed where he was going or how he had reached home. He sighed and went up the steps to let himself in. Dawn was breaking and in five hours' time he was to call for Miss Kingslake and escort her and her cousin to join the others in Hyde Park. Already crowds were making their way there to find a good place from which to view the parade and the arrival of the king and his young wife. George III was far more popular than his Hanoverian predecessors, having been born in England and speaking English as his native tongue, which they had not.

He went up to his bedchamber, then stripped off all his clothes, which would certainly need the attention of his valet if the smell that clung to them was to be eradicated. He ordered Mortimer to wake him at half past eight with a dish of hot chocolate and plenty of hot water, then threw himself naked on his bed. He had learned over the years that to deprive oneself of sleep because one had a problem that needed solving was not the way to do it. By sleeping on it, he very often found when he woke he had the solution in his head. Consequently he was soon gently snoring.

From the window of her room Pippa saw the crowds already making their way along the street to the park, hundreds of them: men, women and children in all manner of garb from the glorious creations of London's best mantua makers and tailors, to the colourful uniforms of soldiers and sailors, from the fustian clothes of the artisan to the rags of beggars and street urchins. This was going to be a huge affair, much bigger than she had realised and her hopes fell; the chances of finding her brother among them was like finding a needle in a haystack. Not even the Piccadilly Gentlemen could do that.

She dressed in a pink-and-white striped muslin round dress without a train so that it would be easy to walk and the hem would not become soiled. She had a matching parasol, though she was not sure she would need it; the day was overcast, as so many had been this summer.

When Ash arrived at ten o'clock, she was waiting with Eleanor in the drawing room. He was dressed simply in a plain cloth coat, waistcoat and small clothes, all in grey, with a plain white shirt and simply knotted muslin cravat. Simple it might have been but it had been put together by one of London's finest tailors and no one could mistake its elegance. He wore his own hair tied back and carried a tricorne, which he flourished in a bow to the ladies. 'Good morning, ladies,' he said cheerfully. 'The crowds are already gathering, so shall we go? Keep very close to me, I beg you, or you will be trampled underfoot. I have arranged for two footmen to accompany us with staves. It will be safer.'

'Sir Ashley, you are alarming me,' Eleanor said. 'Is there danger?'

'It is but a precaution,' he told her. 'And when we meet the others at the Hyde Park Gate, we will be a large party and not to be trifled with. Do not bring money or valuables—that would be inviting trouble.'

They made their way to the street where he offered both his arms. 'Now, ladies one each side of me.'

They took his arms and the footmen ranged themselves alongside and thus they merged into the crowds moving westwards along Piccadilly. There was a great deal of good-humoured pushing and shoving, but Pippa and Eleanor clung to Ash and he was like a bulwark, taking the knocks for them.

'I am certainly glad to have your escort, Sir Ashley,' Pippa said. 'We should never get through this without you.'

'Glad to be of service,' he said cheerfully. His sleep had not produced the answer to his dilemma he had hoped for. In truth, it had been beset by bad dreams in which he was searching for something he could not find and becoming more and more panic-stricken as something hideous and dark threatened him and those he loved. Nor had he decided whether to tell Pippa what he knew about Nat. That all had to be put to one side in order to act the gallant and make sure the ladies enjoyed their day safely.

The other Piccadilly Gentlemen and their wives were waiting as arranged. 'I have reserved seats for us all,' James said, indicating tiers of wooden seats, which had been hastily erected and would give a good view of the proceedings. 'Shall we take our places before the crush makes it impossible?'

Pippa did not think the park could get any more crowded, but she was wrong. Thousands upon thousands crammed in, trying to push their way to the ropes that would give them a good view. And they were noisy, too, shouting and screaming at each other, struggling to keep their feet. Safe above them Pippa, between Ash and Eleanor, could look about her, searching for Nat, and though she thought all of London must be there, she realised it was hopeless. She turned to look at Sir Ashley, but he had left his seat and was standing at the end of the row talking earnestly to a lady in a rose-pink gown whose generous padding made her much too wide for the narrow space.

'What do you think you are at?' Ash demanded angrily.

'Looking for you, Ash, dearest,' she said sweetly, smiling up at him. 'I felt sure you would be here.'

'I thought I made it clear to you that our arrangement is at an end,' he said.

'All over a green boy.' She reached up to touch his cheek with her gloved hand. 'Ash, darling, I did not think you could be so jealous. I am truly flattered, but there is no need, really there is not. I will be good from now on, I promise.' She looked up the row to where Pippa sat. 'Is that…?' Her lip curled. 'Is that what you have been reduced to? No, you would not insult me by attaching yourself to a dowd like that.'

How Ash stopped himself from shaking her and tumbling her down the steps to the ground, he did not know. 'Miss Kingslake is worth a thousand of you,' he said angrily.

'Really? Miss Kingslake—I must remember that name.'

Too late he regretted mentioning it. 'What do you mean by that?'

'It is useful to know where the opposition is coming from. Does she know about you and me?'

'What is there to know?'

'Why, that we are as good as married already. It wants only the little matter of a church and a parson. You cannot deny that.' It was said loudly so those about them could hear her.

'If I had been so foolish as to make you an offer, then certainly I would not deny it,' he hissed at her. 'But you know perfectly well no such offer was made. Now you can make it known that we have decided amicably to part or I shall be obliged to publish the truth. The choice is yours. Now, oblige me by returning to your seat.'

Whether she would have gone if someone behind them had not shouted that they were blocking the view and the carriages were arriving, he did not know. She went back to her place and Ash rejoined Pippa.

She longed to ask who the woman was, but did not dare. Whoever she was, was on intimate terms with him, judging by the way she reached up to touch his cheek. Could it have been Mrs Thornley? Her heart seemed to contract into a tight little ball and she found breathing difficult. As for Sir Ashley, he was looking decidedly uncomfortable and well he might. Eleanor's expression was one of disapproval and the other ladies were chatting among themselves pretending not to have noticed, although they undoubtedly had and there would be more gossip. It quite spoiled the outing for Pippa.

She watched the king's entourage of carriages draw up

and the occupants leave them to take their places. And then the sound of music heralded the arrival of the marching troops. It was a colourful parade, with the soldiers in uniforms of almost every colour of the rainbow, their accoutrements sparkling in the weak sunshine that dared to peep out from behind the clouds. The crowds stood and cheered. As those sitting in the grandstand rose, the whole edifice wobbled and the next minute it had collapsed like a pack of cards, taking its occupants with it in a tangle of splintered wood, torn clothes and broken limbs, accompanied by screams. There was nothing they could do to save themselves.

Pippa found herself on the ground with Ash's body stretched across hers. Nearby someone was groaning and a little farther off a man was cursing. She lay there, unable to move, wondering if she had been badly injured for she could feel no pain. Ash's face, so close to her own, looked grey and his eyes were shut. 'Ash,' she whispered, fearing the worst and realising at that moment if he were to die, she would want to die too. 'Ash.'

He stirred and his eyes opened. 'Pippa.'

'Thank God,' she said, breathless because his weight was bearing down on her chest. 'You are alive. Are you hurt?'

'I don't think so. Not badly, anyway.' There was a lump of wood across his back, which was pinning him on top of her, and he could not move it. 'I'm sorry I cannot relieve you of my presence. Are you hurt?'

'No, I do not think so. What of the others?'

'I don't know.'

People had run from all around to extricate those who had been sitting in the stand and were hauling at planks of wood and broken seats and freeing those who were trapped.

And all the time the music and the marching went on. The wood, which turned out to be one of the main supports of the stand and very heavy, was taken off Ash's back and he rolled off her and lay on his back on the grass, trying to get his breath.

Pippa, who had seen the beam the rescuers had carried away, was convinced Ash's back had been broken. No one, however strong, could have that weight on them and not be badly injured. She was acutely aware that if he had not thrown himself on top of her as they fell, she would have been crushed. All she had suffered were bruises. She knelt up and leaned over him. 'Ash, oh, Ash, what can I do? How can I help you? You saved my life.'

He grinned, though his back was hurting like hell. 'Humbug.'

'It is not humbug. That great beam would have killed me. I wonder it did not kill you.'

'I am not so easily got rid of, my dear. I will be as right as ninepence as soon as I have my breath back.'

That proved to be on the optimistic side. When he tried to sit up he found he could not. The only other injured among their friends was Captain Carstairs who, like Ash, had tried to save the ladies and been hit by a falling seat. He was wandering about in a daze with a lump the size of an egg on the back of his head, unsure where he was. The others were badly bruised, the men more than the ladies, whose padded skirts and tight stomachers had saved them from worse damage. Pippa saw Mrs Thornley pick herself up and replace her wig, which had fallen off, before rushing over to Ash, throwing herself down beside him, all solicitous concern. 'Ash, Ash, darling, how bad is it? I am here, I shall look after you.' She looked up at the men. 'Take him to my house.'

'Madam,' James said, addressing her in his most imperious voice, which, if the situation had not been so serious, might have made Pippa laugh, considering his wig was askew and he had blood and bits of grass stuck on one side of his face, 'leave the gentleman to us and go about your business.'

'He is my business and I will not leave him.'

There followed a most undignified scuffle in which James and Harry tried to hustle her away and she struggled to remain. Ash was too hurt to take part and simply stared at them. Pippa, watching, wondered if he would have defended the woman if he could.

'Come, Pippa,' Eleanor said. 'Let us ladies find those footmen and go home. I could do with a strong restorative. The men will look after Ash.'

Ash was carried off on a stretcher by James and Harry, accompanied by Jonathan and Alexander. Mrs Thornley had gone off in a huff, so Pippa allowed herself to be led away.

'I said you might have something to write about, did I not?' Rosamund commented, taking Pippa's arm. 'But we could not have foretold this, could we?'

'No. I am truly worried about Sir Ashley.'

'Of course you are. We all are. When the men have taken him home and he has been seen by the sawbones, they will come and tell us how he does.'

'He saved my life.' She could not get what he had done out of her head. How could she consider him her enemy now? And yet Mrs Thornley's words echoed in her brain. She never felt more confused in her life.

Rosamund squeezed her arm. 'My dear, it may be that you will be the saving of him.'

'How can that be?'

'Wait and see.'

And on that enigmatic note, they all went into Trentham House to be provided with baths, have their bruises tended to and be dosed with medicinal cognac, after which they waited for the return of their menfolk, debating the events of the day in some detail, blaming the poor construction of the viewing platform, which was not sturdy enough to hold all the people who had crowded onto it. They were also scathing about the behaviour of Mrs Thornley. 'It was bad enough when she called him from his seat to talk to him,' Eleanor said. 'But to come rushing over as he lay on the ground and demand he be taken to her house was the outside of enough.'

'Do you think he really offered her marriage?' Louise asked.

'No, of course not,' Rosamund said. 'He has more sense.'

'But he did not deny it.'

'He was too hurt to know what was going on and too much the gentleman.'

Pippa did not want to listen to them gossiping about Mrs Thornley and was on the point of excusing herself and going to bed, when the men returned. They reported that Ash had been seen by a doctor who assured them Sir Ashley's back was not broken, but it was badly bruised and he must lie abed until it healed. 'It might take weeks,' James told them. 'And the doctor would not commit himself to saying there would be no lasting damage. He said only time will tell.'

Pippa was the least hurt of any of the ladies and that served to make her feel more than ever guilty that she had survived only because of Ash's heroic action. The thought of that strong, handsome, eminently desirable man whom she loved, never being able walk again, was enough to keep her awake and in tears the whole night long.

Chapter Eight

Pippa was not the only one awake. Ash's sovereign remedy of sleep would not relieve him. For one thing his back was too painful, even though the doctor had said it was not broken, and for another, he had realised in the precise moment he had thrown himself on Pippa, that he had met his match at last. He had fallen in love. Oh, he had already acknowledged to himself that she would make someone a loving and lovely wife, but not until today had he known what it was to be in love, really in love. It was nothing like his feelings for his mistresses, the light dalliance, the playfulness, the intransigence; this was serious, stupendous, a huge explosion of emotion such as he had never experienced before, mixed with great tenderness. Now he understood the difference. He knew Pippa's life and happiness was more important to him than his own and he would readily die for her.

Once he was able to get about again, he would tell her he loved her, try to convince her his days of rakedom were over and he truly wanted to settle down as a married man. He smiled inwardly, imagining the comments of his friends when they heard he was a changed man. Sir Ashley Saunders, a determined and committed bachelor, marrying and for love at that, would furnish them with no end of amusement. But it did not solve the problem of Nathaniel Kingslake and he really must put his mind to that before he said anything to Pippa. But how to do so, when he was laid up, he was not at all sure.

'But, Pippa, you cannot go to Sir Ashley's lodgings,' Eleanor said next morning when they met for breakfast. 'It simply is not done for a lady to visit the apartments of a bachelor. It would cause no end of scandal. You do not want to be tarred with the same brush as Mrs Thornley, do you?'

'No, of course not.' Pippa could not subdue the little green god who sat on her shoulder and prodded her uncomfortably, even though she knew she was being irrational. She wanted to find out the truth about Mrs Thornley. Was she more than a mistress? Even that was hard to bear. It was foolish of her; she had no expectation that Ash thought any more about her than that she was a profound nuisance. Except for his kisses. She could not forget the tenderness in them. 'All I want to do is see for myself how he does and thank him for what he did for me and see if anything can be done to make him more comfortable. Is that so very bad?'

'Perhaps if we both went, properly escorted, we might go,' Eleanor ventured. 'I will ask William.'

William agreed and that afternoon he accompanied both ladies to Pall Mall. They were asked to wait in the vestibule while a footman went to see if Sir Ashley would receive them. While she waited, Pippa looked about her.

The house was modest compared to its neighbours, but it was elegantly furnished. What struck her most was that it seemed cold and impersonal and had none of the warmth and ambience of Fairfields. She concluded that Sir Ashley used it only as somewhere to stay when in town and did not look on it as home.

'Fine kettle of fish this is,' Lord Cadogan said. He had come to visit his nephew directly upon hearing that he had sustained an injury the day before. Ash had had his servant help him to a daybed in a small sitting room adjoining his bedchamber from where he could see the park and the people walking and riding there. His lordship had pulled up a chair beside the bed and was surveying him with a jaundiced eye. 'You could have got yourself killed.'

'But I did not, did I?' Ash grimaced. Being told to lie still was frustrating, but every time he tried to move, he was racked with pain and had to desist. 'And how did you find out about it?'

'My dear man, it is all over town. You threw yourself on top of Mrs Thornley and she was so overcome, she collapsed beside you. What were you doing in a public place with her? You told me you had given her the bag.'

'As usual the tattlers have made much of nothing. I did not throw myself on Mrs Thornley. She was nowhere near me at the time. Nor did I ask her to rush over and fall on her knees beside me. If I had had the use of my legs, I would have walked away.'

'Hmph,' Lord Cadogan said, as if he found that hard to believe. 'How long before you are on your feet again?'

'The sawbones would not conjecture, but if I have my way, it will not be long.'

'You would do better to go to Fairfields to recuperate, away from all this speculation.'

'I intend to do so as soon as I can travel.'

'Good. I need you fit and well and free of gossip. I cannot leave my estate to a cripple. It needs a strong, healthy man who is held in the highest esteem. And what have you done about finding a wife?'

'Uncle, I cannot possibly go courting as I am, can I?'

'No, I realise that,' the old man conceded. 'But I hope you will not use it as an excuse to give up and remain a bachelor. Men of property cannot afford such luxury.'

'I will give it serious consideration,' Ash said, his thoughts on Pippa. How badly hurt was she? She had said it was only bruises, but supposing it was more serious than that? How could he find out? He was hardly aware that his uncle was on his feet, preparing to leave.

'Good. I will come back in a day or two to see how you go on. If you need the use of my travelling chaise to convey you to Fairfields, you are welcome to it.'

'Thank you, sir, but I can send for my own carriage.'

On the stairs his lordship met the footman on his way to announce the latest callers. 'I will see myself out,' he told him. He had reached the hall and was picking up his hat and gloves when he recognised Lord Trentham. 'My lord, you have come to see the invalid, have you?'

Pippa, who had seen the man descend the stairs, longed to hide herself. She turned to examine a picture on the wall and prayed he would pass without noticing her.

'Yes, indeed,' William answered. 'May I present my wife, Lady Trentham.'

'My lady.' His lordship swept Eleanor a bow and she curtsied in response.

'And my wife's cousin, Miss Kingslake. Philippa, Lord Cadogan...'

There was nothing for it. Pippa turned to face his lordship. 'Lord Cadogan and I have met,' she said, as calmly as she could manage, given that her knees were knocking and her hands shaking.

His lordship stared at her, in astonishment and then anger. 'What are you doing here?' he demanded. 'Is there no end to your effrontery?'

William and Eleanor looked at Pippa and then at each other in bewilderment. 'Is it effrontery to visit a man who has saved my life?' Pippa demanded. 'Especially as he was injured in doing so?'

'It was you he saved?' His lordship did not bother to disguise his surprise.

'It was.'

'I suppose you are that Thornley woman's replacement.'

'How dare you, Cadogan,' William interrupted angrily before Pippa could frame a reply. 'My wife's cousin is a lady. I demand you withdraw that statement.'

'I withdraw it,' he said, though there was no remorse in his tone. 'For Miss Kingslake's ambition is above being a mere mistress. She is after the Cadogan inheritance.'

'That is arrant nonsense.' Pippa was too angry to observe the niceties of polite conversation. She was determined not to let him browbeat her, though she was still shaking. Her love for Edward had long since dwindled to nothing more than a slight feeling of nostalgia that something which had seemed so good had turned so sour. She had even, since she had come to know Sir Ashley, been glad they had parted. 'I do not want your son. You did me a favour putting that connection to an end.'

'My son, madam, is dead.'

'Edward, dead?' Pippa was so shocked she took a step backwards; finding the seat of a chair behind her knees, she thankfully sank onto it. Edward's death was not something she had ever envisaged; he had been a slight young man, not athletic at all, but he had been fit and well. 'How?'

'Do not tell me you have not heard of it.'

'I have not. I have neither seen nor heard from Edward since…' She paused. 'It must be six years.'

'Six years in the pestilential heat of India. The climate killed him in the end.'

Pippa pulled herself together and stood up again; she would not let him see how much he disturbed her. 'Then I am sorry for you, my lord. Please convey my condolences to Lady Cadogan.'

'I will not do that. She blames you.'

'Me?' she queried. 'Why? I did not ask Edward to go to India.'

'He would not have gone if it had not been necessary to sever his connection with you.'

'Because your foolish wife thought my red hair meant I had made a pact with the devil. Such superstitious beliefs went out over a hundred years ago.'

'Nothing to do with the colour of your hair, more to do with the colour of your money or lack of it, lack of breeding too, which was more important. We simply pointed out to him that he was putting his inheritance in jeopardy if he married an eccentric like you, and he realised it would not do.'

'Whatever are you talking about?' Eleanor asked, looking from one to the other.

Pippa turned towards her. 'I was once engaged to be married to Lord Cadogan's son, six years ago it was, the summer you spent with William in the Netherlands. The breaking of it off caused a scandal, but Aunt Augusta took me back to Norfolk and Edward went off to India. I had no idea he had died.'

'Forgive me for doubting that,' Lord Cadogan put it. 'Why otherwise would you attach yourself to my nephew, if not to continue your assault on the Cadogan estate?'

'Your nephew?' Pippa asked, puzzled.

'Ashley. The man lying upstairs, unable to stir a limb. Not content with depriving me of my son, you have managed to make a cripple of my next heir.'

'Oh.' Sir Ashley was Lord Cadogan's nephew and heir. She could hardly credit it. Why, oh, why, had Ashley not told her?

'I tell you now,' his lordship said, stepping forwards and wagging a finger in her face. 'If he is so foolish as to shackle himself to you, he can kiss his inheritance goodbye.'

'Lord Cadogan,' William said, 'I do not know the rights and wrongs of it, but I deplore the uncivil way you have spoken to my relative. I am sorry you have lost your son, but that is no excuse. Miss Kingslake is upset enough that Sir Ashley has been injured saving her without having to listen to your ramblings.'

Lord Cadogan gave an angry snort and the whole encounter might have ended in one calling the other out if a discreet cough had not made them all turn to see the footman had returned. 'Lord Trentham, Sir Ashley is ready to receive you now.'

Pippa did not feel like going up, she felt more like fleeing, but one look at Lord Cadogan's thunderous face was enough to put steel into her backbone. She would be damned if she would allow him to dictate to her and keep her from her visit, even though any hope that Ash would love her as she loved him had gone. She rose unsteadily and followed William and Eleanor up the stairs. The banging of the front door told them his lordship had left.

She could not help thinking about his remark that she was a replacement for Mrs Thornley. How many other people thought that? she wondered. Did Sir Ashley think it? How humiliating for her if he did. There was a chair outside the door of the room to which the footman was taking them and Pippa, unable to face Ash, subsided onto it. 'I will wait here for you,' she said, handing Eleanor the small parcel she had brought for the invalid. 'Give him this with my good wishes for his speedy recovery.'

If Eleanor was surprised, she did not show it, but took the package and followed her husband into the room.

Ash had been shaved, had his hair brushed and tied back and there was a shawl about his shoulders. A colourful rug covered his legs. 'Forgive me if I do not get up,' he said. 'As you can see I am somewhat indisposed.' He looked past them, expecting to see Pippa. 'But where is Miss Kingslake? Was she injured after all? Is she, like me, unable to stir?'

'Philippa sustained a few bruises, but nothing to worry about,' Eleanor said, handing him the little parcel. 'She sent this to help you while away the hours.'

He took the paper off it to reveal Pippa's latest book. '*Held to Ransom*,' he said, reading the title, his lips twitching at the irony of it. If ever anyone was being held to ransom it was he. 'I shall read it with pleasure, but why did she not come with you? This is not a bedchamber and I am decently clad.'

'She came, but she is a little upset. We met Lord Cadogan in the hall. He was excessively rude to her.'

'Damn the man. I hoped they would not meet, at least not before I had broken the news to her.'

'I wish you would explain,' William said.

'I have, on the recent demise of my cousin, Edward, become Lord Cadogan's heir. It was totally unexpected. I would not have Miss Kingslake upset over it for worlds. Where is she? Has she left?'

'She is sitting outside the door.'

'So near and yet so far,' he murmured. He raised his voice. 'Miss Kingslake, I wish you would come in. I want to see for myself that you are well and none the worse for your fall.'

Pippa rose and walked slowly into the room. Ash lay on his daybed, grey with pain and fatigue, nothing like the strong, cheerful man he had been, and it was all on account of her. If she had not come to London and involved him in her search for Nat, if he had not felt he had to escort her out and about, then he would not be lying injured. Her heart, already his, ached with sorrow and remorse and the misery of knowing nothing could come of her love for him. There were too many obstacles. She could not bring herself to upbraid him for not telling her about Edward, especially in front of Eleanor and William. Her pride would not let them see how much it mattered.

She approached the bed, close enough for him to grasp her hand. His grip was surprisingly strong. 'How are you, Pippa?' he asked, eliciting a gasp from Eleanor for not only using Pippa's Christian name, but its diminutive.

'I am perfectly well, thank you, Sir Ashley.' She was still shaking from her encounter with Lord Cadogan and her answer was stilted. The use of her name hardly registered on her conscious mind. 'More importantly, how are you? If you had not thrown yourself on top of me, it would have been my back that was broken and I am truly grateful for your intervention. It was a very gallant thing to do.'

'My back is not broken,' he said firmly. 'I shall be my old self in no time at all.' He paused. There was so much he wanted to say to her, but it was difficult to have a personal conversation with Lord and Lady Trentham present. It would have to wait. 'Thank you for your gift. I shall read it with interest. Is it the one about the pirates?'

'Yes.'

'And how is the smuggling book coming along?'

'I am afraid I have done nothing since I came to London. There has been too much else on my mind.'

'I am sorry for that,' he said, searching her face. 'If I could relieve your mind, I would.'

She understood he was speaking of her search for Nat. 'I know.'

The gulf that had opened up between them had widened since her encounter with Lord Cadogan and, though her heart was full, there was nothing more she could say. She withdrew her hand from his.

'We must not tire Sir Ashley,' Eleanor said. 'Come, Pippa, we will leave him to rest.'

It was better that way, Ash told himself as he watched them depart. Until he had recovered his health and, more importantly, solved the mystery of Nat Kingslake, he could say nothing to Pippa of what he felt. But she had been looking bleak and he cursed himself for not telling her about Edward as soon as he heard the news himself. Lord Cadogan was the most tactless man in the world to accost her in that way. No wonder she looked forlorn. If they had been alone, he could have explained, could have reassured her in more positive ways than simply taking her hand.

Being in love was not the easy ride he had supposed it to be; it was as bumpy as a pot-holed road.

His valet came in bearing a tray on which was a small glass of a brown liquid, which had been prescribed to deaden the pain in his back, but the few doses he had taken had turned his brain to wool and he could not think straight. And he had to think. He refused the medicine. 'I want you to take a message to Captain Carstairs,' he told Mortimer, who was making disapproving noises. 'I would welcome a visit from him at his earliest convenience.'

Pippa knew she would be in for a quizzing as soon as they were on their way, but that was only fair, so as the carriage took them the short ride to Piccadilly, she told William and Eleanor what had had happened in the past. 'I have come to look on it as a blessing,' she ended. 'I had no idea that Lord and Lady Cadogan bore me so much ill will.'

'We heard that an engagement had been broken, but not the name of the young man, nor the reason behind it,' Eleanor said. 'You have been ill served.'

'Now I must find Nat without Sir Ashley's help,' Pippa went on. 'Then we must go back to Narbeach and take up our lives again as they were before the *Sally Ann* arrived.' She did not tell them about Sir Felix's blackmail. That was something she would have to deal with on her own. The prospect of marrying him filled her with revulsion.

'Do you know where he is?' Eleanor asked.

'No.' She thought of telling them that the *Sally Ann* was docked in London, but decided against it. They would never let her visit it.

'I would help you try to find him,' William said. 'But it is a question of the law. I am part of his Majesty's government and must stand apart.'

'I know, William, and I thank you for even having me in your home. I will not burden you with my presence any longer than I can help. When I visited my publisher the other day, he told me how to go about making enquiries. I shall ask him for his assistance.' She said it more to reassure him than because she meant to do it.

The carriage drew up at Trentham House and any further questions were postponed as they went into the house and repaired to their rooms to rest before dressing for dinner.

Luckily there had been no guests and it was easy to plead fatigue and retire early soon after the meal finished. Instead of going to bed, she changed into Nat's clothes and crept from the house by a back door. She was shaking with nerves and wishing she had the cool strength of Sir Ashley at her elbow. It was all very well to don the clothes of a man and pretend independence, but she was only too aware of her vulnerability. She found a chair for hire and was conveyed to the berth where the Sally Ann had been docked. It had already sailed. Was Nat on board?

She stood looking about her, as if trying to conjure her brother up from the air. It was a cloudy night and the moon appeared only fitfully. She could make nothing out except the looming buildings of the warehouses that lined the shore and the masts of hundreds of ships lying at anchor in the river. She heard scuffling and squeaking close at hand and recognised the sound. There were rats everywhere. She put her hand to her mouth to stop herself shrieking, and took a step or two towards the sound of laughter and singing in a nearby tavern and then changed her mind; she might be safer with the rats. Which way had Ash taken her to find a hackney? She turned to try to find it.

A man appeared out of the gloom and strode towards her. She took to her heels and ran. He pursued her. She had no idea where she was going and was afraid she was running round in circles. A few moments later a large hand fell on her shoulder and she shuddered to a halt. 'I had no idea you were so athletic, Miss Kingslake. You can certainly run.'

She twisted round to see Captain Carstairs smiling down at her. She let out her breath in a huge sigh of relief. 'What are you doing here? How did you know it was me?'

'Your attire was described to me very accurately, so I had no trouble identifying you. Shall we go? I am sure you do not wish to stay here.' He kept his hand on her shoulder as he spoke, admitting of no discussion. 'I have a hackney waiting nearby.'

'Who knew I was here and what I would be wearing?' she asked. 'Was it Lord Trentham?'

'Surely he did not know what you intended? I cannot imagine he would have allowed it.'

'No, no one knew.' She paused. 'Oh. It was Sir Ashley.'

'Yes, Miss Kingslake. He sent me to intercept you.'

'Supposing I had not been here?'

He chuckled. 'Then I would have returned and reported my failure and he would have been obliged to admit he did not know you as well as he thought he did and I would have been the richer by ten guineas.'

They had left the river and were in one of the noisome streets behind the docks. He stopped beside a hackney, opened the door and ushered her in before ordering the driver to take them to Pall Mall and getting in beside her.

'Pall Mall,' she echoed, as they began to move.

'Yes, Ash wants to speak to you and as it is dark and you are dressed in male attire, no one will think anything of it.'

There did not seem to be any answer to that and she fell silent. She knew if she were seen and recognised, her reputation, already shaky, would be gone for ever. But what did it matter? She would soon be back in Narbeach where the gossip of the capital hardly reached the inhabitants' ears. And she did have a bone to pick with Sir Ashley Saunders.

The carriage drew up and Alex opened the door, but did not offer his hand; a man would never help another out of a vehicle unless he was drunk. 'Pretend to be a little foxed,' he said. Obligingly she staggered and he grabbed hold of her and they rolled unsteadily towards the door and were admitted by Mortimer, who manfully concealed his disapproval as he conducted them upstairs. There was no sign of any other servants.

Mortimer threw open the door of the room Pippa had been in earlier in the day. 'Captain Carstairs and a…' he paused '…a young gentleman, Sir Ashley,' he announced.

'Good,' Ash said. 'You may retire, I shall not need you again tonight.'

'But, sir…'

'Go to bed.'

Reluctantly he left and Pippa advanced into the room, followed by Captain Carstairs. Ash was still lying on his daybed, wearing a dressing gown, his legs covered with a rug. He was pale, but he was smiling. 'Alex, you owe me ten guineas.'

The Captain piled ten coins neatly on the table beside the invalid and stepped back. 'I'll leave you. Shout when

Miss Kingslake is ready to be taken home.' And he too left.

'He has left us alone,' Pippa said in consternation.

'So he has.' He indicated a stool beside the bed. 'Sit down. I find it uncomfortable craning my neck to look up at you.'

'But…'

'But nothing. If it were not for this troublesome back, I would dust those elegant breeches of yours. You knew I did not want you wandering about town on your own and yet you still went.'

'I am sorry about your back,' she said, sitting down. It surprised her how close they were, so close she could see could see the lines of pain around his eyes. She resisted the temptation to reach out and stroke his brow and give herself away. He must not know how much she ached for him; it would be too humiliating. 'Is it very painful?'

'I can bear it, especially when you are here to take my mind off it.'

'I should not be. It is very improper.'

He laughed and then winced as pain shot through him. 'You are surely not concerned with what is proper or you would not go about looking like that.' He eyed her up and down, smiling. 'Someone less like a young gentleman would be hard to imagine.'

She felt herself blush. 'I could not go out alone dressed in a gown, could I?'

'You should not have gone out alone in any guise. You were lucky not to be attacked and robbed. Raped, even.'

She would not tell him she had been terrified. 'How did you know I would be there?'

'I am incapacitated, not brainless, and am perfectly capable of adding two and two,' he said. 'I reasoned that you would think you had to go on with the investigation without me and, knowing you as I do, it was not difficult to surmise you would begin with the *Sally Ann*.'

'She has sailed.'

'Has she? Do you know where?'

'No.'

'No matter, Captain Carstairs will find out for us.'

'You have confided all to him?'

'Not quite all,' he said with a wry smile. 'That would be ungentlemanly of me.'

'Oh.' She was thoughtful and then decided to have it out with him while she had the chance. 'Do you look upon me as a replacement for Mrs Thornley, Sir Ashley?'

'Good God, no! Whatever gave you that idea?'

'Lord Cadogan.'

'He is a scoundrel and if I were not laid up I would make him eat those words. When I look for a mistress I do not look among the ranks of respectable single ladies. It would be the worst of bad *ton*. There are plenty of demi-reps, those on the periphery of society from whom to choose, women on the lookout for protectors, usually widows looking for a little dalliance to liven up their lives, or married women tired of their husbands. In no way could you be considered one of them.' He paused to smile reassuringly. 'You are perfectly safe. I will not fall on you with my ardour.'

A wicked imp inside her was not sure whether to be glad or sorry about that. To have him fall on her with his ardour would, she was sure, be a very pleasurable experience. 'You must think me very ignorant,' she said.

'On that score I am glad you are,' he said, suppressing his own wicked imp. 'I hope I have set your mind at rest.'

'Yes, thank you.'

'Then let us talk about our search for your brother.'

'But we are no further forwards.'

'We are a little. I returned to the *Sally Ann* myself the evening before last.'

'You did?' She leaned forwards eagerly. 'Why didn't you say?'

'I was waiting until we were alone, but we have not been alone, which is why I decided to have you kidnapped and brought here.' He smiled. 'Very wicked of me, I know, but I am glad I did if it has cleared any misunderstanding between us.'

She ignored that. 'Tell me what you discovered.'

'I am afraid it is not good news. I was told your brother was indeed on board the *Sally Ann* and employed by Sir Felix to negotiate for cargoes. He was given money to pay for them—'

'Legitimate cargoes,' she said. 'I am sure he would not have anything to do with contraband.'

'Let us hope you are right,' he said, unwilling to shatter her faith in her errant brother.

'Do you know where he is now?'

'On board the *Sally Ann*, I imagine. We will perhaps discover the truth when we go back to Norfolk.'

'But you are not fit to travel.'

'Unfortunately no, but if, as I suspect, the *Sally Ann* has gone to Amsterdam, then it will not return for a week or so and by that time I hope to be on my feet again.'

'Why did you not tell me you were Edward's cousin?' she demanded suddenly.

'Was there any reason why I should? Until a few days ago, I knew nothing of what had happened. And I certainly did not expect to become the Cadogan heir.' He decided not say anything about Ben's and her aunt's earlier confidences, which would have been humiliating for her. 'I would have told you when a suitable moment presented itself, but as things turned out, I had no chance.' He paused. 'My footman told me what Lord Cadogan said to you and I am truly sorry that he should have been so venomous. I would not have had it happen for the world.'

'I thought it was all over and done with,' she said. 'How could he blame me for his son's death? I was not the one to break off the engagement. If Edward went abroad, it was because he was ashamed…'

'Did you love him very much?' he asked softly.

'I thought I did, but I realise I was wrong. It was no more than a youthful infatuation, which would not have lasted. We had so little in common. I was not the wife for him.'

'No, I can see that,' he said, feeling his spirits rise, even though nothing had been solved. 'So you are not pining for a lost love?'

'No,' she said firmly. She might not be pining for Edward, but that did not mean she was not yearning for another lost love, for lost it was. 'Nor have I any designs on the Cadogan estates. Heaven knows where Lord Cadogan got that idea.'

'I do not know that, either.'

Their words seemed to confirm the hopelessness of their situation and yet they were bound together with ties neither could break. He reached out and took her hand. She let it rest in his and thus they remained in companionable silence for several minutes.

'It will soon be dawn,' he murmured at last. 'You must go back to Trentham House before you are missed. Captain Carstairs will see you safely indoors. If you would be so good as to go onto the landing and call him.'

She rose and did as she was asked. Alex was lounging

in a chair in the hall and bounded up the stairs when she called him. Goodbyes were said and in no time at all she was on her way back to the world of Eleanor and William and the social round and gossip.

Eleanor would not hear of her returning to Narbeach so soon after the accident, when Pippa suggested it. 'You may not have been badly hurt,' she said, 'but you have sustained several bruises and I cannot believe you have not been considerably shaken by the ordeal. Stay a few more days. Besides,' she added, 'how can you think of leaving when Sir Ashley is lying prostrate on account of saving you? It would be hard-hearted to abandon him. We can visit him again and take some sweetmeats.'

'I thought you disapproved of him.'

'Oh, I have quite changed my mind. He is the hero of the hour. And he has broken off his liaison with Mrs Thornley, which is a good thing. I am persuaded he is going to become the very essence of a respectable gentleman, especially as he is now Lord Cadogan's heir. Mark my words, in a little while he will be looking for a wife and settling down.'

'I expect he will.'

'He likes you, you know. If you were to make a little push, you could attract his attention.'

'I have already attracted his attention, Eleanor, and for all the wrong reasons. If you plan to matchmake, you will fail. I am not in the marriage market, nor do I wish to be.'

'If you are referring to that business with Lord Cadogan's son and the disgraceful way his lordship spoke to you yesterday, I should put it out of your mind. I doubt Sir Ashley will allow himself to be browbeaten.'

'I am sure he will not, but you are in error if you think he will marry me simply to defy his uncle. He is not that foolish. And nor am I—but you are right, it would be uncivil to leave town while Sir Ashley is so ill.'

They visited Ash each afternoon during the following week and watched his strength gradually returning. His doctor said his recovery was a miracle, but bade him take care not to walk about too much and bring on a relapse. Pippa did what she could to help him, running errands, fetching and carrying, bringing him books which they discussed in some detail. They were always chaperoned by Eleanor and sometimes other people arrived too and made up a lively party round his daybed. The conversation was light-hearted and impersonal.

'The sawbones has said I am fit to travel,' he told them on the eighth day. Only Pippa and Eleanor were present. 'I plan to go to Fairfields to recuperate. I have had enough of London for the moment. I will not be much use as an escort, but it would please me, Miss Kingslake, if you and your maid would consent to travel with me. I am sure you wish to see your aunt and cousin. You can go from there to Narbeach and perhaps you will find your brother there waiting for you.'

Pippa had only been waiting for him to be back on his feet before leaving, but she was doubtful about the wisdom of travelling with him. It was not so much the impropriety of it, but the realisation that if she were alone in his company for any length of time, she would give herself away. If she were wise, she would decline and make her own way home, but she was not wise where he was concerned;

she was weak as water. 'How will you travel?' she asked. 'You cannot possibly go by public coach.'

'No, and neither can you. You are more knocked up than you realise. I have sent for my carriage, we can travel in comfort in that.' He turned to Eleanor. 'Lady Trentham, what do you think?'

Eleanor smiled. Although she knew she ought to disapprove, she felt Ash and Pippa were made for each other and if there was any way she could make them realise it, she would take it. 'I can see no harm in it,' she said, pretending to consider the matter. 'After all, Pippa, you are not a giddy miss just out of school and you will have Teresa for a chaperone. And I am sure Sir Ashley can be trusted.'

And so Pippa agreed to be ready by eight o'clock the following morning.

That night Ash had another visitor. 'There is a rough-looking cove downstairs asking for Thomas Smith,' Mortimer said. 'I told him there was no one here of that name, but he would not leave.'

'For God's sake, man, send him up,' Ash interrupted him. 'And see we are not disturbed.'

Mortimer went away grumbling and was soon back with the visitor. Ash stared at him. He was younger than Pippa, but uncannily like her. And he had a mop of curly red hair. No wonder the seaman had thought Pippa looked like him. Far from cowed, he bounced into the room and swept Ash a bow. 'Am I addressing Mr Thomas Smith?'

'For the purposes of this interview, you are. And you, I conclude, are Mr Nathaniel Kingslake. You do not need to deny it. I am acquainted with your sister.'

'I imagined you were,' he said. 'Josh Stone said my brother was looking for me and described the fellow so carefully I knew it had to be Pip. Up to every rig, she is. How did she meet up with you?'

'In Narbeach when I was staying with Sir Felix.'

'So you know that rogue, too. Friend of yours, is he?'

'I am acquainted with the gentleman,' Ash said, deliberately vague.

'You told my friend you were betrothed to my sister. If that is true, it is bound to put Sir Felix in a temper.'

'I care nothing for Sir Felix's temper, but I imagine you do.'

'Not at all. I wish you good luck.'

'Where have you been? Pippa has been beside herself with worry.'

'I am sorry for that, but it could not be helped.' He paused. 'Josh said Ben had been arrested.'

'Yes, he has. He was caught on the beach when the dragoons came. He seems to think you will testify that he was not one of the smugglers.'

'How can I do that without admitting I am one myself?'

'Quite.'

'Do you think I am fool enough to do that?'

'Then why did you come here?'

'Curiosity, sir, curiosity. And when I asked at your door for Thomas Smith, your man told me this was the residence of Sir Ashley Saunders. Are you he?'

'That is of no import.'

'Indeed it is, if we are to part on good terms. I have heard of you. I believe you are a member of the Piccadilly Gentlemen's Club.'

That the boy knew this surprised Ash though he did not show it. 'Whether we part on good terms or not depends on what you have to tell me. I could send for the Watch and have you arrested.'

'That would not please my sister.'

'You are an insufferably opinionated puppy,' Ash said, losing patience with him. 'If you had an ounce of feeling for your sister, you would not consort with smugglers. They are not the romantic heroes of Pippa's novels, but dastardly criminals who do not stop at intimidation and murder. Not only do you risk your life and liberty, you risk your sister's reputation, for she is fierce in her defence of you.'

'Is she? Bless her. But I know the risks. I am not a green fool. It is precisely because I love my sister that I joined the band at Narbeach.'

'You have a strange way of showing your affection. Be so good as to explain.'

'Are you asking as Pip's friend or as one of the Piccadilly Gentlemen?'

'The two are indivisible. The law is the law and if you are going to tell me that you do it for the money to make a more comfortable life for her, then your reasoning is wide of the mark. You have made it infinitely more uncomfortable.'

Nat laughed. It sounded so like Pippa that Ash winced. 'Only temporarily, sir, and you seem to be doing well as her protector. And for that, I thank you.'

'Come to the point, man.'

'Pip has always been the one to look after me. She gave up all idea of marriage to do it, a huge sacrifice since she would have been in clover if she had married Edward Cadogan, for all she assured me in the end they would not suit. I owe everything to her. I could not let her throw herself away on Sir Felix Markham, could I? He is a devil.'

'What do you know of him?'

'Oh, more than he would care for me to know, but to discover it I had to get in with him. Smuggling is only a small part of it. I know, for instance, that he murdered his first two wives '

'You don't say so.' Ash was shocked, even though Ben had already told him the man had been cruel to his wives.

'I do. It was done for their money. He came into the ladies' portions when they died and he needed the blunt to finance his extravagant way of life.'

'And to buy contraband.'

'That, too.'

'What proof have you?'

'None that will stand in a court of law. That is why I must stick to my purpose, until I get it.'

'Pippa will be greatly relieved to hear you are not a committed lawbreaker.'

'You are not to breathe a word to her. She would forbid me to go on with it and she might say something to Sir Felix and alert him to his danger. Keep this to yourself. And I don't want any of the Piccadilly Gentlemen poking their noses in.'

'If Sir Felix is as bad as you say he is, you could be in danger and might need help.'

'Not while he thinks Pippa will marry him, so I beg of you, say no more about being betrothed to her until all is resolved.'

'You expect me to stand by and do nothing? That is not my way, Mr Kingslake.'

'You will not be doing nothing. You will be keeping my sister out of mischief. No more wandering about dressed as my brother.'

'That I should endeavour to do in any case. But tell me, what are you proposing to do?'

'I am going back to the *Sally Ann*. We have just returned from the Netherlands with a cargo of Geneva spirit and sail for Norfolk on tomorrow's tide. 'Tis a pity you are laid up. I had hoped you would be there when we landed.'

'I will be there,' Ash said firmly. 'We leave for Norfolk tomorrow.'

'Good.' Nat prepared to leave. 'Remember, we have not met,' he said, then laughed. 'But I fancy I might like you for a brother-in-law.'

And then he was gone, leaving Ash deep in thought. It was a dangerous game the boy was playing and he might very well come to grief. And if he thought he could tell one of the Piccadilly Gentlemen what to do, he was glaringly abroad. But Ash would have to tread very carefully; that is, if he could walk at all. If determination could bring that about, he would.

Tom Davies had arrived with the carriage the previous afternoon and the horses were rested overnight, so they were fresh and ready to go the following morning. Ash hobbled painfully down the stairs and climbed in. Mortimer had put several cushions and rugs inside to make him as comfortable as possible. When this had been done, the valet got in to sit opposite him and Tom was directed to Trentham House.

Ash did not get out when they stopped, but waited for Pippa and Teresa to come out, which they did, accompanied by Eleanor and two footmen carrying her trunk which they strapped on the roof. The rest of the luggage was put in the basket at the back. Goodbyes were said and they set off at a steady pace, so as not to discomfort the invalid. It was not so bad while they were on the toll roads out of London, but on the country roads, which had not improved with the bad winter and wet summer they had had, it was apparent that the jolting was causing him considerable pain. Pippa wanted to stop and allow him to recover a little, but he would not hear of it.

He did not feel like talking, having much to think about, but it was a comfort to have her sitting beside him, even if they could not speak of the things that were closest to their hearts. Teresa and Mortimer were at first wary of each other, but were soon chatting amiably, talking about the latest fashions and the gossip of the court. Ash smiled at their efforts to entertain him and surreptitiously reached out to take Pippa's hand and squeeze it.

On the journey up, Tom had arranged for a change of horses to be ready for them at inns along the route and when they stopped Ash was glad to leave his seat and try to walk about a little. 'Now you know what I shall be like when I am old and infirm,' he told Pippa as she helped him perambulate slowly about the inn yard while the horses were being changed.

'Old age comes to all of us if we are lucky enough to live that long,' she said, wondering if she would still know him that far into the future, when by then he would be Lord Cadogan. She had been trying not to think about that, but it frequently impinged on her thoughts when she least expected it. 'But you are a long way from that yet.'

Sometimes they went into the inns for food and drink, sometimes they had something brought out to them, and then, refreshed with hot meat pies and coffee, they were on their way again. The journey was turning out to be exquisite mental torture, Pippa decided, but she had known from the start it would be. To sit beside him, so close his breeches-clad leg was lost in the folds of her skirt, was enough to send shivers up and down her spine, and to talk of this and that as if they were mere acquaintances making conversation in a drawing room made her want to scream. She wanted to discuss the dilemma they faced, to rail at an unkind fate which had brought them so close and then thrust them apart again, but with valet and maid in the carriage with them, it was impossible. Nor would it have been kind considering he was in so much pain.

'We ought to rack up for the night,' Ash said to Pippa when they had been on the road nearly ten hours and all four were becoming very stiff and the conversation had long before limped to a halt. 'But we are so near Norwich, we will keep going if you can bear it. The Maid's Head will make us comfortable for the night and we can go on in the morning.'

'I can bear it if you can,' Pippa said, understanding his wish to be home and have the torment of the journey over and done with. Once there, he could rest. 'Will the horses manage it?'

''T'isn't the horses we should be worried about,' Mortimer put in. 'It's Sir Ashley. I fear the journey has been too much for him.'

'Will you cease your worrying?' Ash told him. 'And tell Tom to keep going.'

They drew into the yard of the Maid's Head half an hour later and Mortimer went to arrange accommodation for them. When he returned he insisted on helping Sir Ashley up to his room, leaving Pippa and Teresa to fend for themselves, which they had no trouble in doing. They did not see Ash or Mortimer again until the following morning, when they set out again with a fresh set of horses.

The rest of the journey was uneventful and by noon they were drawing up outside Fairfields. 'It is good to be home again,' Ash said, as the front door was opened and Augusta stood on the step to welcome them. Pippa ran to embrace her, while Mortimer helped Ash from the carriage and supported him up the steps.

'Oh, I have missed you,' Augusta said, hugging her. 'And poor Sir Ashley. The servant he sent for the carriage told us what had happened. You must tell us all about it, but first I think Sir Ashley must be put to bed. He looks exhausted.'

There were servants in plenty to take care of Sir Ashley's needs and he was taken from them and carried up to his bedchamber. Footmen saw to the luggage and Teresa followed them to the room Pippa had occupied before. Pippa went with her aunt to a small parlour where they were able to sit, drink tea and talk undisturbed.

'Now tell me how Sir Ashley came to be injured,' Augusta commanded and when that was done, exclaimed at the great debt Pippa owed him. 'We both do,' she added, 'for I have been made so comfortable here, I am quite reluctant to go back to Windward House. But I suppose now you are here, I must.' She paused, then went on to the subject closest to her heart. 'What did you discover in London? Did you see Nathaniel?'

'No, Aunt. But he was definitely on board the *Sally Ann*. According to one of his shipmates he left the ship when it docked in London, but we believe he might have boarded it again before it sailed.'

'Whatever is the boy playing at? He must know we are worried to death about him.'

Pippa sighed. 'I don't know, Aunt. I wish I did. Sir Ashley believes the ship sailed to Amsterdam. According to Sir Ashley's informant, Nat was in possession of money given to him by Sir Felix to buy cargo.'

'Sir Felix? Not contraband surely?'

'I don't know. I would like to think it was legal. I told Sir Ashley I was sure it was, but I do not think he believed it. And to be honest, I am not sure I do. It puts us very firmly on opposite sides.'

'We are not at war, Philippa.'

'It feels like it.'

'I am sure Sir Ashley will find a way out. Ben is sure he will.'

'What does Ben know?'

'Nothing. I am persuaded Sir Ashley will arrange his release or why else would he have had us stay here?'

As ever Augusta was really only concerned with her son. If Nathaniel was so foolish as to get himself tangled up with smugglers, it was his own look out and he must take the consequences. She did not realise that the consequences for Philippa would be eternal misery.

'I discovered something else about Sir Ashley that will surprise you,' she told her aunt. 'He is Edward's cousin.'

'Good heavens! And he never breathed a word about that while he was at Narbeach.'

'I do not suppose he felt the need. He did not know my connection with him. But Edward died in India and now Sir Ashley is Lord Cadogan's heir.'

Augusta put out a hand and laid it on Pippa's. 'Oh, my dear, I am sorry. As if you have not troubles enough.'

'It is of no consequence, Aunt.' Pippa tried to sound as

if she meant it, but she could not help being reminded of Lord Cadogan's hateful words. 'The sooner we go home, the better. Perhaps Nat will come to us there and we can put all this behind us.'

'Amen to that. Now, I am sure you are very tired after your journey, so go and rest before dinner. Things will look brighter in the morning.'

Chapter Nine

Pippa's first action on rising next morning was to enquire after Sir Ashley and was surprised to learn he was up and had gone out. 'I told him it was too soon,' Mortimer told her, 'but he would not listen. I might as well talk to myself.'

She left him grumbling and went in search of her host. She found him in the stables talking to Ben. 'I am afraid, without Mr Kingslake's testimony, I cannot set you free,' he was saying.

'I understand.' Ben grinned. 'I'd just as soon stay here. I like working for you.'

'You may do so as long as you wish, but I am sure you would rather work as a free man. I am hopeful that we will find your cousin at Narbeach when we arrive and he will be able to explain all to our satisfaction.'

'We?' Pippa interrupted them. 'You are planning to go to Narbeach yourself?'

He turned to her, smiling. 'Yes, of course. You will need an escort and I am sure you wish to go as soon as possible.'

'When are you planning on leaving?'

'Today. As soon as you are ready. I was just giving instructions for the carriage and some fresh horses.'

She was surprised that he wanted to go so soon. It meant he had not given up on his search for Nat and hoped to catch him red-handed when the *Sally Ann* put in an appearance. How could he be so careful of her one moment, so in sympathy with her in every other way and yet be determined to track down the smugglers, knowing her brother was among them?

'But you are not yet fully recovered.'

'I am well enough and I am persuaded sitting about doing nothing is not the way to a speedy recovery. Exercise, that's the thing.'

She was still very doubtful, but he had obviously made up his mind. At least today's journey would only be of short duration and she could make sure he rested when they arrived and try to keep him off the beach until after the *Sally Ann* came in when, with luck, she would have seen and spoken to Nat. 'Very well,' she said. 'But I insist you stay at Windward House, not the Manor.'

He grinned. 'I hoped you would say that.'

She left him talking to Ben about the horses and went to tell her aunt and give instructions to Teresa.

He watched her go and then sank onto a bale of hay. Standing for any length of time hurt his back, but he would not let her see that. He had to be at Narbeach when the *Sally Ann* arrived and he had to keep Pippa from Sir Felix until Kingslake came with his proof. He wished he could tell her about that, but he was afraid her brother was right; it could put her in danger. Now he knew Kingslake was not a committed smuggler, but on an even more dangerous enterprise, his sole aim was to keep her safe.

They left Fairfield immediately after nuncheon, accompanied by Augusta, Mortimer and Teresa. Pippa was wedged firmly between her aunt and Teresa, while Ash and Mortimer faced them. Stopping in Fakenham for a short time to rest the horses, they were in Narbeach in just over two hours. Joe Sadler came from the stables as the carriage rolled to a stop.

'Miss Kingslake, it's you,' he said, as she opened the door and stepped out. 'And Mrs Whitehouse. Is Mr Nathaniel with you? And Ben?'

'No, Joe. We have not seen my brother. Ben is to stay where he is for the moment.' She turned to see Mortimer helping Ash to alight. He was looking strained again and her heart went out to him. He was certainly not fit to pursue smugglers.

'Sir Ashley,' Joe said, his mouth open in surprise.

'Yes,' Pippa said. 'He has been hurt and is come to take the sea air.'

Joe helped Tom unload the luggage and take it indoors, before they took the carriage and horses away. Pippa led the way indoors to find Mrs Sadler in a panic because she had not been expecting them and she had no beds made up and no provisions in. Pippa gave her the same explanation she had given Joe and then ushered Ash into the drawing room to rest while Teresa and Mortimer went off to help to make beds and find refreshments. Mrs Sadler rushed off to the village to buy food.

'I am sorry no one was ready to receive you,' Pippa told him when she had settled him on a sofa. 'But it was your own fault for rushing off so soon. We could have sent ahead, given time.'

'It is no matter. We are here, that is the main thing. I shall be perfectly content with whatever is available.'

The news that Sir Ashley was staying at Windward House had spread through the village like wildfire as soon as Mrs Sadler had explained to the shopkeeper why she needed extra provisions in a hurry. And in no time it had reached the ears of Sir Felix. He called the very next morning, dressed in a pale-green satin coat and a long yellow waistcoat with huge pearl buttons. His fat calves were encased in white stockings with yellow ribbons at the knees.

'My dear Miss Kingslake,' he said, rushing into the room to bow over her hand, before she could arrange for her aunt to chaperone them. 'I am pleased to have you home again. We all are. We have missed you.'

She retrieved her hand. 'Thank you. I am glad to be back. Will you sit down? I will order refreshments.' Sarah, the parlourmaid, came in answer to her summons and was dispatched to bring tea and cake and to find Mrs Whitehouse.

'I hear that Sir Ashley Saunders is come back with you,' Sir Felix said from the sofa where he had ensconced himself.

'Yes, he has sustained an injury and we thought the sea air might do him good.'

'He should have come to me. It is not done for a gentleman to stay with an unmarried lady.'

'Sir Felix,' she said firmly, 'I care not for what is considered done and not done. My aunt is here and there is nothing improper about it. Sir Ashley was injured saving my life and I owe him a debt of care.'

'Then I owe him the same care, my dear, for your life is precious to me.'

Her heart sank. She did not doubt he would renew his proposal and his blackmail, and how could she answer that? Fortunately he could not go on because Ash strolled into the room at that point. She wondered if he had been listening at the door. 'You're here already, Sir Felix,' he said, laconically. 'We have been back less that twenty-four hours.'

'I came as soon as it was proper,' Sir Felix said. 'And am astonished to find you here. Was my hospitality not up to the mark?'

Ash walked over to the window and stood with his back to it, making it difficult for Sir Felix to see his expression. 'I cannot fault your hospitality, sir. But while these dastardly smugglers are in the area, Miss Kingslake needs protection.'

'And I am perfectly well able to provide it. Better than you, I think, when you are not in the best of health.'

'All the more reason to stay here, where the care I receive is excellent. Besides, the view from my bedchamber window looks out over the beach. I can see everything from there.'

'You sound as if you expect another landing.'

'Yes. Don't you?'

Sir Felix did not answer because Sarah arrived with the tea tray. 'I cannot find Mrs Whitehouse,' she told Pippa, setting it on a table at Pippa's elbow. 'I think she may have gone to visit the vicar's wife.'

'No matter. Sir Ashley is here,' Pippa said, busying herself pouring tea. It was clear the men disliked each other and if, as she had been led to believe, Sir Felix was tied up with the smugglers, there could be trouble. And she feared Ash almost welcomed it. But what of Nat? The last thing she wanted to do was give in to Sir Felix's blackmail, but perhaps if she pretended to consider his proposal it might give her precious time to meet Nat and see him safe. How to manage that without alerting Sir Ashley she had no idea

'Now you are back, we must celebrate,' Sir Felix said, as she handed him a cup of tea. 'I am going to give a dance. You shall be the guest of honour.'

'That will be delightful,' she said, looking straight at Ash, daring him to make a disparaging remark. 'When will it be?'

'In two days' time. I had planned it before you went away so suddenly and all the preparations are already made. Is that convenient for you and your aunt?'

'For me, yes,' she said. 'I will ask my aunt, but I do not think she has made any other arrangements.'

'I hope I am invited too,' Ash said genially.

'Yes, come if you want.' With that half-hearted response, he rose to take his leave. Pippa rang for Teresa to show him out. He took Pippa's hand to bow over it and raise it to his lips, gave Ash a perfunctory bow and was gone.

'I will wager the *Sally Ann* is due in on that night,' Ash said. 'We are to be kept occupied.'

'I thought the same thing, but we cannot absent ourselves. I wonder at you asking for an invitation, when you are not yet strong.'

'I could not let you go into the lion's den alone. He is plotting something.'

'I expect he will ask me to marry him again.' It was said with a heartfelt sigh.

'I sincerely hope you are not contemplating accepting.'

'I am not contemplating marriage at all. My life is here with Aunt Augusta and Ben and Nat, if he should free himself of suspicion. I pray for that.'

It was spoken so sadly he stepped forwards and reached for her hands. 'It will all come right in the end, my dear,' he said gently. 'Do not despair.'

'I cannot help it.' With her hands in his and his dear face so close to hers, she was near to tears.

He drew her closer and put his arm about her, so that her head rested on his shoulder. He did not speak. He was afraid that if he did it would all come tumbling out, what he knew about Nat, what he knew about Sir Felix and most of all what he felt for her. One of her tears trickled down his neck and he gulped hard. Never before had he had to hold himself in check in such a way and it was the hardest thing he had ever done.

She sniffed. 'Sometimes I cannot see a way out at all and I am overwhelmed.'

He kissed the top of her head. 'Let us pretend it is one of your books and you have to work out a happy ending. You have done that many times before, you can do it again.'

'But real life is not fiction.'

'No', he said, affecting cheerfulness. 'Sometimes it is stranger than that.'

She stepped back from him. 'I have made your coat wet.'

'No matter. If it helps you to weep, then weep all you like, I shall not mind it, but I would rather you were laughing.' He took her face in his hands and gently stroked away the tears with his thumbs before turning up the corners of her mouth. 'That's better.'

She managed to smile at his nonsense, though his touch

was making her want to throw herself back into his arms. 'If Nat can be persuaded to turn King's evidence, would that save him, do you think?'

'Oh, undoubtedly,' he said, smiling reassuringly. 'There, you have found a happy ending, after all.'

She did not tell him that was not the only happy ending she needed. The other was her secret and not to be divulged to a soul.

The dance was the talk of the village. It was to be a lavish affair according to Sir Felix's servants, who delighted in telling everyone about the preparations. Everything was being done to please Miss Kingslake: her favourite food, her favourite flowers and a visit from a Norwich jeweller who went away looking very pleased with himself. And rooms were being made ready for guests who were coming from far and wide. Narbeach had never seen anything like it and it was supposed that Sir Felix intended to announce his engagement to Miss Kingslake.

Pippa, walking in the village the next day, catching up on what had been happening in her absence and hoping to hear news of Nat, learned nothing except the preparations for the ball, accompanied by hints as to the reason for them. It filled her with dismay, but she smiled and did not comment.

'Have you heard from Master Nat?' John Bristow called out to her as she passed his smithy. He was busy shoeing one of Ash's horses.

'No, have you?'

'No. He's well and truly gone to ground. And I don' reckon you'll see anything of him while you ha' that there gent staying with you.' He paused. 'We thought he had gone, but here he is ag'in. What's he up to?'

'I don't know that he is up to anything, Mr Bristow. He is recuperating after an injury.'

'You wouldn't betray Nat, would you?'

'Certainly not, but if you know something of him, I wish you would tell me. I know he went on board the *Sally Ann*.'

'Tha's all anyone knows, Miss Kingslake.'

She left him, but had not gone many yards when she met Ash walking towards her with the aid of a cane. 'What are you doing out?' she demanded. 'You should be resting.'

He smiled crookedly and turned to accompany her home. 'I am testing out my limbs. I want to be able to dance with you tomorrow.'

All her hopes and fears were centred around what was to happen on the morrow. She was looking forward to it with a mixture of fear and trepidation and hope, hope that Nat would come home and Sir Ashley would see no reason to hand him over to the law. And hope that she would not have to endure Sir Felix's advances.

They went to the dance in Ashley's carriage since it was more comfortable than the Kingslake one. Pippa, whose wardrobe of fine clothes for formal occasions was limited, was wearing the cream silk gown Eleanor had given her, knowing she looked well in it. Teresa had done her best to tame her hair, by pulling it up tightly into a knot on the top of her head with jewelled combs and allowing the ends to curl loosely. But it was still a fiery red, nothing could alter that, except to dye it black. When she mentioned doing this to Ash, he had been aghast. 'I hope you will do no such thing,' he had said. 'You would not be you without your lovely hair…'

'Lovely?' she repeated. 'How can you say so?'

'But it is and I will take issue with anyone who says differently.'

She laughed. 'Even Lord Cadogan.'

'Especially Lord Cadogan.'

What neither realised until they arrived was that Mrs Thornley was among the guests. Pippa would have turned tail and gone home again if Ash had not held her elbow firmly and led her forwards. 'He has done it on purpose to stir up trouble,' he whispered in her ear. 'Do not let him succeed.'

Offering an arm to Pippa on one side and Mrs Whitehouse on the other, he steered them to the other side of the room, where the Reverend Mr Fearson and his wife were standing talking to Dr Witherspoon and his wife, and they were soon chatting amiably to them. Ash pretended to be listening, but he was looking about him, wondering what, if anything, was going to happen. He had found a telescope on the windowsill of his bedchamber and had used it to scan the sea just before they left. He had seen a ship on the horizon, but it was too far away to identify. He needed a closer look. And what on earth was Arabella doing here? He had not been aware she was known to Sir Felix.

The orchestra started to play for a gavotte and their host came and claimed Pippa, leaving Augusta to sit with the parson's wife. They often worked together to alleviate the lot of the poor children in the village and were soon engrossed in ways and means, leaving Ash standing alone.

Arabella sidled up to him. 'Good evening, Ash,' she said. 'You seem to have recovered from your injuries remarkably quickly. I expect it is down to the excellent nursing you have received.'

'Mrs Thornley.' Not wishing to be seen as ill mannered

in public, he gave her a slight bow. 'What are you doing here?' It was said through gritted teeth.

'Why, I am staying with my good friend Sir Felix.'

'I was unaware that you were acquainted.'

She laughed. 'It is not my habit to discuss one old lover with the next, Ash, but I have known Sir Felix many years.'

'In the biblical sense, I assume.'

'Of course.'

The idea that she had been Sir Felix's lover before she had been his did not sit well with him, but it was not jealousy—he was long past that where she was concerned. It was a feeling that they were plotting against him. 'That does not explain your presence here tonight.'

'He invited me. I think he wanted me to witness his betrothal to Miss Kingslake. She will be his third bride.'

'If she accepts him, which gives me leave to doubt.'

'Oh, she will. He has made sure of it.'

He was startled enough to ask her how.

'He has her brother in the palm of his hand. Unless she agrees, the young man is for Tyburn's tree.'

He looked about him for Pippa, but she was nowhere to be seen and neither was Sir Felix. He dashed off in search of them, cursing himself for allowing Arabella to distract him when he should have been watching out for her.

Felix had dragged Pippa off to a small parlour at the back of the house and was detaining her there by the simple expedient of grasping her by her shoulders so tightly that he was making her wince.

'Come now, Pippa, there is no need to be coy with me. You promised me a decision by the end of last week, instead of which you chose to run away. Did you think that would change anything? I need an answer and I need it now. Why do you think I have taken so much trouble with the entertainment tonight? Everyone is expecting an announcement.'

'Then I am afraid they will be disappointed. I have not yet made up my mind.'

'What is keeping you from a decision? The issue is plain enough.'

'I will make up my mind when I see my brother safe and sound and free of all restraint.'

'It is not I who will restrain him, my dear, but your so-called guest. He is a member of the Piccadilly Gentlemen's Club, did you know that? They are thieftakers, sworn to track down criminals and hand them over to the law, so, you see, if you were relying on him to save your brother, I am afraid you will be disappointed. His oath to the Society is greater than any softer feeling he might have for you. You are wide of the mark if you think otherwise.'

She was afraid that was true, but did not betray the fact she knew it already. 'How do you know this?'

'Why, from Mrs Thornley—who else knows all his innermost secrets?'

If he had hoped she would react to that, he was disappointed. She kept her feelings in check. 'Do you know where Nat is?'

He laughed. 'Not precisely. He may be aboard a ship waiting offshore for the signal to come in.'

'And will there be a troop of dragoons lying in wait to catch the men on the beach?'

'I do not know. It is nothing to do with me. You should ask Sir Ashley, he is the thieftaker, not me. No doubt the miscreants, if caught, will be brought before me to be dealt with. I can have them sent to the Assizes or dismiss the charges as I see fit. It is up to you. You do understand me, I am sure.'

Her heart sank, but before she could answer, the door was flung open and Ash stood in its frame. 'Ah, there you are, Miss Kingslake,' he said, amiably. 'I have been looking for you to claim our dance.'

'Go away, Saunders,' Felix said angrily, dropping his hands from Pippa's shoulders and allowing her to step back. 'Can you not see Miss Kingslake and I wish to be alone?'

'If the lady tells me to go, I shall do so,' Ash said, looking at Pippa. 'Do you wish me to leave you, Miss Kingslake?'

'No. I will come and dance.' She turned to Sir Felix. 'I will give you my answer when you have fulfilled the conditions I have made.' Then she followed Ash from the room.

'What conditions?' he demanded as they returned to the ballroom.

She told him, adding, 'I thought it would give me time to intercept Nat,' she said.

'And then what?'

'I shall beg him to turn King's evidence.' She gave a mirthless laugh. 'If he does, he will not only save himself, but rid me of an unwanted suitor. I cannot think why the man wants to marry me when I am so obviously reluctant.'

'Why, my dear,' he said laconically, 'I should think any red-blooded man would be pleased to have you for a wife.'

She was thoughtful as they entered the ballroom and joined the dance, not about his last remark, which she realised she must accept as light-heartedly as it was made, but how to leave the dance. 'I do not feel well,' she murmured after they had taken a few steps of a minuet. 'I fear I am about to swoon.' And with that, her legs buckled under her and she collapsed against him. He caught her in his arms and picked her up as those around stopped dancing to see what was happening and began talking among themselves.

'It is the heat.'

'It is all the excitement. After all, at her age she must have despaired of ever finding a husband.'

'And one of Sir Felix's standing, too.'

'But I would never have said she was the swooning kind.'

'Anyone would faint in the heat of this room,' Ash said. 'Make way, I must take her outside.'

He carried her to the low windows that led onto the terrace and stepped outside, followed by Dr Witherspoon. 'Put her down on that bench where I can take a look at her,' he said.

Ash laid his burden gently on the bench and sat on it himself so he could nurse her head in his lap. 'I am afraid it has all become too much for her,' he said. 'She was injured in an accident in London and though she said she was fully recovered, I always doubted it. The excitement of the ball, together with the heat, caused her to relapse.'

The doctor was feeling her head and arms. 'She does not seem unduly hot.'

'It is much cooler out here.'

'What happened? Someone said Miss Kingslake swooned.' Sir Felix was hurrying towards them.

'So she has,' Dr Witherspoon told him. 'It was lucky that Sir Ashley was able to prevent her from falling to the ground.'

'Bring her indoors and I will have a bed made up for her. She shall have the best of nursing.'

Pippa stirred and began to moan a little. 'Take me home,' she murmured. 'I want to go home.'

'Of course,' Ash said. 'When you are a little recovered. Sir Felix, would you be so good as to order my carriage brought round.'

'She would be better staying here.'

'I want to go home to my own bed,' Pippa said faintly, sitting up, but still leaning against Ash. The pleasure of lying in his lap and feeling his hand holding hers had to be forgone because of the urgency of the moment. The last thing she wanted was to be kept at the Manor.

'It ain't proper for you to be at Windward House with that…that…' Sir Felix looked pointedly at Ash. 'I have the greater claim to look after you.'

'Please,' she begged weakly. 'Send for my aunt. I wish to go home.'

'I fear Miss Kingslake will faint again if we do not do as she wishes,' Dr Witherspoon said. 'The consequences could be serious. Sir Felix, pray send for Sir Ashley's carriage.'

Pippa would have walked to the coach, but Ash would not relinquish his burden. He carried her round the house, followed by an anxious Mrs Whitehouse and Sir Felix, who hovered about, annoyed that all his plans had come to naught and the evening was going to end in anticlimax. Ash put her gently on the seat, Augusta was helped in beside her; before Sir Felix could renew his protests, Ash climbed in and shut the door.

'I will call tomorrow to see how you do,' Sir Felix called out as they rolled away.

As soon as they were out of sight of the house, Pippa sat up, laughing. 'There, that did the trick. I am free of him.'

'Philippa, did you pretend to faint just to get away from Sir Felix?' her aunt asked, as Ash chuckled beside her.

'Yes. I knew he would not take no for an answer, when he has taken so much trouble arranging the evening and hinting about an announcement. It was all I could think of.'

'And you, Sir Ashley, I can tell by your laughter you were part of the masquerade.'

'No, indeed not,' he said. 'I had no idea what Miss Kingslake was about until she fell against me. It was done so neatly and so cleverly, I had to catch her.'

'You have only postponed the decision.' Her aunt turned from him back to her niece. 'You heard Sir Felix, he is coming calling tomorrow.'

'Much can happen in a few hours,' she said, which made Ash look sharply at her and wonder what she was planning.

When they arrived back at Windward House, Pippa said she was going to work on her book for a while before retiring. 'I was stuck, but now I have suddenly thought of a way to go forwards,' she said. 'I must write it down while it is still fresh in my mind.'

'And I shall retire,' Augusta said.

'In that case, I will go back to the dance,' Ash said. He had noticed no activity on the beach as they drove up to the house, which had surprised him. Perhaps he had been wrong about there being an imminent landing. 'It will allay Sir Felix's suspicions about me. I shall tell him you have been put to bed with a strong sedative and are unlikely to wake again before morning.'

He had no intention of going back to the Manor, but he could not go wandering about on the beach in his evening finery. Although he had, at the time, no idea how he would leave the dance, he had taken the precaution of putting his broadcloth suit, plain shirt and brown stockings in a bag and leaving it in the corner of the stable. He hurried to change, listening out for Joe, but that young lad was either down on the beach or asleep in his rooms.

The ship he had seen was closer in and even as he watched he saw a lantern being swung to and fro and an answering light from the darkened ship. And suddenly from holes in the sand, behind dunes and out of the marshes figures began to appear. Carts rumbled down the only road to the beach, while out at sea two boats had been lowered and were pulling towards the shore. Ash concealed himself in one of the channels of water that ran down from the marshes and watched. He was not intent on apprehending anyone—he could not succeed without substantial help from the military—but looking for Nathaniel Kingslake. Unless he had misjudged her, Pippa would also be on that errand and she really had no comprehension of how dangerous that could be. He was there as much to protect her as for any other reason.

He could hear voices coming close and ducked down lower into the water. 'We gotta get him afore he gets us,' one was saying. 'According to Sir Felix, he's fixed on hangin' the lot on us. Tha's why he's at Windward House.'

'I can't mek that out,' his companion said. They had stopped close to where Ash was hidden and seemed in no hurry to go forwards to the water's edge as everyone else was doing. 'Why would Miss Kingslake have him there, if that be the case? She wouldn't betray us, would she?'

'Who knows, but I reckon tha's why Nat cut and run. He won't come back while that cove live and breathe, but he hen't got the stomach to do away with him.' Ash was not sure, but he thought he recognised the blacksmith's voice.

'It'd save us a job if he did.'

'Hev you ever, you know, done away with anyone afore?'

'No, but I seen it done. Tha's why I hatta do it now, if it mean my wife and little 'uns be safe. I got no choice.'

Ash was wet and shivering and wished they would move away. He wanted to see what was going on down by the water's edge. While he was pinned down where he was, he might miss Nat coming ashore. He risked taking a peep at them. They had their backs to him and were apparently watching what was going happening on the beach. One had a pistol in his hand, the other a heavy wooden stave. He moved carefully backwards, hoping to get out of the ditch behind them.

He was almost out when he thought he saw Nat coming along the sand. Exposed as he was, he could not retreat and dare not go forwards. And then he realised it was not Nat, but Pippa in her brother's clothes again. He held his breath.

'There's Nat,' one of the men said, spotting her. 'I didn't see him get out o' the boat.'

'No more you did.' This was accompanied by a laugh. 'That ain't Nat, that's his sister. Miss Kingslake, go you on home,' he called out. 'This i'n't no place for you.'

She moved closer to them and Ash slid back into the ditch. The splash he made sounded loud in his ears. 'I go where I please, John Bristow, you know that,' she said. 'I came to meet my brother. It is not safe for him to come home yet.'

'Ah, you mean on account of that man you've got stayin' with you.'

'Yes. I must find Nat and warn him.'

'Don' you worry, miss,' the second man said. 'We'll tek care on him for you.'

'Nat? Have you see him? Where is he?'

'Not Nat. He kin look arter hisself. The other.' He held the gun up to show her. 'I ain't got this for show, you know.'

She gasped and ran forwards. 'No, no! Joseph Fletcher, how could you even think of doing such a thing? It's wicked. You will hang for it.'

'We stand to hang anyhow if we're caught smuggling, you know that. Might as well hang for a sheep as a lamb.'

'Give yourselves up, turn King's evidence against those who give you your orders and you will be pardoned.'

'Hev you any idea who give us our orders?' John Bristow asked, laughing.

'I believe it is Sir Felix.'

'But ain't you about to marry him?'

'Not if I can extricate Nat and the rest of you first.'

'And how do you propose to do that, eh?' John Bristow asked.

'Go home,' Fletcher put in before she could answer. 'Leave us to do what we have to do.'

'No. I cannot let you.' She stepped forwards and tried to take the gun from him.

Ash could stand by no longer and scrambled from the ditch to fall on the man from behind. He was cold and shivering and not at full strength and there were two of them and more likely to come to help them if they shouted. It was lucky for him that silence was the order of the day during a landing and so they struggled for possession of the gun without speaking. Pippa was pushed to one side and fell in the sand. Her tricorne hat fell off and her hair cascaded about her shoulders.

'If you fire that gun, you will have a platoon of dragoons down here in no time,' Ash said, wishing he could go to Pippa, who was kneeling in the sand, sobbing.

'The dragoons are on the other side of the bay,' Bristow said and landed a blow to Ash's ribs, which winded him for a moment. 'Sir Felix ha' seen to that.'

'I do not think so,' Ash was gasping for breath. 'They were warned they were being sent on a wild goose chase.'

'Traitor!' Fletcher attempted to point the gun at Ash. 'You deserve to die.'

Pippa could not let that happen. She scrambled up and grabbed the barrel of the pistol and in doing so, it went off, luckily into the air. Immediately the men on the beach took it as the usual warning signal and set about concealing their goods and themselves. John Bristow and his companion jumped into the ditch in which Ash had been hiding and waded upstream as fast as they could. Ash ran to Pippa, who had flung the pistol down and subsided onto the sand. 'Are you hurt?' he asked, kneeling beside her.

'No.' She was shaking at the thought of what might have happened, but her fear manifested itself in anger. 'Why did you have to come onto the beach? Couldn't you have let well alone for once? The men have all disappeared just as they did before, and I still do not know where Nat is. And Sir Felix will come tomorrow and crow and… Oh, I could almost hate you for it.'

'Almost?' he queried with a quirky smile.

She answered by kneeling up and pummelling his chest with her clenched fists, but he gave no sign that it was hurting. 'You…you…'

'Come, my dear,' he said calmly, rising and holding out his hand to her. 'Let me take you home before the dragoons come and arrest you for your brother.'

She got to her feet without taking his hand. She knew that if she did, she would soften and for the moment she wanted to savour her anger and bitterness.

'You know,' he said, as he walked beside her. 'It was a foolish thing to do to try to take a gun from a desperate man. You could have been killed.'

'And so could you. They were going to shoot you.'

'I know.' He paused, smiling in the darkness. 'I was hiding in the ditch and listening to their plans for my demise. Sir Felix is prodigiously anxious to have me put out of the way.'

'Of course he is. He knows you are one of the Piccadilly Gentleman and intent on putting an end to his smuggling game.'

'How does he know? You did not tell him, did you?'

'No, Mrs Thornley did. He told me so. I imagine he thought to surprise me. He said your one aim was to arrest Nat and he was the only one who could save him.'

'Damn the woman. I beg your pardon,' he added hastily. 'No wonder he sent those men to dispatch me. You saved my life.'

'Then we are quits,' she said sharply.

'Oh, there is more to it than that.'

'Yes, not only your life. If you had seen Nat, would you have had him arrested?'

'No. How could I? There must have been a hundred men on the beach, every one of them against me.'

'Then why…?'

'As soon as you pretended to faint I knew you were up

to something and it was easy to guess what. I couldn't let you go out alone, could I?'

'Oh.' They were approaching the house and heard horses being ridden along the road behind them. 'There go the dragoons,' she said. 'And as usual, they will find an empty beach and no sign of contraband.'

'Isn't that what you wanted?' He opened the door and ushered her inside, shutting it behind them. A small lamp glowed on a table, otherwise they were in darkness.

'I don't know what I want. My head is in such a muddle.'

He followed her up the stairs. Outside her bedchamber door, he turned to take her shoulders in his hands. 'Have you forgiven me?' he asked softly.

'What for?'

'For spoiling your little adventure.'

'Oh, I suppose so. No doubt you thought you were acting for the best, but Nat is still missing.'

'Yes. Go to bed, Pippa, and try to sleep. We will discuss this again in the morning.'

'And in the morning Sir Felix will come and I have no answer for him.'

He took her face in his hands and tilted it up so that he could look at it. 'Then you, my love, will be too ill to receive him.' Then he gently lowered his mouth to hers.

She did not struggle. She felt the warmth of his lips on hers and let it spread all over her body. She had no defence against this gentle onslaught. If he had carried her off to bed there and then, she would have made not a single protest. In spite of everything, in spite of what he was, who he was, she was in his thrall, a helpless mass of boneless flesh. A low moan in the base of her throat alerted him to what he was doing. He lifted his head, tilted hers downwards and kissed the top of her head. Then he gave her a little push towards her bedchamber door. 'Go to bed, my red-haired witch, or I will not answer for the consequences.'

Without speaking, she went into her room and shut the door behind her. Then she collapsed onto the bed, her emotions and brain so confused, she did not know what to think. Did he love her? Or was her red hair more compelling than she thought and she had unwittingly bewitched him? After all, he had called her his red-haired witch. That was nonsense, she told herself. He knew perfectly well what he was doing, he was a practised seducer, so he must have been trying to lull her into trusting him. The trouble was it had worked. While he was with her, talking to her, touching her, kissing her, being gentle and understanding, she trusted him implicitly. It was only after they parted that her brain took over and remembered his motives as a thieftaker and his reputation as a rake and she began to have doubts. She did not want to doubt him. Oh, what a mull she was in!

In spite of being up half the night and his back and ribs aching, not only from his injury but the pummelling he had been given on the beach, Ash rose early next morning and walked into the village. He wanted to find out if anyone had been arrested the previous night and was shocked to discover John Bristow and Joseph Fletcher had been taken into custody and were being held in the Customs House until they could come before the magistrate. The Customs men on duty were the same two he had spoken to after the riot and they willingly answered his questions.

'We were tipped off by Sir Felix's coachman,' one of them told him. 'So we went to their homes and found contraband goods in their sheds. A barrel of Geneva and a quarter of tobacco in each. They swore they didn't know how they got there.'

'I am not surprised. I was with them last night and they were nowhere near the contraband. Someone wants them out of the way.'

'We can't let them go just because you say so.'

'No, but will you let me talk to them?'

He was shown into a tiny room, where the only light and air was through a grating high up in the wall. Fletcher was half-lying on a truckle bed against the wall, Bristow was sitting on a stool, his empty hands dangling between his knees 'Come to crow, hev you?' Bristow growled, when he saw who their visitor was.

'Not at all. I know you didn't take the spirits and tobacco off the beach last night. You would not have had time.'

'No, so you had someone put them in our sheds.'

'If I had it would have served you well, for you were bent on killing me, but I did not. Someone else wants you out of the way.'

'Who?' Fletcher queried. 'Miss Kingslake?'

'Good heavens, no! She would never do such a thing.' He looked from one to the other. Both looked truculent. 'You were sent on an errand last night and you failed to carry it out. This is your punishment.'

'Sir Felix?'

'Why not? You do not think he would hesitate to have you arrested and sent to the Assizes if you displeased him, do you?' They still looked doubtful, but they were listening. 'With you out of the way, he has no one to testify against him. Or so he thinks.'

'You want us to turn ag'in our mates, do you?' Bristow asked. 'People may do that where you come from, but not round here, they don't.'

'Not against the other villagers. After all, in the dark, all cats are black. Would you know who was on the beach with you?'

'Course I know them.'

'Would you swear to it?'

'No, what do you take us for?' This from Fletcher.

'I reckon I know what you're drivin' at,' Bristow said. ''Tis only Sir Felix you've a grudge ag'in. It's personal, i'n't it?'

Ash smiled wryly. 'It was Sir Felix made it so, sending you after me.' He banged on the door and one of the Customs men came to let him out. 'You might like to think about why that should be and let me know what conclusion you reach.'

He walked back to Windward House by way of the beach, but there was no evidence of any contraband, yet he knew in the next day or two it would have to be moved. If only Nathaniel Kingslake had come to him as he had said he would, he could organise troops and excise men to intercept it. Where was the man? Sir Felix would not have had him done away with while he hoped Pippa would agree to marry him. Pippa. Oh, how he loved every obstinate, loyal, contrary inch of her! And how he longed to tell her so. 'Nat Kingslake, if you do not put in an appearance by this evening, I shall tell her anyway,' he murmured. 'We cannot go on like this.'

He arrived back at Windward House at the same time as Sir Felix rolled up in his carriage, accompanied by Mrs Thornley. He growled a reluctant good morning to them and they went into the house together.

Mrs Whitehouse hurried forwards to greet them. 'Sir Felix, good morning.'

Sir Felix gave her an elaborate bow. 'Mrs Whitehouse, good day to you. You were not long at my little entertainment last night, so I do not think you met Mrs Thornley.'

'No, how do you do? Won't you come into the drawing room?' She curtsied and led the way, followed by Ash.

'How is Miss Kingslake this morning?' Sir Felix said. 'Her sudden indisposition upset us all and quite put a damper on the evening. I hope she has recovered.'

'She is still not herself,' Augusta said, while Ash hoped Pippa would not choose that moment to appear. 'I have advised her to stay in bed today.'

'I am sorry to hear that.' Sir Felix said. 'I had hoped we could take her for a drive.'

'Another day, perhaps.'

'You did not return to the dance, Sir Ashley,' Arabella said. 'I expected you back in time to join us in the country dances at the end.'

'I did not feel like dancing,' he said curtly. 'I went for a walk instead.'

'Dangerous at night,' Sir Felix commented. 'You never know whom you might meet.'

'That is true. I saw a great many people on the beach, but unfortunately, being alone, I could do nothing about them.'

Sir Felix laughed. 'No matter. Another time, eh?'

'Ash, do watch your step,' Arabella said. 'I should hate it if you came to harm.'

'Thank you for your timely warning,' he said and bowed.

'You would do better to finish your recuperation in your own home,' Sir Felix added. 'I fear the people here are all against you.'

'Yes, do, Ash,' Arabella said. 'You can take me with you. I should like to visit Fairfields. You have told me so much about it.'

'I am perfectly comfortable here.'

'Miss Kingslake will marry me, you know,' Sir Felix said. 'We have so much in common and it is the wish of her brother.'

Augusta gasped. 'You have spoken to him?'

'Of course. He is the head of the house, is he not?'

'Where is he now?'

'Best I do not know. I would not like to be obliged, as a magistrate, to have him taken into custody.'

Arabella laughed. 'He won't come home while you are here, Ash. Miss Kingslake knows that, but she is too polite to ask you to leave. Why not save her the trouble?'

'If Miss Kingslake requests me to go, I will go,' Ash said slowly.

'Then shall we ask her?' Sir Felix turned to Augusta. 'Mrs Whitehouse, can she not come down for a short time?'

Ash looked meaningfully at Augusta, who seemed to be hesitating, unused to going against Sir Felix. 'I am afraid not,' she said, understanding him. 'Doctor Witherspoon said she must have complete rest.'

Thwarted in their intention of seeing Pippa, the visitors reluctantly took their leave, promising to return as soon as Miss Kingslake was well enough to receive them.

'I do not know how much longer we can hold that man off,' Augusta said, after they had gone. 'Did you see anything of Nathaniel last night?'

'Unfortunately, no. I had hoped…' He stopped, unable to explain why he had put so much faith in Nathaniel Kingslake, faith he feared had been misplaced.

'Oh, I nearly forgot. A letter came for you while you were out.' She fetched it from behind the clock on the mantel.

He broke the seal and began to read. He read it twice while she waited, his expression dropping as he did so.

'Not bad news, I hope?' she queried.

'Yes, I am afraid it is. My uncle Cadogan has died. I must go to London at once.'

'Oh, dear, my condolences. Of course you must go.'

'I am worried about Pippa if I leave.'

'I shall look after her, Sir Ashley,' She paused and hurriedly corrected herself. 'I mean, my lord. She shall not stir from the house without me.'

'Is she really in bed?'

'No, resting in a chair.'

'I must speak to her.' He bounded up the stairs, knocked on Pippa's door and entered without waiting for an answer. She was at her desk writing, but put her pen down and turned towards him. 'Have they gone?'

'Yes, Mrs Whitehouse told them you had been advised by Dr Witherspoon to rest and could not have visitors.' He dropped to his knees beside her chair and took her hands. 'Pippa, I have some bad news. Lord Cadogan has died.'

'Died?' she repeated.

'Yes. He had a seizure. I have had a letter from Mr Davison, the family lawyer. I must go to London at once.'

She suppressed her dismay. Ash was now Lord Cadogan, further from her reach than ever. She felt as if her whole world was collapsing about her. The last tiny flicker of hope she had had the night before, when he kissed her, died inside her. 'Of course you must. I am sorry for your loss.'

'I am worried about leaving you. Sir Felix will not give

up and there is no sign of your brother. I fear if he meant to land last night, he was put off doing so by the pistol shot and everyone scattering.'

'Yes, I am sure that was the reason.' She spoke flatly. 'He will find another way. Please do not worry about us.' She attempted a smile. 'After all, we managed before you came. We will manage again.'

'Oh, my brave and beautiful girl, I do not want to leave you here. It will seem as if I am abandoning you. Sir Felix is up to something and I fear for you. Will you consent to stay at Fairfields with your aunt and cousin until I have concluded my business in London? I can take you there on the way.'

'But you are Lord Cadogan now.'

'What difference does that make? Sir Ashley Saunders, Lord Cadogan or just plain Ash, I am still the same man. I did not ask for the elevation, nor do I particularly welcome it, since it has such unhappy memories for you, but I must do my duty and go to London.'

'I understand.'

'So will you come to Fairfields? It would set my mind at rest. We can leave a message for your brother with Mrs Sadler and Joe, so that he knows where to find you, if he should come. But we will tell no one else.'

She thought about living in Narbeach without him. She thought about Sir Felix and his determination to have her one way or another. She thought about her recalcitrant brother and all the men who had broken the law, for whom she seemed able to do nothing, and found herself agreeing. 'If my aunt consents.'

Mrs Whitehouse was overjoyed at the thought and rushed about giving instructions for an early meal and packing and exhortations that no one was to say where they had gone, while Ash saw to his own preparations. They left in the middle of the afternoon.

The journey was a silent one and they arrived in time for a hastily prepared dinner. As soon as they had eaten it, Ash left again. 'I will be back as soon as I can,' he told Pippa. 'And then we will have a long talk. I have things to tell you, things to explain.' He took her hand and kissed the back of it and then turned it over and kissed the palm, which sent shivers down her whole body. 'Cheer up, sweetheart. We shall contrive a happy ending, you'll see.'

He left the servants to put the house into mourning and to conjecture about what it might mean to them. Sir Ashley, now Lord Cadogan, had inherited considerable estates, far grander than Fairfields and they wondered if he would keep it going.

Pippa and Augusta sat and talked well into the night. They relived every single minute of their lives since Ash had come into them and what he meant to them. Pippa was in tears and confessed how she felt about him, which did not surprise her aunt at all. Augusta was equally convinced that Sir Ashley—she found it hard to think of him as his lordship—entertained the same feelings towards Pippa. But Pippa would not be comforted.

'He is a lord, far above my touch even without his connection to Edward,' she said. That was the cruellest blow of all. Old Lord Cadogan might be dead, but his widow was alive and well and she was a strong-minded woman. Pippa feared she would never see Ash again or if she did it would be under far different circumstances. There would be no more gentle kisses, no more risky adventures, no more hearing his soft voice calling her Pippa. He would be the grand gentleman, even wealthier than he had been, able to take his pick of brides and one would be chosen to fit his new rank.

'If that were so,' her aunt said. 'Why did he take the trouble to bring you here?'

'To keep me out of Sir Felix's clutches because he does not trust him. That is what he told me. He promised to explain when he came back.'

'There you are, then!' Augusta said triumphantly. 'All we have to do is wait.'

To which there was no answer and, being exhausted, both mentally and physically, they went to bed.

Ash, with mourning ribbons on his coat sleeve and hat, called at Cadogan House in Hanover Square as soon as he arrived in town. There were black ribbons on the knocker and the curtains were closed. He was admitted by a long-faced footman and conducted to his aunt. Dressed from head to foot in black, she seemed tinier than ever. She held out her hand to him and he took it and bowed over it. 'Aunt Gertrude, I am so sorry. My uncle will be sorely missed.'

'It was so sudden,' she said. 'We had no idea there was anything wrong with him. He went to the Lords in the morning for a debate and in the afternoon he was telling me about it and just fell down dead.' She gulped and dabbed her eyes with a lace handkerchief. 'I cannot believe he has gone. I am in such a state I cannot think. There is so much to do. You must call on Mr Davison. He is arranging everything.'

'I will do so. Is there anything I can do for you in the meantime?'

'You can make sure the servants are about their work. They will need to provide refreshments for after the funeral.

I really cannot bring myself to talk about it.' She waved him away with her handkerchief.

He went to talk to the servants, who were creeping about in stockinged feet and talking in whispers, then took himself off to Mr Davison's chambers. There were no real surprises. Lord Cadogan's affairs were in order, though his will had been made before the death of his son and he had not altered it. 'I advised him to make a new will as soon as we heard the bad news,' the lawyer said. 'But he said there was plenty of time.'

'Does that make any difference?'

'To your inheritance? No, my lord. There is no dispute you are next in line. The stipulation that his son was not to marry Miss Philippa Kingslake does not relate to you.'

Ash was curious enough to ask, 'What would have happened if Edward had defied him?'

'He would have become Lord Cadogan, nothing could have changed that, but he would have forfeited the Holbeach estate and all its income. It would then have been sold and, after provision for his widow, including the deeds to the Hanover Square house, the remainder would have been distributed piecemeal to all his relatives, however distant.' He gave a weak smile. 'Your share would only have been a few thousand.'

In spite of the solemnity of the occasion, Ash could not help smiling. 'Since I have every intention of marrying Miss Kingslake myself and the stipulation would undoubtedly have applied to me, if my uncle had made a new will, you had better follow those instructions.'

'But, my lord, you will be forfeiting a fortune and there is no legal necessity for it.'

'No matter. Do it, please. You do not need to say anything to Lady Cadogan until after the funeral.'

'Very well.' It was said with a reluctant sigh. 'I will notify all those with a claim.'

Thus it was that Lord Cadogan's funeral was attended by aunts, uncles, cousins and cousin's children, all milling about making wild guesses about the extent of the fortune to be divided up. 'I don't know why they are all here,' Lady Cadogan complained as they sat about drinking tea and gobbling up the refreshments. 'They never bothered about him when he was alive.'

She was soon to discover and her fury overcame her mourning. She called Ash an ungrateful cur and worse, but he simply smiled and said he was content to help others who needed the blunt more than he did.

He left the so-called mourners talking excitedly among themselves and went home to Pall Mall where he dined.

Later, Ash went to Trentham House for a meeting of the Piccadilly Gentlemen's Club.

'We did not expect you,' James told him. 'Our condolences on your loss and congratulations on your elevation.'

'Thank you.'

'How goes the lovely redhead?' Alex asked him with a grin. 'Been into any more scrapes, has she?'

'Yes, the situation in Narbeach is serious. I think I may need help to bring it to a satisfactory conclusion.'

'Are you not more concerned about seeing to your new estate?' Jonathan asked. 'I had heard Lord Cadogan had not lived at Holbeach for some years and the place is run down.'

'It is to be sold and the proceeds distributed among the family,' Ash said. 'I inherited little more than the title.'

'I am sorry for that,' Harry said. 'It is always a great shame when estates are broken up.'

'It was my wish,' Ash said. 'Let us not talk about that. There are more important matters to discuss.'

'Go on,' James said quietly. 'We are listening.'

So he told them everything from the beginning: his involvement with Pippa, though not his feelings for her; Nat Kingslake's disappearance; the strange behaviour of Sir Felix and, at the end, Nat's visit and his accusations against Sir Felix. 'Unfortunately, he had no proof, though he said he would get it. I begin to wonder if he has perished in the attempt,' he said. 'And how else are we to obtain it?'

'Sir Felix Markham is a respected magistrate,' James said. 'Are you sure you can believe your informant?'

'I think so. I also know Sir Felix was worried about my presence in Narbeach. Someone told him I belonged to the Piccadilly Gentlemen and he set two men to murder me. I heard them talking about it.'

'That is evidence enough to have him taken up.'

'No, for they are so frightened of him, they refused to give evidence and mine alone will not stand.'

They were silent for a moment, a silence broken by the arrival of Lord Trentham. 'Gentlemen, I have a visitor,' he told them. 'A young relative. I think you should hear what he has to say.' He turned and beckoned to someone in the corridor and Nat came into the room.

He swept them a bow. 'Gentlemen, your servant.'

'Kingslake!' Ash exclaimed. 'Where the devil have you been?'

'Trying to evade Customs and Excise,' he said with a grin. 'I could not get ashore at Narbeach and was carried off on the *Sally Ann* again. We docked in London this morning. I believed you to be in Narbeach and so I decided the next best thing was to speak to Lord Trentham, seeing as he is a relative by marriage.'

'So what have you to tell us?' James asked.

'What do you know already?'

'I have explained everything to them,' Ash said.

'About the murders, too?'

'Yes, but are you sure that is not your fancy?' This from James, who was still reluctant to believe.

'Not my fancy, no. I have proof or I would have if you could persuade a certain Joseph Fletcher to tell what he knows.'

'Fletcher is in custody,' Ash told him. 'Sir Felix had him and John Bristow arrested for smuggling. The Customs found contraband on their premises. I am, however, convinced it was done because Sir Felix had employed them to murder me and they had failed to do so.' He stopped suddenly, remembering the conversation he had overheard. 'I heard them talking and Bristow asked Fletcher if he had ever killed before, and he said no, but he had seen someone else do it.'

'So he had,' Nat told him. 'Sir Felix killed his first wife by bludgeoning her to death with a hammer in a fit of temper and it was made to look as if it had been done by an intruder. He did not know Fletcher had seen him at the time, but later, when Fletcher was taken up for smuggling, he told Sir Felix what he knew and Sir Felix dismissed his case. The second wife simply disappeared. Her body was found two years later when it was impossible to say how she had died. Fletcher knew, though, because Sir Felix fetched him to help dispose of the body.'

'This is incredible,' James said.

'It is true. Fletcher told me himself when he was maudlin drunk and afterwards denied it. He is afraid of being taken up as an accessory and his wife and children left to starve. You need a way to get him talking. And there is the second Lady Markham's maid, Jane Patterson. She was sent away to Lincolnshire, but I tracked her down. She told me Sir Felix often beat his wife black and blue and she had been fearful that one day he would go too far and kill her. Her mistress was convinced that was how his first wife had died. And when she disappeared, Jane was sent away at once. Sir Felix was afraid she would talk.'

'Will she talk now?' Harry asked.

'I believe she can be persuaded as long as she can be sure Sir Felix will not be free to take his revenge—the same for Fletcher, of course.'

'And he wants Pippa for wife number three,' Ash said. 'Thank God, she is safe at Fairfields.'

'We must do something about this,' James said.

'You need to be quick,' Nat told them. 'If Sir Felix gets wind of your intentions, Fletcher won't last long.'

'Right,' James said. 'Alex and Harry, go to Narbeach and stay at the local hostelry. Let it be known you are there because you have heard you can purchase an anker or two of brandy, but keep an eye on our man so that he does not disappear or harm our witnesses. Jonathan, you go and charm Miss Patterson into giving evidence and bring her to London. Can you accommodate her until she is needed?'

'Yes, of course. Louise will make her welcome.'

'Will you go with him, Mr Kingslake? She knows you.'

'With pleasure, so long as I know my sister is safe.'

'What about me?' Ash asked. 'You do not think you can leave me out, do you?'

'It would be best if you stayed out of it, my friend,' James said. 'Sir Felix knows you and he knows you are a member of the Society. If cornered, there is no telling what he is capable of. And are you not busy with Cadogan business?'

'No, that is being dealt with by the lawyer, nothing to do with me. And my aunt is angry with me and forbidden me the house.'

'Then I suggest you go to the Thetford and warn the judiciary to expect Mr Fletcher at the Assizes and to handle him carefully until he is needed to turn King's evidence.' He smiled, knowing Ash's impatience. 'Then go to Fairfields and wait. I am sure you can find a way to pass the time until you hear that you are needed.'

'I think I will warn the Lord Chief Justice,' William said. 'This is going to cause quite a stir.'

The meeting broke up and the men went to make their preparations. Ash dashed back to Pall Mall and instructed Mortimer to pack again. 'We are going back to Fairfields,' he said.

'Tonight, my lord?'

'Yes. Tonight. We can cover a few miles before it becomes too dark to see, then rack up somewhere and go on by way of Thetford in the morning.'

Mortimer went off grumbling that he never knew what his master was going to do next and it was about time he stopped racketing around and behaved like the lord he was. Ash was in far too good a mood to scold him and in an hour they were on their way.

Pippa loved being at Fairfields. The house was comfortable and the servants anxious to please. She and Augusta took walks in the countryside and talked to the villagers from whom they learned that everyone respected Sir Ashley and were pleased for his good fortune, but expressed the hope that he would not abandon Fairfields for Holbeach Hall. Sometimes they took sketching pads out into the gardens to draw some of the unusual plants growing there. Sometimes they sat on the terrace reading or sewing. It was an idyll that Pippa knew could not last.

It was shattered in the worst way possible about a week later when Pippa was walking along the lane that led to the village, carrying a basket of eggs which the housekeeper had given her to take to the rectory. The dreadful early summer seemed to be behind them at last and the day was warm. She was wearing a gingham round gown, with three-quarter sleeves and a light gauze scarf about her shoulders. She wore no hat, but carried a parasol to shield her face from the sun. The lovely weather lifted her spirits, though her worry about Nat and her disappointment over Ash would not go away.

She heard a carriage behind her and stepped to one side to allow it to pass. Instead of passing, it stopped. The door opened and Sir Felix jumped down in the road beside her. 'My dear, you should not be walking in the sun,' he said, taking her arm. 'You will be overcome with the heat. Allow me to take you back in my carriage.'

She tried to pull herself away from him. 'I am enjoying my walk, Sir Felix. What are you doing here?'

'I have come to claim my bride. Please get in the carriage.'

'No. I am not your bride, Sir Felix, nor ever will be.'

'Then you give me no choice.' He pulled her towards the carriage. She resisted as fiercely as she could and was roughly manhandled for her pains. Her basket went flying and the eggs broke all over the road. She was aware, as she struggled, that the driver had jumped down from the box and come to his master's aid and Mrs Thornley had left the carriage to help bundle her into it. She had no defence against three of them and was deposited roughly on the seat. Sir Felix and Mrs Thornley got in with her and the driver climbed back on the box and they left the scene at a brisk trot.

'Where are you taking me?'

'Somewhere I can keep you safe. If you want to see your brother alive again, you will not resist. Did you think I was boasting when I said I held his life in my hands?'

She was shaking like an aspen, but more angry than frightened. Or so she told herself. He must not see her cringe. 'You are not as powerful as you think you are. When Sir Ashley—'

'Lord Cadogan, you mean,' he interrupted her. 'You would be unwise to put your faith in him. He has other fish to fry. I have it on good authority he is busy placating his uncle's widow.'

'I insist you take me back to Fairfields,' Pippa said, pushing the thought of Ash as Lord Cadogan out of her mind and concentrating on her own predicament. 'Everyone will wonder what has happened to me and search for me.'

'And fail to find you.' This from Sir Felix. 'At least, not until you appear as Lady Markham.'

'I cannot understand why you wish to marry me at all,' she said, 'I have nothing to offer. The late Lord Cadogan himself said that and he was right.'

'But you are a valuable commodity, my dear. Nathaniel will do as he is told while I have you and you will obey me while I decide whether your brother lives or dies.' He laughed suddenly. 'And I have a fancy to own Windward House. The easiest way to do that is to marry you.'

'Why do you want Windward House?' she asked in

surprise. 'It is nothing like as big or as elegant as the Manor. And my aunt always complains it is draughty and cold.'

'I do not intend to live in it, my dear, but it commands an enviable view of the shore and the sea beyond. And ideal spot for signalling. And it has a deep cellar. I am told there is a tunnel from there all the way to the beach.'

'You have been misinformed. I have never seen such a thing.'

'No doubt it has been blocked up. We will soon rediscover it.'

All the time she had been talking, she had been looking about her, hoping for a way of escape. Perhaps when they passed through Fakenham she could shout for help or try to jump out if they had to slow down. But the coachman avoided the town and they took a circuitous route through countryside with few inhabitants. When she put her hand on the door handle, he noticed it and roughly wrenched it away. 'Do that again and I shall have to tie you up.'

She sat back and put the back of her bruised hand to her mouth. Her situation seemed hopeless.

Chapter Ten

Having called at the justice's home in Thetford, Ash arrived at Fairfields that evening to be met by a distraught Augusta with the news that Pippa had disappeared.

'When? How?' he demanded.

'She left to walk to the rectory with a basket of eggs and did not return. We went looking for her and found the basket on the ground and the eggs all over the road. Her parasol was hooked up in the hedge, but there was no sign of her. Something dreadful has happened to her, I know it.' And she began to wail so loudly Ash had to beg her to be quiet and let him think.

'This is Sir Felix's doing,' he said furiously. 'God damn the man. Could he have found out what we were planning?'

'What are you going to do?' she asked.

'Go after them, of course.' He did not doubt Sir Felix had abducted Pippa, nor did he doubt what would happen to her when he had her safely indoors somewhere. She would be a ruined woman. The man was counting on that.

'Show me the spot where you found the eggs.' He shouted at Tom who was leading the carriage horses away, 'Have my riding horse saddled. I will be better on that.'

Ten minutes later he was squatting in the road, examining the mess of eggs. 'There are tracks of a carriage here,' he said. 'And hoofmarks of four horses.' He looked along the road. The eggs had marked the carriage wheels and he could see the direction it had taken. 'Go back to Fairfields, Mrs Whitehouse. I will track them down, never fear.'

Then he mounted up, followed the tracks as far as the crossroads and then galloped off across country towards the coast. His horse was put to jump ditches and hedges and scattered farm animals as they fairly flew along. He was in too much of a hurry to take care, but it did not stop him thinking.

When Pippa had asked why Sir Felix was so anxious to marry her, his answer had been flippant, but it was a question he had often asked himself. Pippa had something he wanted. She was not wealthy, so it had to be something other than money. Did Nathaniel know? It was too late to ask him now. Once, he dismounted to lead his horse to rest it, but was soon in the saddle again, making for Narbeach. It had to be his first port of call.

At the edge of the village, he left his exhausted horse with a farm boy to rub down and water for him and walked the rest of the way. He approached the Manor cautiously and made his way to the stables. The men and boys were idling in the yard, a sure sign that Sir Felix and his carriage were not there. Had he arrived ahead of them, or had they gone elsewhere? He returned to the centre of the village just as a carriage rolled to a stop outside the Cross Keys and Harry and Alex tumbled out, laughing at some jest. Harry was, as usual, colourfully overdressed and Alex was in naval uniform. If they were surprised to see him standing in the road, they gave no sign of recognition as they went into the inn. A few moments later Ash followed them.

'A quart of ale and a tot of your best cognac for me and my friend,' Alex was saying to the landlord.

'I hear there's night-time sport hereabouts,' Harry said.

'Night-time sport?' the landlord said. 'Don' know what you mean.' He turned to Ash. 'Do you know what they mean, Sir Ashley? I don' understand that Lunnon talk.'

'No, can't say I do,' he said, warning them with a look not to recognise him. 'Unless they mean fishing.'

'Yes, fishing, that's what we mean,' Harry said quickly.

'You will need to hire a boat and equipment,' Ash said, trying not to betray his desperate haste to the innkeeper. 'I saw a boat and tackle at Windward House. I will take you there, if you like.'

They swallowed the last of their drinks and followed him outside. 'What in heaven's name do you mean by fishing?' Harry demanded as soon as they were out of earshot. 'I ain't dressed for fishing. And what are you doing here? James sent you to Fairfields.'

'Sir Felix has got Pippa. We've got to find them before…' He could not bring himself to put his fears into words.

'And you think fishing will help?' Harry said, laughing.

'No, of course not, but I had to get you out of there. I need your help.'

'Go on.'

'He nabbed her at Fairfields and bundled her into his

carriage, but where he has taken her I don't know. As far as I can see he has not returned to the Manor, but I may be wrong. Harry, will you pay a call on Sir Felix, see if you can find out where he is? I can't go, the servants know me and I am sure they have been given instructions not to admit me. Alex, can you pretend to be some sort of official and go to the Customs House and ask to interrogate Fletcher. Ask him if he has any idea where Sir Felix might hole up. Promise him a free pardon if he talks.'

'I have no authority to do that,' Alex put in.

'Do it anyway. This is no time for exactitude.'

'What are you going to do?' Harry demanded.

'I am going to see if I can get into the Manor by a back way, while you keep the servants occupied. I am sure you can think of a way of doing it.'

'Where shall we meet? Back at the inn?'

'No. Windward House.' He pointed towards the headland. 'There, that's it.'

They went their separate ways. Ash turned down a lane that ran alongside the Manor wall, looking for a place to climb over and into the grounds. He groaned when he saw the Reverend Mr Fearson driving his trap towards him.

The vicar pulled up alongside him. 'Good to see you back, Sir Ashley,' he said. 'I trust you have fully recovered?'

'Yes, I thank you, sir.'

'And Miss Kingslake is also well? We have missed her, but now she is back—'

'Back?' Ash repeated. 'You have seen her? Spoken to her?'

'Why, no, but I saw Sir Felix's carriage outside her house not an hour since on my way back from visiting a dying parishioner. I assumed he had been to fetch her.'

Ash sprang into the trap and seized the reins from the astonished cleric. 'I am sorry, Reverend, but it is imperative I get to Windward House as swiftly as possible. I fear Miss Kingslake is in danger.'

Ash was driving the pony so hard, the trap was swaying from side to side and all the poor man could do was hang on to the sides and pray. Down the village street, they went, scattering children and chickens and leaving the women standing with their mouths open. Up the slight incline towards the headland they went with the pony breathing hard, and pulled up outside Windward house. Sir Felix's carriage stood outside.

Ash threw the reins to the parson and jumped down almost before the wheels had stopped turning. He did not bother to knock, but rushed into the house. He was met by Sir Felix, Arabella and Sir Felix's coachman. 'Where is she?' he demanded. 'What have you done with her?'

'Done?' Sir Felix asked mildly, though his tone belied the furious look in his eyes and the way his shoulders stiffened. 'Done with whom?'

'He means Miss Kingslake, I do believe,' Arabella said, coming to Ash's side and taking his arm. 'Do calm down, Ash, and tell us what is troubling you.'

'You have abducted Miss Kingslake from my protection, taken her by force, and I demand you release her.'

'If that is so,' Felix said, with a sneer, 'your protection fell short of what it should be.'

'Darling Ash,' Arabella said. 'No one has abducted the lady. If she left your house, she left it of her own free will.'

'If that is true, she will tell me so herself. Where is she?' He rushed from room to room. There was no one in any of them, not even Mrs Sadler or Sarah who had been left behind to look after the house. The kitchen fire was cold and the house had a neglected air. 'Where is she?' he demanded, coming back to the hall where Sir Felix stood tapping his boot with his cane.

'My dear fellow, how can I know what was in the lady's mind?'

'Then what are you doing here? And where are the servants?'

'I am here because I expect to own this house soon. And the servants have been dismissed.'

The vicar came in the front door. 'What is going on?' he asked, looking from one to the other. 'I cannot keep my pony standing outside—'

'Then take it home,' Sir Felix said brusquely. 'You are not needed.'

It was a side of Sir Felix the poor man had not met before and he was shocked. He retreated in confusion. Ash did not think he would be much help in any case. He looked about him. Surely there was some clue as to what had happened. It was no good repeating, 'Where is she?'—he would not receive an answer. He searched the rooms again, more thoroughly. It was in the kitchen he saw it: a tiny scrap of gauze caught on the latch of the door to the cellar. 'Pippa!' he shouted. 'Pippa!'

'It is no good making that noise,' Sir Felix said, following him into the room. Hastily Ash snatched the incriminating evidence and put in his pocket.

He was sure Pippa was in the cellar, but he had to draw Sir Felix and Arabella away from the kitchen. He went back into the hall and pretended to leave. 'I shall find her,' he said.

Sir Felix laughed. 'You will not need to look far. She will be in church on Sunday to hear the banns read. I advise you to make your peace with Mrs Thornley and get your own banns read as soon as may be.'

They went outside. Harry and Alex were coming up the lane towards the house. They appeared to be drunk. Sir Felix stared at them. 'Who are you?'

'They are friends of mine,' Ash said. 'Alex, what have you to tell me?'

'The person in question is on his way to Thetford.'

'Agreeable?'

'Yes.'

'Good. Then be so good as to arrest Sir Felix.'

Alex and Harry ranged themselves on either side of Sir Felix and took his elbows to propel him towards his carriage, while he blustered angrily, 'How dare you! I am a magistrate and squire of this village. I will not be manhandled.'

'Not even a magistrate is above the law,' Harry said cheerfully, bundling the man into his coach, while the stupefied driver looked on.

'Get up there and drive us to the lock-up,' Alex commanded him.

'This one, too,' Ash said, taking Mrs Thornley's arm and forcing her towards the carriage. 'She is an accessory.' He did not wait to see if they obeyed, but dashed back into the house, along the hall and into the kitchen. 'Pippa!' he shouted. 'I am coming.'

It took him a minute to find something to break the lock, but then he was dashing down stone steps into darkness. 'Pippa?' There was no answer. His heart sank. Had she been made unconscious? Knocked out? Drugged? Killed, even? He was close to panic and had to stand a moment to calm himself. And then he began feeling his way round the walls. The cellar was definitely empty. Where was she?

Was the whole thing a masquerade on the part of Sir Felix to put him off the scent? How he must be chuckling. He was about to give up when he felt a ring set in the wall. Half-expecting her to be chained to it, he felt all round it. No Pippa.

But his eyes were becoming accustomed to the dark and from the little light penetrating down the steps behind him, he saw a small door with the ring in the middle of it. He pulled the ring and the door swung outwards. Whatever was on the other side was as dark as pitch. He put his head inside and yelled. 'Pippa!' Her name echoed round and round, but there was no reply.

He dashed back up the steps to the kitchen, found a lantern and fumbled with the flint to light it. Then he carried it down to the hole. There was a second cellar behind the first. It was dark and damp, but also empty. Even in his anxiety he realised this was an excellent hiding place for contraband and Sir Felix knew that; if he married Pippa, it would be his. Ash explored it and found a second door on the far side. Surely not a third cellar?

He stepped towards it and nearly fell over a bundle on the floor. 'Pippa! Oh, my darling.' He knelt down, took the gag from her mouth and undid her bonds. Then he gathered her into his arms. 'I thought I'd lost you.' She was crying and shivering. He held her close and chafed some warmth back into her hands. 'Darling, darling Pippa, you are safe now. It's all over. All over.' He picked her up and carried her back up the steps into the house and put her on the sofa. She was still very cold. He ran up to her room, dragged the clothes from the bed and took them downstairs where he wrapped them round her and sat with her head in his lap.

'You are safe, my love,' he murmured. 'Sir Felix has been arrested. He will trouble you no more.'

'Oh, Ash. I prayed you would come.'

He smiled. 'And here I am. But what a fright you gave me. I was in despair. If anything had happened to you, I think I should have wanted to die. You are my love, my life, the reason for my existence.'

Her heart, so cold before, was singing with joy at his words, but she was still puzzled. 'How did you find me?'

'It is a long story, my love, and I have to confess to keeping something from you. It tried my conscience sorely, but Nat swore me to secrecy.'

'I don't understand. You have spoken to my brother? Where is he?'

So he told her everything: Nat's first appearance in London, his accusations and search for proof, and the arrangement to meet in Narbeach, which was thwarted when that pistol had gone off. 'He was carried away again,' he said. 'And so I was in no position to expose Sir Felix and then my uncle died at the most inopportune moment imaginable.'

She smiled. 'The poor man could not help that. So you took me to Fairfields and went to London. I thought I would never see you again.'

'But, my sweet, I promised to come back.'

'I know, but I knew it would be different then.'

'It is not different. I love you as much as ever—more, if possible.'

'Love me?' Her eyes lit up.

'Of course. I thought you would have guessed. I hardly troubled to hide my feelings.'

'Sometimes I hoped; other times I thought you were simply playing some rake's game. After all, you fall in love at least once a month, you told me so.'

'I was bamming. I have never been in love in my life before until now. I am past being a rake. That life is all behind me.'

'Because you are Lord Cadogan.'

'No, nothing to do with that. I may be Lord Cadogan, but I have waived my claim to the estate.'

'Why? Surely that is a foolish thing to do?'

'Not at all. It was a very wise thing to do. You see, I have fallen in love for the first and last time in my life, with the most beautiful, most contrary, most mettlesome redhead in the world. Pippa, I want you for my wife. Please say you love me as I love you and will marry me.'

'But how can I? Nat...'

'Your brother is on the side of the law, he always has been. He has found proof that Sir Felix murdered both his previous wives. Smuggling is only part of the man's crimes.'

'Good heavens! And Mrs Thornley?'

'She has been arrested, too, as an accessory to abduction. The best she can hope for is deportation to the colonies.'

'Oh, Ash, what a tangle it has all been.'

'But it must have a happy ending. No story should finish without a happy ending. So, my love, will you answer my question and make me the happiest of men? Will you marry me?'

'Oh, yes, Ash, yes, please.'

He kissed her then and went on kissing her; her forehead, her nose and ears, her cheeks and neck, her lips, hands and arms all received his attention. She flung her arms about him and kissed him back until both were breathless. And that was how Harry and Alex found them, locked in each other's arms.

'Another of the Piccadilly Gentlemen bites the dust,' Harry said with a grin. 'Come, Alex, let us leave them. There will be time enough for explanations later.'

* * * * *

Author's Note

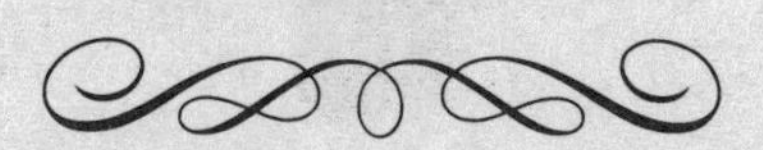

Although I live in Cambridgeshire now, my roots are in Norfolk and I often use Norfolk and the Fens as backgrounds to my books, as I have in this one. The idea for the smuggling background came from a book about Norfolk smuggling called *The Lawless Coast* by Neil Holmes and I would like to record my thanks to him.